HER FATHER'S DAUGHTER

HER FATHER'S DAUGHTER

ALISON BROWNSTONE™ BOOK ONE

JUDITH BERENS   MARTHA CARR   MICHAEL ANDERLE

DISRUPTIVE IMAGINATION

HER FATHER'S DAUGHTER TEAM

Thanks to the JIT Readers

Nicole Emens
Keith Verret
Misty Roa
John Ashmore
Daniel Weigert
Larry Omans
Paul Westman
Angel LaVey

If we've missed anyone, please let us know!

Editor
SkyHunter Editing Team

DEDICATIONS

From Martha

To everyone who still believes in magic
and all the possibilities that holds.
To all the readers who make this
entire ride so much fun.
And to my son, Louie and so many wonderful friends who
remind me all the time of what
really matters and how wonderful
life can be in any given moment.

From Michael

To Family, Friends and
Those Who Love
To Read.
May We All Enjoy Grace
To Live The Life We Are
Called.

T he Light Elf banged on the pane, shouting, his voice
swallowed by the soundproof glass.

On the other side, a human stood, a smile on his face as he watched the elf. "He can still see us, correct?"

"Yes, sir," responded a man in a lab coat next to him—his chief researcher. "We felt the more the test subjects could see us, the more it'd encourage the advanced-stage subjects to use magic to escape. A few of the subjects managed to escape, but security disposed of them. This one though is our best success up to date. His natural magical capability has been completely crippled despite high initial levels."

His employer nodded, a satisfied smile on this face. "And you're sure there's nothing about this cell that counters magic? The last report didn't impress me, considering an anti-magic deflector was involved."

"No, sir. It's just a room." The scientist shrugged. "It'd be trivial with normal magic to escape from this room. It's proof of concept for the advanced-stage subjects. It was difficult to capture this subject to begin with due to advanced magical potential."

His employer rubbed his chin. "But you've not been able to get it to spread. This whole effort might be for nothing if we can't spread it easily. What good is a weapon you practically have to shove down your enemy's throat?"

"No, sir. We can't yet fuse the magic with a virus that spreads easily and maintains the same anti-magic potency." The scientist shook his head. "It's been difficult. You have to understand. We can't use the same magicals to aid us for any length of time. We have to change often. They all become suspicious too quickly. It's been slow going accordingly, sir." He sighed. "We've had to dispose of several already when they started asking too many questions."

His employer nodded at the elf banging against the window. "Look at him. So powerful, yet reduced to nothing. The arrogance of their kind, of all magicals. To take an unnatural power, a perversion of nature, and encourage its spread to a new planet. I don't care what the past was like. We didn't have much magic for thousands of years and did fine."

"Of course, sir. I agree wholeheartedly, sir."

The man shook his head. "I've spent decades of my life trying to ensure humanity's safety. I thought the path to that was mixing technology and magic, but the more I've delved into it, the more I've found that it is a dead end, only more perversion." He took a deep breath. "But I have something most people don't have: the resources and influence to do something about it."

The scientist nodded and tapped a few notes into his tablet. "Yes, sir. Of course, sir."

"You don't understand. What we're doing here is this world's last line of defense. The governments of the world have given up. They're content to let magic pour back into Earth." He shook his head. "At least before, humanity understood magic's danger. Even if it had to exist, it was kept hidden, controlled, but the portals to Oriceran are fully open and the magic of that world is corrupting Earth. It makes a mockery of humanity." He stared at the elf. "It reduces the glories of mankind's minds to nothing but cheap parlor tricks compared to magic. If I can do anything with my wealth, I will protect this planet, no matter the cost. First, though, we need to advance our research. We need to see if the truly powerful can be weakened, their magic stripped. Otherwise, this is another dead end."

"Of course, sir, but it's difficult to accomplish that in a laboratory setting. Just getting the titer necessary for infection to take root is hard enough, and our supply of the transformation elixir is limited for logistical reasons. You have to understand, as much as this is a virus, it's a kind of curse as well."

The man laughed. "Of course. That's what it makes it so fascinating. We're turning their own weapons against them." He walked over and sneered at the elf. "Fine, then. Don't concern yourself with laboratory conditions. It's time for some field tests. Maybe a small number of subjects, based on what I've read from your earlier results. Half-breeds might be easier."

The scientist nodded. "Yes, sir. We're still working out

all the immunology, but again, we're hobbled by the difficulty in being open with our magical contractors."

"That's nothing additional tests and money can't solve." The man stepped away from the glass, watching as the elf slumped to the ground, pleading in his eyes. "What you really need is certain test subjects, powerful ones who are far more likely to have their abilities pushed to the limit. As long as we spread the test subjects across the world and avoid pure Oricerans for the field tests, we can avoid the Oricerans looking too closely into it. All the money and years of effort can't go to waste." He rubbed his chin. "But a little *more* money can keep things quiet, as long as we're subtle about this. I'm willing to take the time. Patience was what got me my wealth to begin with. I do have one suggestion, though."

"Of course, sir. What is it?"

"Hiding a test in the noise." The man smiled. "I have a perfect field test subject in mind. Powerful, and a symbol of everything that's gone wrong since the return of magic. High-profile enough that we'll be able to keep an eye on her with ease, but also so prone to trouble that it'll be difficult for her to ever figure out where she got the virus, even if she can find someone to help her understand the magical components."

The scientist furrowed his brow. "Who might that be, sir?"

"Oh, you know her. After all, her adoption hearing was worldwide news." His lips curled into a sneer. "Alison Brownstone."

CHAPTER ONE

Alison's boots thudded on the asphalt, the sound echoing in the narrow alley. The noise mixed with the desperate footsteps of her prey, a puffing thug in an ill-fitting suit. The power of fear, desperation and longer legs let him pull away from her.

The sight might have looked bizarre to anyone else: a large thug wearing a mask of panic fleeing from an attractive and fit young woman in her mid-twenties. Only her stark white long hair suggested she was more than a normal young woman, something easily misinterpreted as a fashion statement.

With a grimace, Alison considered her options. The bastard was getting away, but using too much magic early might prove a problem once she found his buddies. She pushed the thought out of her mind. The scumbag was her only lead, so it wasn't time to hold back.

"Whatever," she muttered. "I haven't used any yet."

Alison threw up her hands, narrowing her eyes and

concentrating. Shadows flowed together, murky circles lining the walls to her left and right.

"I bet those Drow never thought I'd use it this way," Alison mumbled. She pushed her glasses up her face.

An errant can sent her prey tumbling to the ground as she jumped toward the left wall. Her foot landed on the first shadow disk, then pushed off and flew toward the next disk on the right wall faster than she had been running. She alternated between the walls, speeding up with each bounce.

The thug scrambled to his feet and broke into a new sprint, his face red and beaded with sweat, his breathing ragged.

Alison reached her last acceleration disk and pushed off, now barreling toward the escaping criminal. A quick movement of her hand summoned a shimmering field of light around her. Being fit didn't mean the smaller woman wouldn't hurt herself crashing into a much larger man.

She slammed into the man's back, her energy shield flashing. The thug yelped and fell face-first only a couple of yards from the street. The hard collision knocked the air out of his lungs, and he gasped for oxygen, Alison's knee in his back.

"You bitch," the man rasped. "I think you broke something."

"Aw, poor baby I hope I did." Alison patted him on the shoulder, pulled out her 9mm, and jammed it in his back. Magic had its place, but a gun was often easier. "A bullet might break a lot more."

The man gritted his teeth. "You don't know who you're fucking with, little girl."

She ground the gun into his back. "I think it's kind of the other way around. Speaking of girls, where is she?"

"You'll never find her." The man grunted.

Alison laughed. "If you don't tell me where she is, I don't have much reason to keep you alive, now do I?"

"You kill me, you'll never find her. Go ahead. Shoot me."

She lowered her gun-free hand in front of his face and turned it so her palm was up. "How much do you know about me?"

He snorted. "You're that bastard Brownstone's daughter. You're half-elf or some shit."

She chuckled. "That sounds about right. I want you to think about that. My dad doesn't have a reputation for restraint, and I have a lot of respect for my dad." She sighed. "And I have a lot of magic, including hungry shadow magic."

A writhing mass of twitching shadowy tentacles appeared in her palm.

The man's eyes widened. "What the fuck is that?"

Alison leaned over to whisper into his ear. "Do you want to find out? Want to see what it might do to your brain? So hungry. So *very* hungry."

She almost laughed. It was nothing more than a party trick, but a little misdirection might expedite the interrogation.

The thug trembled. "You can't kill me. If you do, you'll never find her before they ship her out of the country."

Alison sighed. "That's the thing. If you're not going to tell me anyway, then you're just an asshole helping traffic girls. And I don't think the police are going to call the

Paranormal Defense Agency because some piece of trash like you ends up dead under mysterious circumstances."

He rattled off an address in the Union Market area of northeast D.C. "That's a restaurant supply warehouse where they've got the girl stashed. Please, don't let that thing eat my brain. I'm just an errand boy. I'm nothing, really."

"Huh." Alison nodded. "Less brave than I thought." She fished handcuffs out of her red denim jacket and secured the man's hands. "It's your lucky day. Since you cooperated, nothing's going to eat your brain. I'll have the police come and pick you up, and just keep in mind, it's a good thing for you that you're not going to be at that warehouse when I show up."

She slammed a fist into his head, which smacked into the hard asphalt of the alley. His eyes rolled up as he passed out.

"I doubt your friends will be as cooperative," Alison murmured and dusted her hands off. "I almost hope they aren't."

Alison parked her red Fiat Spider in front of the loading door to the warehouse. She loved the car, even though the city kept threatening to pass an anti-internal combustion engine ordinance that would make it expensive for her to keep it. It might be an older vehicle, but it was a gift from her mother.

She stepped out of the car and slammed the door. No obvious cameras stood out, but one security drone circled the area. The kidnapping gang now knew she was coming, and she liked the idea of them sweating a little.

"Saving a little magic power earlier might have helped, but it wasn't *that* much. Better be careful this time in case I run into something serious," she muttered under her breath. "But what's the worst these guys could have? Guns? A merc wizard?"

Alison would use the magic she needed, even if there was pain in her future. She didn't have time for self-pity. She had a little girl to save.

"Wish that damned wizard hadn't blown away my Aegis Pendant."

She shook her head. Even if she'd often neglected the defensive artifact until recently, it'd been helpful in conserving her personal magical energy. Now it was gone —a victim of a dark wizard's spell, like so many other people and artifacts.

Alison marched over to the loading door of the warehouse and narrowed her eyes. No reason to be flashy until she had a better idea of the number of opponents.

Sometimes the best way to do things is Dad's way, but sometimes it's Mom's way.

She continued toward a side door and with a quick tug, she pulled it open, half-surprised it wasn't locked. Laziness or arrogance on the part of the kidnappers?

The door squeaked as it opened, but no gunfire erupted. No one shouted. Warmth seeped out from inside and dissipated in the crisp November air around her.

They have to know I'm here, so why aren't they doing anything? Not even a peep?

Alison furrowed her brow. No use wasting magic

until she was sure. She crept inside, gun in hand as she stepped onto the vast warehouse floor. Rows of pallets piled with boxes filled most of the room, forming a maze of wood, cardboard, and boxed silver-ware, from the looks of things. Metal stairs ran up to a partial second floor formed of metal railings and grates.

Dust choked the air, and Alison wrinkled her nose. She knelt near a tall stack of pallets near the door, listening. No yelling. No footfalls. No teen girl crying.

Time to turn a disadvantage into an advantage.

Alison pulled off her glasses. The warehouse and its contents vanished, replaced by darkness with hints of color in the distance, including aura light leaking around the edges of the pallets and highlighting what would have otherwise been invisible to her unaided vision. Soul light.

Okay, so they're hiding among the pallets. Of course they are. Thoughtful thugs. Just what I needed.

She stared at her glasses for a few seconds, the magical energy of the artifact bright under her natural vision. People had suggested to her she wasn't blind; after all, since she could see magical energy and the souls of living things. Unfortunately, most cars and buildings weren't alive, even thirty years after the return of magic to Earth and the portals to the magical planet of Oriceran starting to open.

Alison slipped her glasses back on.

Thanks, Mom. Wouldn't be able to do my job without these glasses you got for me.

Multiple men lurked in the loading bay, and they were waiting in ambush. She inhaled deeply.

They might not be dark wizards, but they were criminals preying on children. That was almost worse.

She shook her head. The last several years had taught her there was nothing worse than a dark wizard. Even as she tried to concentrate on living a normal life in college, they were never far from her thoughts. Attending a non-magicals' college instead of a magic school as she'd done in high school might have thrust her into fewer conflicts with dark wizards, but she hadn't avoided them entirely.

Visions of mangled bodies and tortured innocents flashed through her mind—the handiwork of dark wizards she'd encountered. She had hoped after she left the School of Necessary Magic that she'd seen the worst of what evil men with power would do, but too many encounters with depraved assholes had convinced her that wolves always lurked in the shadows. Someone had to protect the sheep. Might as well be her.

Alison stood and gritted her teeth. Letting her past affect the current job might not have been professional, but she didn't care. At least the wizards could claim they were tempted by magical power, not petty cash.

"I'm Alison Brownstone," she shouted. "And I know you're hiding in here. All I want is the girl. You give her to me, I walk away, and you can escape before the police come. You resist, I'm going to give you a little taste of the family legacy, assholes."

A man chuckled and stood. She followed the sound and spotted a tall man standing by a crate on a railing upstairs.

He shook his head. "Having that last name don't mean shit, little girl. I don't know how you found us, but you're gonna regret coming here."

Alison sighed. "I'm giving you one last chance to surrender. I can't guarantee your safety otherwise."

The man laughed. "Get a load of that shit, boys! One little bitch thinks that because she's got a famous daddy and a little magic, she can take us on. Stop hiding. Show her why she's fucked."

Dark chuckles filled the warehouse as a dozen men emerged from behind pallet stacks, all holding guns.

"I think," the man replied, "that you're going to be—" He screamed and collapsed, holding his leg.

She'd put a bullet in him and rolled behind a pallet before the rest of the gang had registered what had happened.

"A little magic and a gun, asshole," Alison shouted.

She inhaled and raised a hand, concentrating. A shimmering nimbus of white light surrounded her body. "I'm going to keep shooting you people until you give me the girl. I'm going to get her in the end, so why not cut yourself a break?"

"Kill that bitch!" the man on the second floor shrieked.

Alison popped up and put a bullet into a man a few rows down, and he collapsed with a groan. Serpentine sprinting sent her to a new pallet stack as the other men opened fire, the echoing cacophony of their shots overwhelming. Most of the bullets zoomed past her, but a few struck her shield, bouncing off with flashes.

She fired a few more rounds. Two ended up in a thug's chest, and another bullet found a man's head.

That asshole was cocky, but this is all he's got?

After a few deep breaths, she rushed around the corner and emptied her magazine, taking down several more thugs. The enemy's fire concentrated on her, the bullets striking her energy shield but not making it through before she leapt behind more pallets.

Alison hissed as pain shot through her body. She wasn't hit. Not a single bullet had come close to piercing her defenses. No, the now-familiar pain was from a different cause.

"Come on," she muttered. "I'm not even overdoing it yet." She rolled her eyes. "Whatever. Suck it up, Alison."

In open defiance of her body, she reloaded and holstered her pistol and raised both hands. A slight hum filled the air despite the continuing loud gunshots and the bullets pelting the metal, wood, and cardboard around her.

A pulsing orb of white light grew between her hands, and a grin spread on her face. The gunfire died as several men slapped new magazines into their guns. She continued to feed the orb building in her hands.

Alison jumped around the corner and thrust her hands forward, and the orb shot off with a roar toward several men. They leapt out of the way as the magic struck the tower of pallets behind them, but a white-blue explosion of energy consumed the area, blowing the screaming men into the air. The nearby pallets buried a few and the jumbled pile of boxes and pallets smoldered, smoke rising into the air.

She nodded in satisfaction before retrieving her gun. Marching forward, she put quick shots into the few remaining thugs who were standing there slack-jacked.

"Pay more attention," Alison suggested.

The groans of the surviving men filled the area.

Alison brushed a few strands of her white hair out of

her face. "I've been pretty nice about this, and I think you understand now that I'm not leaving here without the girl. Considering I've kicked your asses, time to start talking."

"Fuck you," shouted the man on the second floor. He groaned and crawled forward. "You haven't won, bitch. You just got lucky."

She sighed. "Just tell me where the girl is, asshole."

The man spat, "You're dead, bitch. He's gonna show you. We're not done yet." He groaned and fell unconscious.

"Okay, so we have one vote for brave but stupid stubbornness." Alison waved her gun a few times. "How about a vote for cooperation from any of the people still alive? Anyone?"

A loud clang echoed in the warehouse, and Alison narrowed her eyes. She leapt for cover.

"Somebody new to the party? Take a look around. Your friends didn't last."

More clangs were followed by a mechanical whirring.

"Oh, damn it."

She peeked around the corner and holstered her 9mm. It wouldn't accomplish anything against the new arrival.

A man in eight-foot-tall thick black power armor advanced across the warehouse floor, its black visor concealing his face. He held a massive rotary machine gun in his right hand, the gun belt fed directly from a huge backpack. He approached the burnt remnants of the pallets she'd destroyed with her magic.

The machine gun roared to life and spat rounds Alison's way that shredded the wooden pallet and boxes around her, blasting the contents all over her in a shower of forks, knives, and spoons. After the bright flashes of the first few impacts from bullets and silverware on her shield, she dropped to the ground and crawled around the other side of her cover.

The torrent of bullets continued for a few seconds before the gun whirred down.

How the hell do these local losers have military-grade power armor?

Alison took a deep breath and raised her hands. A few quick movements helped her feed more strength into her energy shield. She hadn't tested her magic against a machine gun before, and she wasn't eager to find out how long it'd hold.

Every historian said the same thing. The chaos accompanying the return of magic to Earth thirty years prior had led to economic and technological stagnation for years, but humanity's remarkable adaptation had won out in the following decades—especially in the last ten years, and now everything was advancing again at a rapid pace.

Alison would have been proud of her planet if a man in power armor hadn't been trying to kill her.

The machine gun roared to life again and blew the rest of her cover into confetti, then the deadly hail met her shield. After a few seconds, spikes of pain blasted through her body. The bullets weren't reaching her, but her shield wouldn't hold under the punishment.

She swung her arm to the side. A porous and twisted line of shadow shot from her hand and struck a wall. The line jerked her from her position, dragging her through the warehouse as her foe trailed her with his bullet storm.

Shadow wings might have given her more mobility, but her strategy let her escape while using less magic overall.

Arriving at the wall, she turned the corner and ran into a hallway. The wall behind her exploded in a shower of dust and drywall as bullets ripped into it.

Alison wiped some sweat off her forehead and took a few deep breaths. Science and engineering might now be producing wonders on par with magic, but that didn't mean they were invulnerable.

Her enemy kept up his barrage, and his heavy footsteps sounded nearby. If he caught her in a narrow hallway he might win, even with her magical shield.

"Okay, they've got power armor, but maybe it's not shielded. It's worth a shot."

She pulled a small notched black sphere out of her pocket, pressed the button on top of it three times, and then waited for it to beep. With a quick spin around the corner, she hurled the device, an EMP grenade, toward the advancing power armor.

A few bullets struck her shield during her quick retreat, but her defenses held. Seconds later, there was a loud buzz and the hail of bullets died. A massive thud echoed down the hallway.

"Guess it wasn't shielded."

Alison grinned and rushed around the corner. The power armor lay face-down a few yards from the entrance to the hallway. She released her shield, the light around her dissipating over several seconds, and continued toward the armor.

With a pop, the back of the armor separated. Grunting, a man pushed it open and lifted his head in time to see Alison's gun pointed straight at his face.

She smiled. "They say every weapon has a counter, but

your problem is you bought shitty power armor. Don't feel too bad. If the EMP hadn't worked, I would have carved you up with magic." She shrugged, and her smile disappeared. "Now, tell me where the girl is or I'll blow your damned head off."

Ten minutes later, Alison kicked in the door to a broom closet. A gagged teen girl sat in the corner, her legs and hands bound with nylon rope and blood running down her bruised and battered face.

Alison's stomach tightened.

That could have been me if it hadn't been for Dad. She's around the same age as I was back then.

The girl tried to shout through her gag, tears running down her face.

Alison rushed over to the girl and pulled the gag down. "Are you okay? Can you walk?"

The girl shook her head. "My ankle. They hurt it earlier. I think it's broken."

Alison reached into her pocket and pulled out a blue glass vial. She yanked the stopper out and held it in front of the girl's face. "Do you know what this is?"

The girl shook her head. "No."

"Healing potion, now open wide. It tastes like ass, but it'll fix your ankle."

The girl complied, and Alison poured the potion down her throat.

About a half-minute passed before relief spread over the girl's face. Her bruises disappeared, and her cuts closed.

Alison untied the girl.

"I feel...*fine*," the girl murmured.

Alison offered her a hand. "The cops will be here soon to handle the few guys I left alive. Let's get out of here before they arrive. I think it's better you see your family before they make you answer any questions."

The girl nodded, her eyes wide. "Thank you, but who are you?"

"Me? I'm Alison Brownstone."

CHAPTER TWO

Alison kicked her legs as she sat on the edge of the examination table, the paper crinkling beneath her. She rubbed her forearm where the phlebotomist had drawn blood earlier that morning. All her tests results were supposed to have been passed along to the doctor's office, and the nurse had allegedly confirmed that when she'd taken Alison's vitals twenty minutes earlier.

"They better not make me try and give my blood. It took her enough tries to find the vein this morning," she muttered. "It's like she was enjoying it."

She pulled out her phone to check the headlines. Twenty minutes of brooding over her bruised arm were more than enough.

DISTRICT ATTORNEY'S DAUGHTER SAVED FROM TRAFFICKERS

Alison smiled. Not only had she saved the girl, but the girl's father was making sure that no one would come sniffing around her alleging use of excessive force. Letting her bounty hunting license expire had made certain things more complicated, but it wasn't like she needed an excuse to kill every bad guy on a job.

Her name had been kept out of the news. She didn't mind a little good press, but her dad's experiences during his bounty hunting career had taught her the value of maintaining a low profile when possible. No matter how badass the reputation a person earned was, somehow there was always someone or something who thought it was an invitation and not a warning.

It's a good thing to not have the license. I need to follow my own path. Private security jobs don't require a bounty hunter's license. I'm Alison Brownstone, not just James Brownstone's daughter.

She laughed, thinking of her mom. Shay might not be as active in her career as she had been years ago, but it wasn't like she needed an official tomb raider license.

How would they even decide what an official tomb raider license required? Take a test about what magical artifacts are acceptable to pull out of ancient ruins?

There was a light knock, and Alison pocketed her phone.

The door opened, and a white-coated elderly man with a stethoscope around his neck entered. He held a tablet.

"Good evening, Miss Brownstone. I'm sorry for the delay, but there was a bit of a technical problem with your test results. I'm Doctor Olsen."

"But you've got everything now?" Alison glanced at her savaged arm. "Or am I going to need to give more blood?"

Fighting a man in power armor with a machine gun worried her less than an incompetent phlebotomist.

"No, we've got everything we need." Doctor Olsen extended his hand and Alison gave it a firm shake.

"Nice to meet you, Doc."

Doctor Olsen smiled and sat on a stool on the other side of the small examination room. "Nice to meet you, too, Miss Brownstone. Before we discuss your case, I just wanted to confirm a few things. I apologize if this seems unusually intrusive, but some of my questions are needed because of your slightly complicated background."

Alison nodded. "Whatever you need, just ask."

"You're half-human and half-Oriceran, correct? More specifically half-dark elf?"

"Yeah, they go by Drow." Alison shrugged. "It's not like a Drow's going to be horribly offended if you call them dark elves, but you know, it's more accurate and polite."

Doctor Olsen tapped his tablet. "Of course, of course. I'll remember that. According to your intake form, you've spent more than six consecutive months on Oriceran in the past ten years?"

Alison nodded. "Yeah. I was born in Los Angeles and I lived there most of my life, but I've spent a little time over there. I was doing magical training with the Drow. Nothing long-term."

He looked her up and down for a moment. "Can you describe to me what you feel your problem is? I know you've written some things down, but I want to hear it in your own words."

She shrugged. "I've never had to be careful to not overuse magic, but for the last six months, I've had pain and fatigue when I use my magic, even when I'm nowhere near the levels of what I've used in the past. It's a lot harder for me to do things that were super-easy before. I kept thinking it'd get better, but it's been getting worse. I don't always notice, but what I did during the job I was on should barely have strained me. I figured I should get checked out, first with a human doctor, then maybe an Oriceran healer when I had time. This problem with my magic makes my job more difficult."

"And you are a…" the doctor frowned and looked at the tablet, "private security contractor? Is that like a bounty hunter?"

Alison shook her head. "No. I focus on client protection and retrieval. Some of the bad guys I run into might have bounties, but I don't actively hunt bounties. Not anymore."

Doctor Olsen smiled. "Didn't want to follow in your father's footsteps? Braver than me. I thought I was being clever by not being a thoracic surgeon."

She chuckled politely. "Oh, you've heard of my dad?"

"He hasn't lived a quiet life." Doctor Olsen returned his attention to the tablet. "Speaking of your family, I'm a bit confused by the family history on your intake form. Could you explain the situation in your own words? Again, I'm not trying to be intrusive. It's just important that I have a complete understanding of all the factors that might contribute to your medical condition."

Alison chuckled. "Yeah, I get that." She shrugged. "It's kind of straight-forward actually. My biological mother was a full-blooded Drow from Oriceran. My biological father was a normal human, no magical ability unless being an extreme asshole is considered a magical ability."

Doctor Olsen blinked. "I see."

She wasn't about to explain the horrible betrayal of her

biological mother by her father, so she continued. "Anyway, he wasn't a wizard or anything like that. James Brownstone is my adopted father. Shay Carson-Brownstone is my adopted mother, but I call them Mom and Dad and have for a long time." She shrugged. "Does that make it clearer?"

"Yes, much clearer." Doctor Olsen nodded. He held up a finger. "Of course. I just remembered the hubbub about your adoption. I have to admit I watched all the coverage on it. Funny how much things have changed in such a short time. No one blinks at cross-planetary adoptions anymore. You're a trailblazer, Miss Brownstone."

"Yeah, it's funny now." Alison smiled. "Wasn't all that funny at the time. A lot of the media were pretty harsh on both my dad and me."

"Of course, of course. It's all ratings for them; just the way they are. I wouldn't take it personally." The doctor tapped a few more times on his tablet. "Okay, has your biological mother ever exhibited any of the symptoms you mentioned? Although we're still learning a lot about Oriceran biology in terms of scientific medicine, it does seem basic principles of heredity and genetics apply in most species, particularly the humanoid ones, such as elves. Numerous inherited conditions have been identified by both human doctors and Oriceran medical specialists."

Alison shook her head. "She never mentioned anything like that." She frowned.

"Have you double-checked with her recently?" Doctor Olsen inquired. "Sometimes parents conceal certain conditions to avoid stressing their children but will be more honest when they are older."

Alison took a deep breath. "She's not around to ask anymore. My biological mother died when I was fifteen. She was…killed."

Doctor Olsen blinked. "I'm very sorry to hear that, Miss Brownstone. I wasn't aware. I'm terribly sorry to bring up unpleasant memories."

Didn't read about that during the adoption-hearing media circus? Kind of surprised, Doc.

Alison blew out a breath. "But you're right. It's not like I'd know if she had this problem. I didn't even know she was Oriceran until right before she died, so it wasn't like we were discussing unique magic-related medical conditions."

The doctor furrowed his brow. "But according to your intake form, you were born with an unusual disability that is magical in nature and affects your vision?"

"Sure, but I just kind of rolled with it." She laughed and tapped her glasses. "These take care of it now."

"I understand that. I was more saying that I'm surprised that you didn't realize one of your parents might have been magical, given the situation with your sight."

Alison shrugged. "It all makes sense in retrospect, but at the time I didn't think it was unusual. I'm not sure, but I think my mom did everything she could so I wouldn't think I was strange, and compared to a lot of the stuff that people had to get used to when I was younger, I wasn't. I kind of assumed it had something to do with like background magic radiation or something like that."

"I see, I see. That makes sense." Doctor Olsen ran his tongue along the inside of his mouth. "And have you tried contacting the Drow and asking them about the medical condition? Please don't take offense, but many Oriceran races aren't forthright about sharing information, particularly information that others might perceive as weakness."

Alison chuckled. "Yeah, that sums up the Drow. I haven't talked to them yet. I've been avoiding going to see anyone about this. I thought it might go away on its own; that it was just some weird temporary thing. I guess I have the bad Oriceran habit you just talked about."

Doctor Olsen tapped a few additional notes into his tablet and nodded. "But it didn't go away, and now you feel you had no choice but to see a doctor?"

Alison shrugged. "The weeks became months. I think I got used to restraining my power usage, but I can't put this off anymore. Right now it's manageable, but if it gets worse, I won't be able to do my job."

Doctor Olsen gazed at her. "I think it's a good thing that you came in, and I can provide some insight into your condition."

Alison's eyes widened. "Wait, you know what's wrong with me?"

He sighed and set the tablet on the counter. He folded his hands in front of him. "Yes, only because I recently attended an emerging diseases conference focused on the threat of emerging trans-planetary diseases. While you're my first patient with this problem, you're not the first patient to display these symptoms."

"What are you saying?" Alison leaned forward, her heart rate kicking up. "What's wrong with me?"

"It's very rare, Miss Brownstone, but your bloodwork and symptoms are consistent with it. You have a condition called Advanced Magical Deficiency Syndrome. It's as you described. You'll continue to have increased pain and fatigue associated with magic, along with difficulty using higher levels of magic. It's a very rare problem, and thus far only a small number of patients have been diagnosed with it. Currently, it only seems to affect half-human/half-Oriceran patients. At least, we've received no reports that it's an issue on Oriceran or any reports of full-blooded Oriceran patients with the problem on Earth, and it seems distinct from other diseases and conditions that can affect magic."

Alison shook her head. "That doesn't make sense. I've been exposed to healing magic and anti-disease magic in the last six months. It would have cleared out any disease."

Doctor Olsen shrugged. "And that is also consistent with case reports from other patients who have engaged in extensive anti-viral and magical therapies but achieved no relief for this particular condition. We have identified the virus responsible, but genetic and anti-viral therapies targeting it are currently ineffective. A doctor in Maine partnered with some Light Elf healing specialists, and they were also unable to cure the disease despite the application of extensive healing magic. It's really quite perplexing, and unlike anything seen before on either Earth or Oriceran."

"But that doesn't make any sense. How can a virus be immune to both technological and magical healing? That's impossible, isn't it?"

Doctor Olsen sighed. "We honestly don't know. There's so much about it we still don't understand, like the inter-face between magic and biology, and so little we *do* under-stand about this disease, including its progression and exact molecular biology. Its mutation rate is incredible. To the best of our knowledge, it's the single fastest-mutating virus ever observed. The Light Elves involved in the Maine research suggested there's a magical component to it, but even *they* don't understand the exact nature of the magic. It's also unlike anything they've ever seen.

"There are some indications that it's a magical virus." He picked up his tablet. "We don't even know how it's transmitted, but it doesn't seem to be airborne or sexually transmitted, based on the case reports we currently have. Given the magical nature of the disease, it might be more complicated than traditional diseases, and given that it is currently affecting only half-human, half-Oriceran patients, that's strongly indicative of a genetic component to it as well."

He managed a smile. "I know I've just delivered a lot of gloom, but we do know *some* things. We at least know it's caused by a virus, and we can identify the virus in patients. That gives us a target."

Alison stared at her hands. "So how does this end? Does this get worse until I die?" She blinked several times.

"The earliest case we've identified is in a woman who first exhibited symptoms five years ago. Genetic studies of sequencing databases provide little evidence that the virus was extant in existing Earth populations before then, but we can't rule it out. Nor we can rule out zoonotic transmission."

"Zoonotic?" Alison furrowed her brow.

The doctor nodded. "Species-to-species. Traditionally, this has meant Earth-based animal to human, but given the many unusual creatures on Oriceran, the virus could have hopped over from one of them."

"So, what, some dragon coughed and infected people with this thing?"

"Possibly." Doctor Olsen reached over to pat Alison on the arm. "There's hope, though. That patient I mentioned—she's still living a healthy life, although her magical capabilities are severely curtailed. They've been reduced to about five to ten percent of what she used to be able to do, but she doesn't exhibit other negative health symptoms as long as she avoids magic."

Doctor Olsen sighed. "Other than that, we can't say. I will note that current data doesn't support a conclusion that excessive magic use aggravates the course of the disease. It seems to be a simple function of time, but as the disease progresses, magic use becomes more and more dangerous, carrying potential neurological complications."

"So the clock's ticking," Alison replied. "Right now I can still do most of my magic, but there's no cure, so I have four or five years now before I'm useless. That's what you're saying, right? That if we can't cure this disease, I'll effectively lose my magic?"

"Now, now, Miss Brownstone. We don't know that. A therapy might be found, and you can still live a rich and full life without magic. Billions of humans do, and have for the history of our species."

Alison stared at the wall as the doctor rambled on about her options and his desire for her to participate in a clinical study of AMDS patients. One possibility of cure presented itself in her thoughts—a legacy of her birth mother. It was a magical wish, something bequeathed to James Brownstone even before he'd adopted her.

Her dad had controlled the wish for many years, but

with the help of the current Drow queen, the wish had been transferred to Alison.

She'd thought about using it before. Curing her blindness so she didn't have to rely on magical glasses had been tempting. She'd also thought about using it to help a few other people in desperate situations. Each time, though, she had decided against it, waiting for a critical moment where she'd truly need it and had no other option.

Is it even my wish anymore? This disease isn't killing me, from the sound of it, just limiting my magic. I should save the wish for something special; something that can help a lot of people. Could I wish away the entire disease for everyone? When I visited Oriceran, the Drow acted like there were limits to the wish.

No. I can't use it for this. Not yet. They could find a cure tomorrow, and I'll have wasted the wish on something selfish.

"Miss Brownstone?" Doctor Olsen prodded. "Are you listening?"

Alison blinked. "I'm sorry. It's just a lot to take in. I'm sorry, but I don't think I want to participate in the study. I get that it's for science, but for now, I think I'm going to explore different solutions."

Doctor Olsen smiled. "I understand. If you change your mind, you know where to find me. I'm sorry to have been the one to tell you this. If it's a small comfort, you're not alone."

She shrugged. "Not your fault. At least I know what's going on. So, for now, just live my life and don't strain my magic unless necessary?"

The doctor nodded. "That's the only real advice I can give you, other than exercise and eat right. We can treat the symptoms when they become more advanced, but avoiding unnecessary magic use is preferable."

Alison managed a chuckle. "Thanks, Doc. At least you gave me a name for it. I feel like if I know the name of my enemy, I can beat it."

CHAPTER THREE

Alison lay on her bed and sighed. It should have been a great week. She had kicked trafficker ass and rescued a girl, but discovering she had a disease affecting her magic put a cloud over everything.

"I've got time," she mumbled. "Years, maybe. Just because they don't have a cure now doesn't mean they won't have one in a few years, and I'm not dying. Besides, can't be in the Brownstone family without some sort of weird thing hanging over you. At least I don't have weird people trying to kill me."

Her phone rang, and she grabbed it from her nightstand.

SHAY CARSON-BROWNSTONE.

Alison accepted the call. "Hey, Mom. Wasn't expecting a call from you."

"Well, I *was* expecting a call from you. I thought you were going to call me after you finished up your job." Annoyance colored Shay's voice. "I had to read about it on the news, and your name wasn't even in there. If I hadn't known what you were up to, I wouldn't even have known you were the one who saved that girl." She laughed. "And killed a bunch of guys."

"To be fair, I offered them a chance to give up first."

Shay snickered. "You're more merciful than your dad or me. Still, what's with all the secrecy?"

Alison laughed. "Come on. For a woman who has done most of her jobs under a fake name, it's a bit much to be complaining about me not announcing it to the world. Sometimes I want people to know; a lot of other times, I don't."

"I'm just saying," Shay grumbled. "I want to brag to my friends about how my daughter is mowing down shitbags. It'd be a nice little point of conversation when we're having lunch."

"Seriously, Mom?" Alison rolled her eyes. "This is what you talk about with your friends, or is this what you talk about with your department head? 'Oh, by the way, here's a lecture on the true nature of Atlantis, and my daughter annihilated a warehouse full of terrorists and a guy in power armor?'"

"Well, I couldn't have the conversation with you hiding everything. Look, when I kick ass myself, it's not like I can tell everyone about it since I'm supposed to just be a normal college professor. Your dad's kind of on the bench unless something really extreme happens, and in that case, the whole damn world will probably know about it." Shay sighed. "So I need vicarious ass-kicking stories from you, at least for now."

"I'll keep that in mind." Alison swallowed.

Maybe I should tell her about the disease, but then again, what's the point? Mom and Dad will want to do something about it or maybe even tell me to use the wish. It's not something that they need to worry about. They've got other things to worry about.

"How did Dad's last barbeque competition go?" Alison asked, changing the subject.

"He didn't compete." Shay laughed. "Grunted about it for days."

"He didn't compete? But he's been talking up that competition for a month. I don't get it." Alison frowned. "He's feeling okay, right?"

"Oh, everything's fine. The big baby is just being OCD. Somehow he convinced himself, and Mack, for that matter, who should really know better, that if they weren't going to take first, they shouldn't even compete because they'd be risking exposure of their secret new sauce." Shay snorted. "You know him. If it's barbeque, it's the most important thing in existence. I think the only thing that has saved this planet from James taking over and instituting the First Barbeque Empire is that he took that detour into bounty hunting before he could fully obsess over meat."

Alison rolled onto her side. "Detour? He's probably the most famous bounty hunter in history. I still get emails from people I had like a single class with in college. 'Hey, Alison, you might not remember me, but we were in Intro to Philosophy together. I was in the back row, but I never talked to you because you were too hot and intimidating. So, hey, can you get your dad to show up at my bachelor party, or if not that, can you get a recording of him saying 'have a happy fucking wedding?'"

Shay laughed. "Seriously?"

"Seriously, Mom. It's damned annoying, and what I just described happened less than a month ago." Alison scoffed.

"You know I'd tell you to not pump his ego with that sort of thing, but I honestly don't think he cares. Not like anyone messes with us anymore, so he's more obsessed with his barbeque rep than his ass-kicking rep."

"Speaking of ass-kicking rep, I talked to Lily the other day, and she said you guys did a tomb raid together recently." Alison chuckled. "You're mad at me for not talking to you about my job, but you're running off and doing secret tomb raids. I thought you said you weren't going to do another one until next year?"

Shay groaned. "It wasn't a big deal. An opportunity came up, and it's good to keep the skills fresh. You never know when I might need to go find some ancient urn of power or something to save the world. That, and make a shit-ton of money."

Alison smiled. "Sure, Mom. Sure."

"Oh," Shay all but shouted, "I forgot to tell you something I would have trouble believing if it weren't for one detail." She cackled so hard she had to take a deep breath.

"What?" Alison asked.

"Your dad, the man who took you to all those musicals when you were younger but never enjoyed them, is genuinely excited about a traveling Broadway show. He's been constantly talking about it. Already bought tickets. Front row, by the way." Shay snickered. "He's studying up on the cast."

Alison brow shot up. "Dad's interested in a musical? Someone check the temperature in hell."

"Yeah. Can you guess which one? Here's a hint: it won a Tony Award."

"That doesn't narrow it down." Alison blinked. "Oh, wait. Of course: *Nadina: Low and Slow.*"

Her mom cackled. "Yep. The only musical based on the life of an elf barbeque chef. I don't even think he gives a shit that it's about a real-life story, just that it's a barbeque-based musical. I remember how he had to fight sleep every time he took you to a show in the past, and now he's talking about the accuracy of the songs and how they relate to barbeque—like I give a shit."

"Well, this is a good thing. Gives us more to chat about." Alison's gaze cut to a framed picture of her as a teenager with James and Shay. "I don't like to chat about the job, if only because Dad's advice is always a bit…straightforward and I'm trying to do my own thing."

"Yeah, James does love a good, 'Just kick their asses until they stop moving' recommendation, but you sound like you're doing well—especially with that latest job. You don't need his advice or mine either, at least when it comes to tactical shit."

Alison sighed. "I'm not so sure."

"You're not so sure? About what?" Concern crept into Shay's voice.

"Yeah. I've been scoring high-end security jobs for local types, particularly politically-connected rich bastards, but DC makes my skin crawl." Alison shook her head. "I feel like everyone's ready to stab everyone else in the back. I've been trying hard to pick jobs I believe in, but that takes work."

Shay laughed. "It's a viper's nest of politicians and

lobbyists. What did you expect? Hey, you can always go into tomb raiding. Lily's doing a kickass job, but she could use a partner."

"I don't think so." Alison shook her head. "I'm just not into grabbing artifacts. I want to protect people."

"You've always had that tendency. You didn't get that from us."

"How can you say that?" Alison replied. "You and Dad have protected a lot of people."

"Mostly because people were screwing with us." Shay sighed. "But it's not like I'm gonna complain that you want to help people. Let me be very clear, Alison, and in this case, I'm speaking for James too. You should do what *you* want to do, and not worry about what your dad or I have done. You've got your own special talents and a financial cushion, and you can figure out the best way to use those. The only thing we want is for you to be satisfied with your life. Both your dad and I fell into our careers rather than chose them. We want you to choose."

Alison smiled. "Thanks, Mom. I appreciate that, and I'm not trying to say I look down on bounty hunting or tomb raiding. They just aren't my thing."

"We know, and we're both proud of you. You kicked more evil ass than either of us did at your age when you were still a teenager at the School of Necessary Magic." Shay snorted. "Even if you kept that a little too close to the chest in the beginning."

"You're still mad about me keeping that from you?"

"No, you can take care of yourself. You've always been able to. Just keep in mind that we are here for you if you need us, and government stooges aren't going to keep your dad from helping you if you need it."

"Thanks again, Mom," Alison replied.

Guilt stabbed at her stomach.

Just need to keep reminding myself that there's nothing they can do about a disease, and if worse comes to worst, I always have the wish.

Shay blew out a breath. "The only advice I have for you is get organized and get proper backup. Your dad and I spent way too long being lone wolves before realizing the power of a good team. And I'm not just talking about a computer guy. Not saying you have to open an entire agency, just saying if you want to protect people as a security contractor, find people who can fill in holes in your skillset. That'll cut down on trouble for your clients and you."

Alison lay back down. "I'll think about that. Still getting a feel for DC in general and the kind of jobs I'll be taking in particular, so not sure what kind of people I might need to hire or team up with."

"Okay, but forget about work for now. What about friends?"

"Friends?" Alison echoed.

Shay chuckled. "Yeah, friends. Even *I* have friends, and I'm a stone-cold bitch half the time."

"I chat with Lily on occasion. Exchange a few letters with Izzie, but you know it's hard with Lily always on the job and Izzie's...complicated situation." Alison blew out a breath. "It's weird. I get the letters and read them, and they burst into flame once I'm done. Anti-tracking magic on them, too. Makes me worry."

"Given who her parents are, she'll be just fine. I'm sure they'll figure it all out eventually, and she'll be able to come out of hiding. The best thing you can do is keep reminding her you haven't forgotten about her."

Alison sighed. "I hope so. I feel kind of guilty that I get to have a normal life and she's on the run."

"I don't really know if being a half-human, half-Drow magical security contractor is all that normal a life, especially considering that James and I are your parents."

"You'd be surprised, Mom." Alison stared at her popcorn ceiling. "It's not like the world is the same as even when Dad first adopted me. Lots of mixed couples out there. It's like it used to be a big thing, but now a lot of people take it for granted."

"Hrmm. Maybe it's because I'm a tomb raider, but I can't ever take magic for granted. I've seen too much."

Alison sighed. "So have I. Oh, thank you for your and Dad's help with Tanner."

Shay groaned. "Alison, that was a year ago. You don't have to keep thanking us every time we talk. By the way, every time I tell James you thank him, he just grunts and says the same thing."

"Dad promised me he'd get Tanner out of that coma and he did, with your help." Alison sighed. "Even if things didn't work out between us, I'm grateful."

"Do you still love him?" Shay asked, her voice quiet.

"No, not in that way. A part of me always will, but I spent too many years away from him when he was in that coma." Alison took a deep breath. "Too many years obsessing about dark wizards. And he's a man out of time, a man who missed years of his life. It's sad, but it's good that we both moved on, and that he has his life back. The only thing…"

"The only thing what?"

Alison sighed. "Should I have used my wish from the beginning? On him? I know that's weird all of a sudden, but I was just thinking about the wish the other day, so Tanner's been in my thoughts."

"No one can answer that but you, but it worked out, didn't it?" Scratching came over the line as Shay shifted position. "Look, I get that you're a little less self-serving than either James or me, but don't be *too* generous. You can't beat yourself up because you don't personally save everyone. Even your dad couldn't pull that off if he tried."

Alison sighed. "I know, I know, but it's still hard."

"Also remember what that wish is. It's your real mother's legacy."

Alison sighed. "I understand that—and you don't have to talk about her that way. You're as real as my mother as she was."

Shay snorted. "I stepped in when you were almost grown. I love you, but I also get that she did all the hard work."

"But I love you as much as I did her."

"I'm just saying that even as she lay dying, she made sure to pass that wish so you'd have it. I don't think she was worrying about you using it to save the world or something. I think she wanted you to use it for yourself. It's your wish, and I don't think you should feel guilty about using it to help yourself. If anyone else has a problem with that, fuck them. They can take it up with James and me, and we'll kick their ass all the way to that moon base they're building. You use it for what *you* want. Use it for a pile of candy, for all I care."

Alison draped an arm over her forehead. "Like curing my incurable disease."

She wasn't sure why she said it. Something about love and trust in the back of her mind, maybe. She'd kept so many secrets in her life, including about her skirmishes with dark wizards when she was at the School of Necessary Magic as a teen, at least at first. Even if she had been more honest about the battles she'd dealt with in her college years, she couldn't help the tiny piece of conscience in the back of her mind telling her not to lie by omission to the woman she claimed she loved.

Alison took a deep breath and related what the doctor had told her.

"Shit," Shay responded after a good thirty seconds of silence, then sucked in a breath. "I'll be honest, Alison. That sounds like a prime candidate for the wish."

"But they might be able to cure it, and I'll have wasted the wish when I could maybe use it to bring Dad back to life or something."

Shay laughed. "He's got good people keeping an eye on him."

"What about you, then? You might not be as active, but you're also not out of the game."

"I'll be fine. Don't you *dare* keep that wish because you're worried about me." Shay snorted. "I'd consider that an insult."

Alison groaned. "I'm just saying, Mom."

"It's your choice, in the end," Shay replied. "It's your wish. No one's going to force you to do anything with it. If you think the disease situation's under control, don't use it. We'll look around on our end to see if there's anything we can do to help you as well. I'd suggest talking to the Drow when you get a chance. Maybe they'll have insight, unlike the Light Elves the doctor mentioned."

"I will when I get time." Alison pursed her lips. "But for now, I'm just going to take it day by day."

"That's all anyone can do."

"Thanks. I think I'm going to get some sleep now. Give my love to everybody."

"I will," Shay responded. "We love you, Alison. Remember that."

Alison smiled at the phone. "I always do."

The call ended, and she took a deep breath. She felt better about telling her mom about her AMDS. Her family might not be normal, but they had each other's backs.

She didn't want to lean too hard on her parents, but it wasn't like a mysterious new disease was something her dad could solve through the standard Brownstone strategy of gratuitous application of ultra-violence. That fact alone should keep him under control.

A smile spread over her face, and she nodded to herself. "Screw the AMDS. I've got years before it becomes a real problem, and I saved a girl this week. I'm doing damn well. Tomorrow I'm getting myself some victory sushi."

CHAPTER FOUR

Alison smiled and took a seat on an open stool in front of the counter and the conveyor.

The owner of the sushi shop smiled at her. "Welcome to Urashima. Glad to see you again, Alison."

She offered him a polite nod and turned her attention to the white trays of sushi rolls on the conveyor belt running around the counter, through a hole into the kitchen, and back out to the counter.

Urashima might not be the fanciest place for sushi, but it's damned good and cheap.

Alison snatched a few passing plates to start: spicy tuna roll, California roll, salmon roll, and some uni.

She smiled and broke apart her chopsticks. With their help, she plopped a spicy tuna morsel into her mouth, savoring the texture and flavor. Her dad insisted barbeque was man's highest culinary achievement. Her mother argued that New York-style pizza was the obvious winner, but the elegant simplicity of sushi, where the individual ingredients were elevated with careful skill and balance, convinced Alison that it was the true highest cuisine.

Alison glanced around as she downed more tuna. Most of the tables were filled, along with the stools at the counter. Most of the crowd was human, but an elf couple sat at a corner table enjoying their food.

As she chewed on her rice and fish, she considered their presence. Even though she was a half-elf, she looked like any other young woman in her mid-twenties. Her stark white hair might be unusual, but given the number of women wandering DC with bright pink, cyan, green, blue, purple, or other exotic hair colors, white was almost mundane.

Alison moved on to the salmon and looked at the TV in the corner. A news program was on.

The serious-looking gray-haired anchor gazed earnestly at the camera. A graphic of the moon appeared beside his head. "The International Lunar Exploration Consortium, ILEC, announced today that they're satisfied with the results of a pilot program evaluating the effects of magical transportation on electronic components. They will be accepting bids from several different companies for magical transportation of equipment and cargo to the surface of the moon.

"ILEC anticipates that the use of magical teleport and portals to transport cargo will dramatically decrease the cost of the moon base project, in addition to accelerating the completion of Tranquility City. However, no final contracts have been awarded, and there is still fierce competition between several companies, magical and otherwise, for the lunar transport contract."

Alison barely focused on the news report since the chyron riveted her.

RECOUNT FINISHED FOR VIRGINIA 5TH CONGRESSIONAL DISTRICT. ELECTION OF LUCAS SHEPARD, FIRST OPENLY SHIFTER REPRESENTATIVE, CONFIRMED AFTER ACRIMONIOUS CAMPAIGN AND ELECTION.

"Good job, Luke," she murmured. She didn't keep up with a lot of her old friends from the School of Necessary Magic. Most of them had gone their separate ways when they went off to college or jobs, but she wasn't surprised to see Luke entering politics. He'd always been a leader, even at their school.

"Shut that shit off!" shouted a man at the counter. He was red-faced and his suit was wrinkled, his tie barely on. A drained beer sat in front of him, and it likely wasn't his first.

The owner frowned. "Excuse me, sir. Is there a problem?"

The man pointed to the TV. "Shut that magic-loving shit off."

A man beside him, this one in jeans and T-shirt although just as red-faced, nodded. "Yeah."

The owner furrowed his brow. "Is it too loud?"

The man in the suit snorted. "Don't you get it?" He waved at the TV. "Now they're talking about not even doing rocket launches anymore. They're talking about using fucking magic to build the moon base. Don't you think that's ridiculous?"

"I'm not quite following you." The owner grabbed a remote and muted the TV. "But I'll turn it down for now."

Alison sighed as she chewed on the uni.

The drunk in the suit shook his head. "Sometimes I feel like I'm the only fucking sane man on this planet."

The man next to him shook his head. "Nah, I've got your back, bro. I know what you're talking about. You see that shit below? They're letting that *animal* be a congressman. What the fuck is that?"

Alison's heart sped up, and she clenched her hands.

If I start a fight here, it'll just break a bunch of stuff and make trouble for the owner. I can control myself. Just some drunks. They'll wander off soon.

"What are you talking about?" the owner asked, his face a mask of confusion.

"Oriceran," shouted the first man. He shot out of his seat. "Think about it. Think about old people. They lived a long time knowing magic was bullshit. I grew up with elves and shit just being there, but for them, it was like all of a sudden, 'Oh, sorry. It was a big lie. There's this freaky planet that's connected to us through magical portals, freaky land of fairies and elves and shit.'" He slammed a fist on the counter, shaking the nearby plates. "And it was a big fucking lie. The Oris were screwing with us the entire time."

The elf couple in the corner glanced at the man, worried expression on their faces.

The owner shook his head. "Humans also participated in the coverup of magic. It wasn't the Oricerans oppressing us. Get over it."

"Who gives a shit?" growled the suited man. "The point is, humans were on top with our technology. Then the portals opened, and magic came back. Freaks came here, or

46

freaks were born here. Come on." He turned and gestured grandly. Everyone was watching him now. "It's not like it's some big secret. Everyone knows how much Oriceran fucked shit up. All the bullshit happened, magical criminals, and then we needed bounty hunters and anti-enhanced threat teams because you can't even walk down the street without some Ori summoning demons to suck your brains out or some shit. It used to be we had to worry about terrorists getting nukes. Now any person with magic *is* pretty much a nuke."

Alison's stomach knotted. It took a lot to make sushi and sashimi taste bad, but this bastard was doing it.

This is my happy place, asshole. Don't push me.

His friend nodded. "Yeah, I heard on tv that if it wasn't for the Oriceran shit, we would have been way more advanced already. We would have our own moon base already, fancy AI—the whole thing. Magic jacked up the world."

The owner shook his head. "People fear change. That doesn't make it bad. Life is change. You must adapt." He shrugged. "You could say the same thing about the invention of firearms or the Industrial Revolution or the rise of the internet."

The suited man shook his finger. "This isn't just about change. It's an invasion. How are we supposed to compete with those creatures? Oris should stay on their fucking planet. Magic's ruined everything." He flicked his tie with his hand. "I had three interviews today. You know why? Because I've been unemployed for six months. I already know what they're going to say, too, every time. 'Sorry, we don't need you, but thanks for applying.'" He sneered and slapped his chest. "You know why I lost my job? Because of magical automation." He glared at the elf couple. "No one gives a shit about non-magical types if there is money to be made. Maybe the Humanity Defense League has the right idea."

"Nah, bro," his friend offered. He shook his head.

The suited man glared at him, but the other man held up a hand.

"It's not just the Oris causing trouble. I read that the average high-level bounty is someone born on Earth." He snorted. "Think about that. The Humanity Defense League is all obsessed with humans, but the problem is the magic. New Veil's got it right—get rid of the magic. Who gives a shit then?"

The elf couple exchanged a few words with a waitress. After a quick swipe of a card through her portable POS terminal, they rose and headed toward the door.

Alison couldn't blame them. She too was about to leave before she lost her temper and smashed a few racists through the window. She didn't commit violence off the job.

The suited man laughed. "New Veil are a bunch of hypocrites. They say magic is bad, but they use magical artifacts. Fuck them. You can't trust anyone who uses magic, no matter what they say. This planet used to be better thirty years ago before magic came back. Before Oriceran reconnected with Earth and we found out how they'd manipulated history. Ignorance was fucking bliss, man."

The owner sighed and cleared his throat. "If you

gentleman can't control yourselves, I'm afraid I'm going to have to ask you to leave."

The two men snorted in unison. "I'm not paying for shit sushi from some Ori lover."

The owner pointed to the door. "Get out. If you come back, I'll call the police."

"Whatever." The suited man stomped toward the door, a smirk coming to his face. "Maybe we should clean up some Ori trash while we're out."

His friend grinned and nodded. The owner grabbed a phone and dialed. He whispered furtively, and she caught the words "aggressive drunks" and "they are too drunk to drive."

Alison sighed. All she had wanted to do was have some sushi, but the police might not race over to a sushi place because of a couple of drunks. She fished some cash out of her wallet and tossed it on the counter before moving toward the exit.

When she stepped outside, the elf couple were hurrying down the street, the two men close behind.

Alison ran toward them.

You bastards should have just gone to the parking lot.

"Hey, you fucking Oris," called out the suited man. "Where you going? Why you in such a hurry? Have some kid's soul you need to suck out to fuel a spell?"

The elf man frowned and turned around. "We've done nothing to you. Why don't you leave us alone?"

"Nothing to me?" The man laughed. "You've done something to my whole fucking *planet*, you Ori freak. But you got magic, right? Maybe you can blow me away with a spell?" He slapped both hands on his chest. "Show it to me, asshole. Show me the magic."

The elf woman sighed. "Just leave us alone. We only wanted some sushi."

The man's friend cracked his knuckles. "Wonder how quickly they can whip off some magic?"

Alison took a deep breath. "I wouldn't do that if I were you."

The two men spun, their faces twisted with anger.

"Who the fuck are you, bitch?" the suited man shouted.

"Someone who isn't interested in seeing two dumbasses mess with innocent people." Alison shrugged.

"Are you kidding me?" He pointed to the elves. "No such thing as an innocent Ori, and why are you taking their side? If you're a human being, you should take the side of humans, not some fucking elves. Stay the fuck out of shit that's not your business otherwise."

Alison rubbed her chin. "Well, I'd argue that if you weren't a piece-of-shit human being you wouldn't threaten people who've done nothing to you, but if it makes your little racist mind feel better, I'm half-elf. Half-human, half-dark elf. Drow more formally. You ever heard of Drow?" She gave him a hungry grin. "They're a warrior race, and they don't take shit from anyone on Earth or Oriceran."

The suited man narrowed his eyes. "You little bitch. You think you can scare me?"

She angled her arms and smiled. Shadow blades extended from her hands. "One thing you're right about: magic's changed everything. Want to see if a shadow can kill you, asshole?" Alison offered her sweetest smile.

The other man swallowed. "Come on, bro. It's not worth it. Let's head back to my place. No Oris there."

The suited man flipped Alison off. "Fuck you. Earth for humans, bitch."

Alison rolled her eyes. She waited as the men turned around and marched past her with a wide cushion as they headed toward the parking lot down the block. Once they were about ten yards away, she released the energy fueling the shadow blades.

She watched the men until they disappeared around a corner before returning her attention to the elf couple. A sigh of relief escaped her mouth. Beating down people on the job was one thing, but a day without violence was always nice, and in this case, *she* would be the one charged with using excessive force.

"You didn't have to do that," the man offered.

Alison shrugged. "No one said I did."

The woman eyed Alison, suspicion on her face. "I'll admit I'm surprised a Drow, even a half-Drow, would help Light Elves. Who are you, exactly?"

Alison grinned. "Alison Brownstone."

Understanding dawned on the woman's face, and she nodded to the man. "You're probably the only Drow princess who would risk herself for Light Elves. Our magic isn't so barbaric that it's useful in such situations." She sighed. "I apologize. I didn't mean to insult you."

"No offense taken. And it wasn't much of a risk with those two drunken yahoos, but I get it." Alison laughed. "Humans complain about Oricerans and Oricerans complain about other Oricerans." She waved. "Have a good night, and remember, those dicks don't represent all of humanity."

The two elves gave her a polite nod and walked away.

Alison continued down the block, making her way toward the parking lot. She hoped the racists would leave her alone on her way to her car.

Thirty years had passed, and in some ways, Earth and Oriceran were more integrated than ever. Not just space projects, but the large numbers of half-Oriceran, half-humans on the planet, not to mention all the families who found out there was hidden magic in their family lines. It was like the man had said—everyone now took it for granted that Earth was filled with magic.

A police car pulled into the parking lot, and she smiled as she closed on it. Even a half-human, half-elf family was normal in their own way, but she wasn't. Her own family had their own secrets, which were even wilder than the truth of Oriceran and Earth.

I'm doomed to never have a normal life, but that would be kind of boring anyway.

Alison spotted the drunks arguing with a police officer and smirked. Assholes were assholes, regardless of species. They were getting what they deserved without her having to spend a night filling out a statement.

She continued toward her Fiat. Time to head home, relax, and get a little sleep.

CHAPTER FIVE

Alison's eyes snapped open to the harsh sound of her phone ringing. She blinked several times at the blackness. The magical energy radiating off her glasses on the nightstand was the only color she could make out with her naked eyes. She slipped them on to return full vision to her world before picking her phone up and blinking a few times as her eyes adjusted to the phone's light.

UNKNOWN NUMBER.

"Damn it. The election's over. This better not be another damned robocall. All this magic and technology and we still have these spammy calls."

She slid her finger over the phone to answer it.

"Hello?"

Someone took a deep breath on the other end. "I'm attempting to reach Alison Brownstone," replied a male voice. His vowel emphasis was strange, but she couldn't attribute any particular accent to it.

Alison furrowed her brow. "Who is calling?"

"You can call me Mr. D," the man responded.

She snorted. "How very pointlessly mysterious of you."

"I would think a woman who has chosen your vocation could understand why a man might want to be circumspect with his identity."

Alison stifled a yawn and looked out the window. Darkness cloaked the world. Mr. D was an early riser.

"Is this about a job?" she asked.

"Yes," he responded. "One that I think that your unique background and pedigree are well-suited for."

Alison frowned. "Just to be clear, I'm not my dad. I don't make a business of hunting down bounties."

"But you will do item recovery, will you not?" Mr. D took a deep breath and slowly let it out.

"Yes, but I'm not a tomb raider either."

He chuckled. "Don't worry, I don't need anyone to go to far-off ruins. If you're interested, come to the Orange Room." He rattled off an address in Georgetown. "I'd like to meet you there tonight at ten. It's a restaurant, so you might want to avoid dinner. Be aware that this is a restaurant for magically-inclined beings. I'd prefer if you came alone, but if you must bring someone else, make sure they have magic."

Alison frowned. "And if I say no to coming?"

"Then nothing," Mr. D responded. "You're my first choice for this job, but you're not my only choice."

She thought it over for a few seconds. "It won't hurt to talk."

"Generally it doesn't. Not always."

Alison laughed. "Fine. I'll see you there."

Alison crossed the street from the parking lot and approached the building. A simple sign reading THE ORANGE ROOM hung over the orange wooden door. No windows pierced the brick walls, and nothing outside gave any indication what type of business it was.

She moved to the door, and her hand hovered over the handle for a moment before she turned it.

Nothing. That was what she saw. There was an empty, dusty room lit by a single LED ceiling lamp.

Alison frowned and stepped inside. The door slammed behind her, and the entire room blurred. A moment later, a crowded but intimate dining room filled with tables appeared. Light classical music played in the background.

Several Light Elves sat at a table smiling and chatting. A group of witches in elegant evening dresses sat at another table, their expressions serious. A dozen gnomes in matching blue suits were clustered around three small tables.

Alison grimaced. She was in jeans, a t-shirt, and her red denim jacket, not exactly up to the dress code.

She relaxed after looking around some more. One table was surrounded by what looked like Venus Fly Traps with legs and two vaguely humanoid creatures made of crystal.

Huh. Technically, aren't they naked?

A suited elf in a tuxedo and bow tie approached her. He looked her up and down with faint disdain. "Can I help you, Miss?"

Alison glanced at the tables. Anyone in the restaurant

could be her potential client. She didn't even know what species he was.

"I'm here to see Mr. D."

The disdain melted from the elf's face. "Ah." He gestured. "Please follow me."

Alison nodded. Apparently, Mr. D had juice. She could work with that.

She trailed after the elf maître d as he led her to the far side of the room. A gnome sat at a table by himself. Unlike the other gnomes present, he wore a black suit. There was an empty plate in front of him, but a plate with a grilled chicken breast surrounded by microgreens sat opposite him.

Mr. D nodded to the chair in front of the chicken breast. "Please join me, Miss Brownstone." His gaze flicked to the elf. "Do not disturb us."

The elf gave a polite nod before leaving.

Alison took the seat and grabbed a fork from the arrayed silverware. "I'm assuming this is for me?"

"Yes. I took the liberty of ordering." Mr. D's strange vowel emphasis continued.

Alison didn't understand. It wasn't like gnomes couldn't handle normal human speech, but she'd run into a lot of strange Oricerans in her time. Just because someone looked vaguely humanoid didn't mean they had the same psychology as a human from Earth. Oriceran, after all, was a magical planet with a vast number of diverse intelligent races.

After ingesting a forkful of chicken with a perfect balance of salt and thyme, Alison smiled at the gnome. "I thought they were going to throw me out. Didn't mention a dress code."

"There isn't one, as such." Mr. D's gaze cut around the room for a few seconds. "Especially for my guests."

Alison downed some greens. "I'm here. Let's talk about the job."

"Straight to the point, are we?" The gnome overemphasized the T sounds this time in addition to the vowels.

"Yes. You called me, so you obviously know my skills and background." Alison shrugged. "Let me make this clear: because of that, I'm not here to sell myself to you. I'm here to listen to your job offer and decide if I'm interested. Whatever you think you know about my family and me, know this: I'm not in this job for the money, and if I think a job's going to make the world a worse place, I walk."

Mr. D gave her a thin smile, but it didn't reach his eyes. "Then it's a fortunate confluence of circumstances, Miss Brownstone, for both of us."

"What do you mean?"

"The job," Mr. D replied. "There was a certain item stolen from me by a wizard named Terrence McKenna. I'd like to pay you for its recovery."

Alison eyed him. "And you want me to kill the wizard?"

The gnome shrugged. "I don't care if he lives or dies. I think the world would be a better place without him, but that's a subjective judgment. I care about the item—a small gem. Needless to say, it's magical. Not so needless to say, it's very unstable and dangerous. It can enhance magical power, but if overused, it can lead to…destruction."

"Destruction?" Alison frowned. "Like what?"

"Like towns blowing up." Mr. D let out a weary sigh. "I don't wish to go too far into the background, but a cousin of mine with some talent made the gem. I took possession of it from him once I realized its instability. I was preparing to destroy it, but because of its nature, it can't be destroyed through trivial means unless one doesn't care about the area around it being vaporized as well. My research suggests that attempting to send it to the World in Between might set it off, but fortunately, it won't blow up without heavy long-term use. We have some time, even with that idiot McKenna using it, before it's a risk, but I'd rather not leave it be. I'd hate for my cousin to feel guilty about blowing a city up."

Alison shook her head. "If this thing was so dangerous, why didn't you turn it over to the Paranormal Defense Agency?"

The gnome barked a laugh, but after a moment he frowned. "Oh, you're serious. Let's just say that turning dangerous things over to the government doesn't work out so well. Given your family's history, I'd think you of all people would understand that."

Alison shrugged. "Okay, I see your point, but how do I know you're telling the truth?"

He shrugged. "Feel free to use a truth detection spell."

"You might be able to beat that."

"Perhaps, but the offer is there."

Alison smiled. "I've got a better idea." She reached up and pulled off her glasses.

She squinted for a moment as a riot of colors assaulted her eyes. Every inch of the restaurant shone with magical energy. After a moment, she focused on the gnome in front of her, taking in his aura. Ennui, embarrassment, confusion, and annoyance danced together, but only the faintest strains of something more sinister.

"Interesting," Mr. D murmured. "I thought so."

Alison frowned and returned her glasses to her face. "What do you mean?"

Mr. D pointed to the glasses. "I had some contact with the gnome who made them."

"Why am I not surprised?" Alison sighed.

She knew her mom had gotten them from a gnome named Tubal-Cain, but the whole project had turned complicated, and the gnome had kept pushing the delivery date back until years had passed. At least no deposit had been involved.

Alison shrugged. "You look honest to me, but I need more details about the job."

"It's simple. I've tracked McKenna to Seattle, but my magic fails me past that. So I need someone who can hit the street but is also magical. He's a very dangerous wizard, Miss Brownstone, with little regard for innocent life. That makes him a crude boor in my estimation, but he's ultimately a coward, which gives us an opportunity for you to find him and recover the gem before he masters it. If you want to kill him, be my guest, but that's secondary to the recovery of the gem. I will pay you a large fee upfront with the balance upon completion, along with a daily stipend, since I understand this might take some time. I also have a number for a local contact who might be able to facilitate your search."

He snapped his fingers, and a folded piece of paper winked into existence. He slid it over to her. "Is this sufficient to get you started?"

Alison unfolded the paper and nodded. Money wasn't a strong concern, but she didn't want people thinking they could hire her for pocket change either.

"Seattle, huh?" Alison smiled. "Never been there. Okay, Mr. D, I'll get your gem."

CHAPTER SIX

Alison pushed into the Starbucks, turning immediately down the hallway and passing through a wall past the bathrooms. It wasn't like she was there to get coffee. She started down the metal stairs.

She smirked as she considered the ranting racists from the other night. They had gone on and on about magic infiltrating the world, but there were still so many secrets.

Most people believed Starbucks existed to serve coffee, and they did do that, but the truth was the chain had spread for a more utilitarian magical reason.

Alison hit the end of the stairs and smiled. A long line of people waited in an underground train station. A shiny red metal train car was at the platform, doors open, and various magicals filtered inside.

Racist Boy would probably stroke out if he learned there was a network of magical underground trains that go to anywhere Starbucks is located.

"We're beneath your feet," Alison murmured to herself. "Muahahaha."

A gnome bumped into her and scowled, muttering, "Watch it, asshole."

Alison sniffed disdainfully and rolled her eyes. "Drow."

Assholes in every species.

She tugged on her red jacket and made her way into the line. She didn't want to miss her train. People continued filing forward, riders filtering into the seats on either side of the train car. Non-magical people couldn't even touch the car without a nasty surprise, and most didn't even know about it.

She wondered why the various governments still tolerated the magic trains. *Some* non-magical government officials outside of the PDA and their equivalents had to know about them. Perhaps they worried that trying to control something so convenient would lead to pushback they weren't ready for.

In a world of magical criminals, cultists, and terrorists, hassling peaceful commuters had to be low on the list. Various spells and hidden magical security personnel ensured the safety of the underground railways as well, meaning the governments had less to worry about.

Relief passed through Alison as she stepped onto the train and snagged the second-to-last seat. For all the convenience of the magical trains, they didn't run constantly.

She leaned back with a smile as the train lurched forward, steam billowing around them, the tunnel and track becoming a blur. No matter how many times she took the train, the wonder remained.

Alison stepped off the car into a thick crowd. She pushed past several frowning wizards on her way to the stairs.

She sighed. "This is what I get for choosing to go to the original Starbucks. Of *course* it's going to be crowded."

A few minutes of jostling and stern looks let her close on the exit stairs. A Gray Elf stood near the wall playing a glowing lute. In the dense mass of magicals surrounding the train, Alison couldn't make out anything but the cacophony of voices, but a few yards away, the voices vanished and only the music remained, a faint magical residue in the air.

Each strummed note produced cascading and overlapping harmonies. She smiled and paused, taking in the performance. She rarely saw Gray Elves other than her friend Lily, and these days she rarely even saw her.

The elf continued playing for a couple of minutes before stopping.

He looked around, his gray eyes filled with mischief. "I guess you're my only audience at the moment."

Alison chuckled. "You want some money, or is there something else you're busking for?"

"Money." He shrugged and reached into his pocket. He pulled out a card with a QR code.

Alison pulled out her phone and brought up a money transfer app. She scanned the code and sent some cash the man's way.

"Surprised you're not making more." She nodded toward the crowd. "Busy place, and this is the original Starbucks, the place that started the entire railway."

The busker shrugged. "Depends on the day. Today's just not a music appreciation day. Sometimes I make so much money I figure I can move to Mercer Island." He chuckled. "Been to Seattle before?"

Alison shook her head. "Nope. Somehow I've never been here."

He bowed with a grand flourish. "Then let me welcome you to the great city of Seattle. Let me also share a little secret."

"A secret?" She arched a white brow.

"Yeah. It's the original coffee shop, but it's not the original station." He shrugged. "At least that's what I've heard. They just let everyone think it is to help protect the magic that powers the entire system. Especially since, well...the incident."

"Incident?" Alison winced. "Oh, you mean *that* incident."

The busker nodded. "You'd think people would have figured it out, but ever since then, you know, they like to call us the Wild West of Magic."

"Wild West, huh?"

Most major cities had a kemana underneath them. Prior to magic returning fully to Earth with the connection to Oriceran, maintaining magical energy had been much more challenging. In distant millennia past, before the portals had last closed, various underground areas with large deposits of quartz were imbued with magical energy to act as recharging stations. Magical cities and towns had grown up around them to provide a place for magicals to live without fear or risk of exposure.

With the open return of magic kemanas had diminished in importance, but most maintained at least some population, although concerns about the so-called 'Dulled Quartz

Belt' had arisen in the United States, with equivalents in other countries. Younger magicals were not as concerned about special magical towns. If a person could freely walk on the surface and had little trouble maintaining their magical energy, it was hard to convince them of the continuing importance of kemanas.

Seattle's kemana, though, was a special and terrible case. Alison's hands clenched just thinking about it. Fifteen years ago, the magical community of Seattle had been the site of a devasting magical terrorist incident. Galbraithian wizards, disciples of the dark wizard Michael Galbraith, had unleashed a horrific artifact, destroying the kemana. The worst part was that Galbraith had been dead for ten years at that point, but his twisted soldiers marched on with his nihilistic plans.

Alison didn't care about anyone's logic, plans, or creed. She had a very Brownstonian solution to dark wizards: shoot them until they stop moving.

She blew out a breath. "Is the kemana still trashed, then?"

The busker sighed and nodded. "Nothing to see there but rubble."

"What's cool just for basic normal tourism?" Alison shrugged. "I'm here on business, but I'd hate to miss cool stuff. I don't necessarily need to see magical stuff."

He smiled. "The minute you step outside the Starbucks, you're in Pike Place Market. Plenty of touristy stuff there. Heck, go watch the guys throwing fish."

Alison pulled out her phone. "Yeah. Can't check into my hotel yet, so I might as well." She waved. "Thanks for the help and the music."

"No problem. Enjoy Seattle. We're really more than coffee." He winked.

Alison laughed and headed for the stairs.

Watching men throw fish back and forth proved exciting for about ten minutes. Apparently she wasn't in as much of a touristy mood as she'd expected, Alison left the market and made her way toward the old wooden piers extending into Elliot Bay.

She inhaled deeply, enjoying the salty scent of the water. A Ferris wheel stood down the street, along with a massive aquarium complex. A cold wind blew off the water and she shivered, rubbing her elbows through her jacket.

"Huh. Maybe this whole area is a bit *too* touristy," she murmured.

"Can anything be too touristy?" asked a woman's voice behind Alison.

She turned around. A beautiful Asian woman with long black hair wearing a black wool coat stood behind Alison. Her arms were crossed, and she had a faint smile on her face. Her open coat revealed her outfit, which impressed Alison with its audacity given the chilly temperatures and wind coming off the bay: knee-high black boots, a short black skirt, and a midriff-baring red top.

"Aren't you cold in that outfit?" Alison blurted.

The woman laughed and shrugged. "Style before comfort, I always say."

The woman's mouth quirked into a bigger smile. Alison sensed the tingle of magic in the air.

She chuckled and removed her glasses for a moment. She pretended to clean them with the bottom of her shirt while staring at the woman with the full benefit of her magical sight.

Attending a magical high school near a magical creature reserve had allowed Alison to experience a huge number of different types of magical energy signatures—so many that she was rarely surprised anymore.

She barely stopped herself from gasping.

A golden-red hue surrounded the woman, and multiple fluctuating golden tails of energy appeared and disappeared. Different colors spiked the woman's soul, indicative of intense curiosity and amusement but also strong undercurrents of fear.

What the hell are you? And are you thinking the same thing? You afraid of me or something else?

Seeing fear in people's souls had long ago stopped disturbing Alison. In the busy modern world, many people, regardless of magical ability, carried fear.

Alison slipped her glasses back on. "Maybe I'm just jealous because I couldn't rock that outfit regardless of temperature."

The woman thrust out her hand. "Hana."

Alison took her hand. "Alison."

Hana looked Alison up and down. "So you're visiting our fine city?"

"Here on a little business, but was seeing the sights first." She shrugged. "Killing time for a few minutes before I check in at my hotel. It's pretty close to here. Figured I'd take in some stuff, but so far I've visited the first Starbucks and seen some guys throwing fish. I felt sorry for the fish, even though they were dead."

Hana laughed. "Yeah, it's cute the first time you see it, but I can only see so many flying fish." She smiled. "I'm a Seattle native. If you want to see cooler stuff, I could show you around." She shrugged.

Alison stared at her. "Um, not to be a suspicious bitch, but why?"

Hana winked and leaned in. "Look, I get that without a kemana, a lot of newer magical people don't know how to get their bearings. All this magic and people are still afraid of things like the internet."

"That obvious?" Alison eyed the woman again, still trying to figure out what she might be.

Hana nodded and looked around. No one else was close. "Even if I couldn't tell normally, your glasses reek of magic." She tapped her nose. "I can smell it. Besides, you look interesting. I feel like I've seen you somewhere before, too, and that's not just a line."

On one of those stupid documentaries they made about my adoption?

Alison chuckled. "I think I just have one of those kinds of faces."

Hana walked over to her and threw an arm over her shoulder. "So, what kind of things are you into? Consider me your unofficial ambassador to the city. You can be my good deed for the day."

Alison wrinkled her nose at the strong scent of Hana's perfume. The woman seriously needed to dial it down.

"Sushi."

Hana pulled away and clasped her hands together. "Maneki," she shouted, spinning around. "Of course!"

"Huh?" Alison blinked.

Hana stopped spinning and grinned. "Maneki. It's a Japanese restaurant. It's kind of a local institution. It's been here since 1904. Great sushi. Great atmosphere." She pointed at herself with her thumb. "My last name is Sugimoto, by the way. I'm Japanese. Well, Japanese-American." She waved a finger. "The point is I grew up on Japanese food, so I know good Japanese food, including sushi. We should go. Heck, we should go right now. It's only about a mile from here."

Alison rubbed her chin. "It sounds great, but I'm just not that hungry. Hate to go to a great new place and not feel up to eating anything."

"Oh, oh." Hana snapped. "Then let me show you cool stuff until you work up an appetite."

"I don't know. I'm kind of waiting to check into my hotel."

Hana waved a hand. "Come on, Alison. You can wait until tonight to worry about that." She looked at the sky and smiled. "I think it was perhaps fate that I met you to show you around today. Well, that and I was bored and didn't have anything else to do." She lowered her head to look at Alison. "And I'll go back to being bored if you blow me off. Come on, let me show you around. My treat."

Alison sighed. "One second. I need to check on something with a business contact. Even if I can't check in, I might have to do some work stuff today."

"Oh? What kind of work do you do?"

Alison shrugged and pulled her phone. "Kind of a

consulting thing. This is a vaguely non-disclosure type thing, so I'm going to make the call over there."

It was close to the truth.

"Would it help if I stuck my fingers in my ears?" Hana smirked.

Alison chuckled. "It'll just take a second."

She trekked to the edge of the pier and dialed the number Mr. D had given her. It rang three times before someone picked up.

"Yes?" came a smooth male voice over the line.

"Mr. D gave me your number," she replied, her voice quiet. "Assuming this is Vincent?"

"I see. What matter is this concerning?"

Alison took a deep breath. "I was told you could help me find Terrence McKenna."

Vincent let out a disappointed sigh. "Of course. Yes, I've been expecting your call, Miss Brownstone, and yes, I should be able to help you, but I'm in the middle of something. I can meet with you in two days."

Alison blinked at the phone. "Two days? Are you kidding me?"

"No. Two days." A faint hint of amusement colored Vincent's voice.

"There's no way we can meet earlier? This is important." Alison frowned, her hand tightening around her phone.

"Everything's always important to everyone. Two days. Contact me then. If you bother me too much, it'll take longer. Have a good day."

Vincent ended the call.

Alison's head slumped, and she groaned.

"Problem?" Hana asked.

Alison took a deep breath and shook her head. "No, but my business contact can't even meet with me for two days. I wasn't expecting that."

Joy exploded over Hana's face. "Perfect. Then you can hang out with me, at least today. Don't worry, girlfriend, I'll show you the real Seattle."

Alison chuckled. "Why the hell not?"

Hana laughed. "Yes. Some of the best days of my life have started with me saying 'Why the hell not?'" She looked around. "Got a car?"

"Uh, no, I took the train directly here."

"Were you hoping to see something special at the first Starbucks?"

Alison shrugged. "Kind of."

"Lots of magical types do." Hana winked. "Don't worry, I'll hook you up."

CHAPTER SEVEN

Alison stepped out the Currus sedan, followed by Hana. When magic had returned, most people envisioned dragons and turning lead into gold, not so much self-driving cars navigated by spells. She wasn't sure if she trusted them either, and she couldn't quite put her finger on why. Maybe a little of her dad's natural distrust of complicated things had leaked into her personality.

The car zoomed down the street, nearly silent; an electric car controlled by magic, the ultimate fusion of technology and magic.

At least it's not a weapon. They could add a few magical enhancements to power armor and make something very scary. Maybe the black ops guys are doing just that already.

Hana rubbed her hands together and flung an arm to her side. "Behold my surprise! And thanks for not looking until I said to."

They stood underneath the down-angled end of a tall trellis bridge. There was nothing special about that, but the massive concrete giant emerging from underneath the bridge was a bit more noticeable. Concrete dipped over one eye to imply hair, and a polished hubcap provided the visible eye. The statue's hand was large enough to hold an ancient Volkswagen Beetle.

Alison's brow lifted. "Okay, that's cool. I didn't know about this. I didn't exactly read up on all the interesting sites." She tilted her head. Faint magic radiated off the statue. "Or is this more than just a statue?"

Hana nodded, her grin stuck on her face. "This is the Fremont Troll. The official story is that this was part of a revitalization project way back in the '90s. This area was filled with drug dealers and crime."

A dense clutch of expensive-looking townhouses surrounded the Troll, with not a single sketchy person in sight. Alison couldn't say whether that was the result of a magical art project or a half-century of economic growth spilling into all parts of Seattle along with the massive skyscrapers and swarms of drones flowing around the center of the city.

"But it's magical." Alison took a few steps toward the Troll. "Or I can sense magic coming from it anyway."

Hana sniffed at the air. "Yeah. Definitely magical. You really didn't read up on Seattle before showing up, did you? Lazy, girlfriend."

Alison shrugged. "I figured I'd just be here a few weeks and focused on business. I didn't expect my local inf...local contact to blow me off for a couple of days."

Hana pointed to the Fremont Troll's eye. "Here's the deal. It's not just magical; it's an actual stone giant."

"Shit. Seriously?" Alison blinked a few times. "Is he awake?"

The other woman bounded toward the giant and hopped on top of his right hand, which was splayed on the ground. "Nope. Very powerful containment spell is keeping him asleep. Those old-school magic cops were involved—what were they called? Yeah, the Silver Griffins. The rumors say it was some sort of dark-wizard attempt to kind of reveal magic. No one really knows for sure, and it's not like the Griffins are around anymore to explain things."

Alison nodded slowly as she crept toward the Fremont Troll, her gaze fixed on its hubcap eye. "Why did you ask me about if I'd read up on Seattle? Is he about to wake up? If so, shouldn't you get off?"

Hana bounded up the Troll's arm until she stood on his shoulder, her slender arms out to either side. "Nope, he's not going to wake up. Hopefully. The thing is, this area has gentrified a lot over the last ten years. Property values are through the roof, but they say they won't go much higher because there's a worry the Fremont Troll might wake up one day and go on a rampage, so the local HOAs are trying to convince the city council to move him."

Alison couldn't bring herself to jump on the giant. It seemed rude. She wouldn't have liked it if pixies walked across her while she slept.

"Why don't they just move him then?" she asked. "I'm sure they can stick him in a warehouse or something."

"No easy way to do it without disrupting the containment spell." Hana leapt from the top of the shoulder and landed with ease despite the ridiculous height of her boot heels. "Everybody has known about this for thirty years and the city council never cared, but money talks, and they're trying to spin it as a big public safety thing." She walked toward Alison and shrugged. "I'd kind of like to see him wake up. Everyone assumes he's going to be an asshole, but maybe he'd be cool, you know?"

A soft smile took over Alison's face. "Good point. You ever hear of the School of Necessary Magic?"

Hana looked to the side and ran her tongue inside her cheek. "Isn't that the government-sponsored magic high school in Virginia? Wasn't it one of the first magic schools?"

"Yeah. I went to that school, but it was built on top of a large kemana on an old estate. I dealt with a lot of different magical creatures there, which really taught me not to judge." Alison shrugged. "Well, that, and a few other things."

She looked down and smiled softly. Everyone feared her large tattooed father as a dangerous bounty hunter, the so-called Granite Ghost and Scourge of Harriken, but she'd looked into his soul and seen the beauty there long before he'd settled down.

Hana walked over to Alison and placed her hand on her shoulder. A faint tingle spread from Alison's shoulder and the other woman leaned in, her dark hair falling and framing her face—obvious magic. Her dark round eyes changed to slit yellow pupils.

"Let's just relax," Hana murmured in a low, husky voice. "This is fun, isn't it? I told you I'd show you something cool."

Alison stared at Hana. "What exactly are you doing?"

"We're just chatting." Hana fluttered her eyelashes. "And relaxing." A panicked look spread over her face, and she jerked her arm back. "Um, sorry. Forget about that. I...

damn it." She blinked, and her eyes returned to normal. "I almost made a big mistake."

Alison stared at her. "Oh, I'm sorry. I get what this is, and I should make things clear. I didn't mean to lead you on."

Hana stared at Alison for a few seconds. "What?"

"I'm not into girls." She shrugged. "Sorry. You're cute and all, but I'm straight." She thought the situation over for a second, wondering what the hell the tingling was and why Hana's eyes had changed. Maybe it was just a reflection of attraction.

The other woman nodded and shifted from foot to foot. "Oh, yeah, sure. Um. Darn it." She snapped. "All the good girls are taken. Yeah, that's exactly what this is." She laughed nervously.

Wait. I'm being dad-level obtuse here, and not in the way I thought.

Alison narrowed her eyes. "Then again, if you were just hitting on me, you wouldn't have tried to use magic on me."

Hana backed away, her hands raised in front of her. "I think you're misunderstanding what happened. I wasn't trying to use magic on you. Like you said, just a misunderstanding."

"What did you mean about making a big mistake? You were going to do something and then backed off. What, exactly? Put me to sleep? Take over my mind?" Alison narrowed her eyes. "I wasn't totally honest with you earlier, Hana, so let me be honest with you now."

"Honest about what?" Hana kept a smile on her face, although panic screamed in her eyes.

"I'm here on business. Security consultant business." Alison lifted her hand and summoned a shadow blade. "I'm hunting a very dangerous wizard, and now I wonder if he sent someone my way first. Quick lesson on dealing with me, something I learned from my dad: if you want to take me down, you better do it before I know you're coming at me."

Hana sighed. "Guess that explains why you had the gun."

"Noticed that, huh?" Alison took a step forward and scraped the ground with the shadow blade.

Hana grimaced. "Whoa. Just back up, girlfriend. I mean, *whoa*. Let's put the shadow sword away and calm down. I didn't do anything to you. Yes, I *started* to, but I stopped myself, so you know, no harm, no foul, right?"

"I'm going to give you one chance. You tell me what the hell you were just trying to do or we're going to have an unpleasant discussion about it. Extreme discomfort might be involved." Alison pointed the blade at the other woman. "Please don't run."

Something didn't seem right. When Alison had looked at her soul earlier she had spotted fear, but nothing sinister.

The dark-haired woman face-palmed, a frown appearing on her face for the first time since Alison had met her. "I can't believe my damned luck. I thought you were just a stupid business bitch, and I run into some sort of witch assassin."

"Not a witch. You see a wand?" Alison waved the sword a few times. "Half-Drow."

"Oh, fuck my life." Hana collapsed to her knees. "A

damned Drow? Look, this was really nothing personal. I... shit." She let out a strangled laugh. "I'm going to die in front of the Fremont Troll. The worst part is, I'm normally not so sloppy. Look, we can work a deal? I can do something for you. I can make it up to you."

Alison lifted her glasses for a moment. Fear loomed large in Hana's soul now, along with a healthy amount of embarrassment and regret. Other complex emotions and feelings twined together in her energy, but the core was of a good but wounded person.

This isn't the soul of a dark-wizard assassin.

"I'm not going to kill you if I don't have a good reason," Alison explained, still holding her glasses up but keeping her shadow blade pointed at the other woman. "Now, let me talk about how this is going to work. I'm going to ask two simple questions and you'd better damned well be honest with me because that's going to determine how the rest of this conversation will unfold. I'll know if you're lying. Got it?"

Hana nodded quickly and stared at the glasses, understanding dawning on her face. She blew out a breath. "Ask your questions."

"First, question, what the hell are you?"

The other woman stood and curtsied. Nine glowing yellow tails appeared behind her. "Different cultures have different names for my kind, but the most straightforward is nine-tailed fox."

Nothing in her energy indicated she was lying.

Alison nodded. "Then you're a type of shifter?"

Hana shook her head. "No, not like that. I mean, sure, I can turn into a fox, but I don't know all the magic and biology behind it. I just know we're different than, say, a werewolf. We're also rare, even by the standards of magicals. Used to be more of us in Asia back in the day, but a lot of wizards and sorcerers hunted my kind as…spell and potion components or just out of fear of our charm magic." She shuddered. "Lot of slaughters in the 19th and 20th centuries; most nine-tailed foxes were killed then. We kept a lower profile after that. Lot of us emigrated from Asia to avoid the hunters there."

"I've heard of nine-tailed foxes, but just in stories. Never realized they were real. So, you were lying earlier? You emigrated from Japan? What are you like, two hundred or something?"

Hana snorted. "No, I'm only twenty-two. I was born here." She pursed her lips. "My parents came over from Japan before I was born." A wistful expression covered her face. "They were killed when the Galbrathians destroyed the kemana. I know it's not an excuse, but after I lost them, I had to take care of myself. A lot of people didn't want anything to do with some weird creature they didn't understand. Had to make a lot of less than optimal choices to survive. It's a hard world." She shrugged.

"Trust me, I know." Alison furrowed her brow and nodded at the tails. "Those only appear when you want them?"

"No." The glowing tails vanished. "If I use major magic, they do. The charm spell is half-seduction, half-magic, so I can generally keep my fox traits from being too obvious." Hana shrugged. "It's why if I'm going to charm someone, I like to get them alone just in case."

Alison nodded. "Now on to the most important question: why were you trying to charm me?"

The other woman sat there, head down, not saying anything for a long moment before looking up and sighing. "Look, this isn't how I normally do things. Yes, I'm a con artist, but I have limits. I've never believed in going too far, and what I was about to do was way over the damned line. I freely admit that."

Alison kept her attention on her energy. The dark colors of regret spiked, almost overwhelming the rest. She hadn't lied once that Alison could tell.

"Go on."

Hana shrugged. "It was you or me, okay? I don't want to die or become a plaything for sick bastards." She ran a hand through her dark hair and shook her head. "I didn't want to have to deliver anyone to those bastards either, but they gave me twenty-four hours or I was going to end up chained up and whored out in some basement, if not dead."

"Who wanted you to deliver me? Terrence McKenna?"

"Terrence McKenna?" Hana blinked. "Who the hell is that?"

"A dark wizard. Why did you need me if you don't know who that is? You were targeting me, right?"

"No. I didn't even know who you were. You just look like a good...sorry, a good sucker." Hana shook her head. "So not you specifically. The Daimyo said I had to deliver him a cute young woman, preferably magical, for his brothel or I'd either end up dead or taking her place." She pushed herself up. "I know I can't even ask for your forgiveness. You might as well kill me here. I have it coming, and it's more merciful than what he has in store for me."

"Daimyo?" Alison frowned. "Wait, like a Japanese warlord?"

"That's what he calls himself. He's a major player in the Eastern Union. You know about them?"

Alison nodded. "I've heard of them. Fusion of some Yakuza and Russian mafia groups, really into the illegal artifact trade. Newish, right? Popped up mostly in the last ten years, and mostly on the West Coast. I haven't run into them personally before, but I'm from LA originally, and it doesn't have those kinds of groups with major influence anymore."

"Oh, yeah. Brownstone and his guys are down there." Hana shrugged. "Anyway, that about covers it. The Daimyo is the leader of one the bigger Eastern Union organizations in Seattle. I...fucked up recently. I ran up a gambling debt with them. Thought I could charm my way out of it but he was ready for me, so I've been stuck doing all sorts of dirty work." She shuddered. "Charming cops to look the other way, courier work taking who knows what, even petty garbage like picking up his dry cleaning."

Alison blinked. "Seriously? His *dry cleaning*?"

"Seriously, girlfriend, this guy is as petty as he is evil." Hana kicked a pebble toward the Fremont Troll. "It wasn't that bad when I was just charming cops, but then I got the twenty-four-hour deadline."

"Why didn't you just go to the police?"

Hana laughed. "The Eastern Union has its tentacles in the cops too. Not saying Seattle cops are super-corrupt, but if I go to the police, I bet you I get stopped by some random patrol car and get a bullet in my head a day later. And before you ask, I can't run away. He's used oath magic on me. I can't leave Seattle without dying." She pulled up her top. A complex red glyph sat on her skin right beneath her bra. "See?"

Alison frowned. She'd seen dark wizards use this kind of spell before, but was surprised a non-magical human could pull it off. The right artifact could empower even the weakest man, apparently.

Don't know if that's a good thing or a bad one overall, but in this case, this guy might have control over a lot of dangerous people.

Hana shook her head. "I don't even know why I'm telling you all this. Let's just…get this shit over with. Somehow I always knew I'd die a cheap death." She swallowed and knelt. "I'd appreciate it if you could just take my head off cleanly. Better luck next life, I hope." She let out a nervous chuckle and took a deep breath.

Alison sighed and lowered her arm. The shadow blade faded into nothingness. "I'm not going to kill you, Hana. I don't know what I *am* going to do, though. I can't let you wander around tourist traps trying to kidnap women to give as prostitutes to organized crime."

Hana looked away, a hint of a tear in her eye. "I didn't want to do it, but I didn't have a choice. The Daimyo might be a human, but he's got so many artifacts and thugs… It's not like I can do anything. I know that's no excuse, and if you can see that I'm telling the truth, then you know I feel a piece of shit for trying this."

"Maybe I should pay this guy a visit and have a discussion with him about renegotiating your debt." Alison frowned. "And convince him to reconsider his business model."

"You might be tough, but you're one woman. You don't want to mess with this guy. He's a survivor. He used to be in the Harriken. You heard of them? That big gang James Brownstone destroyed? This guy survived facing James Brownstone. He was wounded, but he didn't die. He joined the Yakuza after Brownstone took down the Harriken."

Alison's hands clenched into fists, and her heart thundered. "He's a damned Harriken?"

Hana nodded, her eyes wide. "Yeah. Used to be. The point is, this is a guy who basically survived the equivalent of a nuclear weapon going off around him. You could call that luck or toughness, but if I had to bet, I'd say he's a born survivor."

Alison let out a quiet chuckle that built into a loud laugh.

Hana blinked several times and backed away from her. "You okay there, Alison?"

She stopped laughing and gave a curt nod. "You see, I kind of owe the Harriken."

"Owe the Harriken?" Hana's face scrunched in confusion. "Unless you're a lot older than you look, they were wiped out when you were, like, a teenager, right?"

"Some other time I'll tell you the full story, but the short version is, the Harriken murdered my mother. Tortured her to death. They planned to do the same thing to me, but a man saved me and adopted me." Alison looked over her shoulder at the Fremont Troll. "An already-awakened giant who is one bad motherfucker." She returned her gaze to

Hana. "And that man destroyed the Harriken." She chuckled. "I never did tell you my last name."

Hana's eyes widened. "No way."

"That's right. I'm Alison Brownstone."

"I know I have no right to ask you for help, but if anyone can win against the Daimyo, it'd be a Brownstone." The nine-tailed fox clasped her hands together and pled with her eyes. "I'll do anything. You can bind me with oath magic if you want. Just help me get away. If the Daimyo dies, the oath magic on me dies with him."

Alison snorted. "I don't do that kind of magic, but it doesn't matter because I'm happy to help you. I owe the Harriken and that bastard is Harriken, so this is personal." She took a deep breath. "It's time to have a talk with the Daimyo."

CHAPTER EIGHT

Alison and Hana strolled up the sidewalk toward the four-story office building looming in the distance, the headquarters of the Daimyo's Eastern Union group. They'd come up with something approaching a plan on the way over in another Currus, but there were still a few details to work out.

"How am I supposed to act?" Alison asked. "Should I be acting all zombie-like or something?"

Hana shook her head. "No. When I charm someone, they just like me a lot more. It makes them suggestible, but I can't order them around like puppets." She took a deep breath. "I can't believe we're about to do this."

They stepped toward double-glass doors etched with an elaborate geometric logo and the large etched words KYUSHU SURPRISE IMPORT/EXPORT. The doors slid open, and the women continued inside. Two large men in suits, one Russian and one Japanese, stood on either side of a metal detector. A third man sat at a desk, a computer monitor in front of him.

Hana smiled at the guards. "Remember me? I've got a friend I want the Daimyo to meet." She patted Alison on the shoulder. "This is my new friend Alison."

The Russian guard nodded. "She packing?"

The fox turned to Alison. "Hey, be a dear and give the nice man your gun. He's another friend of mine."

Alison considered refusing. If she needed to clear out the entire building her AMDS might make relying on magic dangerous, but she remembered something Shay always told her.

Hey, if you run out of ammo or your gun jams, just kill a guy and use his.

There was a certain practical value to the advice.

She reached slowly into her shoulder holster and grabbed the weapon. She held it out grip-first and waited for the guard to take it.

The other standing guard marched over to her with a frown. "Spread your arms and legs."

Alison complied and the man patted her down, his roaming hands lingering in a few intimate places longer than necessary.

Oh, I'm going to enjoy kicking your ass later.

He smirked as he finished and nodded at the metal detector. She handed him her phone and stepped through.

The guard at the desk grunted once, and the other guard handed her phone back.

"He's in a meeting on the third floor," the guard explained.

Hana paled. "A meeting? With, like, everyone there?"

"Yeah, but he told us if you came by with any new friends to go straight up." The man leered at Alison.

She forced a smile on her face even as she wanted to put her boot up his ass.

Hana tugged on her arm. "Let's go hit the elevator then, Alison."

Neither of them spoke again until they were in the elevator and rumbling toward the third floor.

"Shit, shit, shit." Hana scrubbed a hand down her face. "I was thinking maybe we'd get him in his office or something, but there's a bunch of the guys there. We can't do this. I can't ask you to do this. You'll die."

Alison snorted. "This isn't about just helping you anymore. It's personal."

Hana rubbed her temples. "I'll tell you the one thing I've learned from this. I'm never gambling again."

"Probably a good thing."

The elevator dinged, and the doors opened.

Hana stepped out, and Alison followed her. The nine-tailed fox led the other woman down the hallway to a black door with a sign reading Conference Room 305. Another door to the same room stood farther down the hallway. Hana took several deep breaths, adjusted her top, and knocked on the door.

The door opened, and a Japanese man with a scar on his chin frowned at Hana.

"What are you doing here?"

She nodded at Alison. "I brought a new friend for the boss to meet."

The man smirked. "We had bets on whether you could do it, you know. Guess you're not as weak as most of us thought." He nodded inside. "Okay, take her in."

Not weak to have a conscience, asshole.

89

Hana smiled at Alison. "Hey, we're going to meet the cool guy I told you about."

Her cloying voice almost made Alison roll her eyes, but she focused on keeping a soft smile on her face instead.

They need to think I'm charmed until it's time to kick ass.

They entered the room. Dozens of dangerous-looking men, both Russian and Japanese, filled three long conference tables surrounded by rolling chairs. A heavily scarred Japanese man in a white suit sat at the head of the middle table.

He chuckled. "Ah, Hana. I was expecting you to come crawling back asking for more time, but you've brought me a gift instead. I'm almost impressed."

Hana shrugged. "This is Alison. She's, um, half-elf, and you can see she's hot, you know? I'm sure she'll be glad to be a new employee in your…business endeavors."

Several men around the table snickered. Alison's stomach tightened, but she kept smiling.

Wait for it.

The Daimyo stood and stepped away from the table. He reached into his pocket and pulled out a small stick carved with intricate lines. "I'll need to have her agree to a few oaths first. Don't want any misunderstandings." He advanced on Alison.

She sighed and rolled her eyes. She couldn't take it anymore. "I just need to know one thing before I agree to anything."

He stopped, a curious glint in his eyes. "What is that, Alison?"

"Hana told me you used to be Harriken. Is that true?"

The Daimyo glanced at Hana. She shrugged.

He nodded. "Interesting. She told you that?"

Alison nodded. "Yeah."

"Yes. I was, before the Scourge. The Harriken were short-sighted. They deserved to die." He shrugged. "But I learned from their mistakes, I'm not short-sighted, which is why I lead these men of the Eastern Union."

A few men nodded their agreement.

Alison narrowed her eyes. "Hana told me all about how she got a gambling debt and everything you've forced her to do. Doesn't sound like you've learned from your mistakes to me."

"Did she now?" The Daimyo cast a baleful glance at Hana. "You've betrayed me, fox." He laughed and pointed at Alison. "Did you think this girl would save you? Who is she, police? Hmm? FBI? PDA?"

Alison glared at the Daimyo. "Hey, I'm talking to you, asshole."

Murmurs rippled around the room.

He laughed. "Such spirit. I like that."

Alison shrugged and her gaze flicked to a man in a chair about a yard away, the bulge in his jacket marking his gun. "I'm going to give you one last chance. If you're willing to turn yourself in to the police right now for all your crimes, you'll live. And I mean *you*, Daimyo. I'm sure your guys are pieces of shit, but I only care about you unless they get in my way. If you don't want to turn yourself into the police, you're not going to live to see the end of the day."

Silence swept the room, and a few seconds later the Daimyo burst out laughing. His men joined him.

"I'm going to enjoy breaking you, Alison." He licked his lips. "Personally." His smile disappeared, and he frowned at

Hana. He held up the stick. "You betrayed me, Hana Sugimoto. There's nothing worse than betrayal, and for that, you need to be punished."

Her eyes widened, and she held up her hands. "Please, I can explain."

He muttered something in a language Alison didn't understand, and the carved lines in the stick glowed bright red.

Hana screamed and fell to the floor, writhing in pain.

Alison looked at the Daimyo. "Let her go, bastard!"

"No, girl. You need to see this. You need to see what defiance brings." He sneered. "She gave an oath and she's broken it, and now she will suffer slowly until I decide if she lives or dies. Fox bitches should know their place, like all bitches."

"Fuck your oath," Alison shouted. "You forced that magic on her, you sonofabitch."

Hana continued screaming, tears running down her face. She twitched onto her back and forced her head toward Alison. "Just…run. My…fault. My…punishment."

The Daimyo took a breath and nodded. "You know what? I am feeling generous." He flicked his wrist toward the door. "Go, Alison. The little fox bitch is right. You shouldn't suffer for her. You're not the one who owes me anything. I'm feeling generous, and I think I'm going to be busy for the next few days playing with Hana until she breaks."

Alison raised a hand and a made few quick movements, chanting a quiet incantation under her breath. A ray of light shot from her hand into Hana before arcing to the Daimyo's artifact.

She hissed as pain shot through her body. The intensity sent Alison to one knee. Hana stopped screaming. Her sobs turned to whimpers, and the lines on the Daimyo's artifact stopped glowing. After a few seconds, the fox slumped and her eyes closed.

The Daimyo's eyebrow lifted, and his smile returned to his face. "Interesting. Foolish, but interesting."

Alison hissed and stood. The disruption spell had taken a lot more out of her than she'd anticipated.

The criminal leader's smile remained. If he was intimidated, nothing about his body or expression showed it. "You're full of interesting tricks, aren't you?"

His men pulled their guns.

The Daimyo held up a hand. "Put your weapons away. How I can claim to lead you if I need your protection from one little bitch?"

The thugs holstered their guns again, watching Alison with frowns.

He gestured for Alison to come at him. "Your eyes scream murder, so kill me, Alison. You're not leaving now and neither is that fox bitch, so the only chance for both of you is to kill me."

Alison locked eyes with the Daimyo and thrust her palm forward. A white bolt of energy shot from her hand and flew toward the man. He didn't even flinch.

The magical bolt closed to within a few inches and dissipated, breaking apart particle by particle as if blown away by a stiff wind. The Daimyo laughed.

That didn't go as well as I would have liked.

Alison gritted her teeth and summoned an energy shield around her body.

"Good, hide. Make me earn my victory." He shook his head. "When you fight, you should know who you're fighting. There's a reason I lead these men." He cracked his knuckles. "Natural selection."

"Whatever, asshole." Alison smirked. "Do you know how the Grandfather of the Harriken died?"

The Daimyo's smile faltered. "No one knows for sure. Brownstone destroyed the entire building, but everyone knows about his magic suit now. He probably used that."

Alison shook her head. "Nope. That's just it. the Grandfather died because he didn't consider the obvious."

"The obvious?"

Alison spun and slammed a fist into a nearby gangster before reaching into his jacket and pulling out his gun. The groaning gangster slumped as Alison opened fire on the Daimyo.

"No one shoot her!" he shouted.

He jerked back as bullet after bullet hit him, his blood splattering the floor and table near him and staining his white suit. Alison kept firing until the gun clicked empty.

The gangster fell to his knees, a smile still etched on his face.

Alison scoffed. "You should have surrendered when you had the chance. By the way, I never told you who I am. I'm Alison Brownstone."

He stood, his wounds closing, and shook his head. "I see. In that case, it's a good day for revenge."

She sighed and glanced at Hana. The nine-tailed fox was awake but not moving, her gaze fixed on Alison.

I should have known this wouldn't be easy.

CHAPTER NINE

Alison summoned twin shadow blades. "Hana, go ahead and get the hell out of here. I'll make an opening for you, and I'll take care of these assholes. Don't worry, by the time this is all over, the Daimyo will be dead and the oath spell will be gone."

Hana took a deep breath and gave a slight nod but remained on the floor, her face still red from her earlier tears.

The Daimyo grinned. He reached into his suit jacket and pulled out a knife. "They say this can cut through everything, but I tire of this. Now you'll see the power of the Eastern Union. Men, now you may join me. We're going to kill this bitch as an example to all who would defy us."

The gathered men pulled their guns and aimed them at Alison.

Yeah, Doc, this is going to involve excess magic, but first I need to clean out the distractions.

Alison rushed toward a gangster and pierced his heart

with a shadow blade. She yanked it out, spun, and slashed another. The room exploded in gunshots, dozens of bullets pelting her shield. She impaled the two men a yard behind her at the same time.

She let the blades vanish and grabbed the guns from the falling bodies, spinning and firing with both pistols. Not aiming might have proven more a handicap in a less crowded room, but man after man fell to gunshots with screams or yells. Their bullets kept bouncing off her shield.

All nine of Hana's golden tails burst into existence, her eyes turned vulpine, and her nails lengthened into claws. She burst from the floor, bowling into a nearby gangster and crashing him into a wall. A swipe ripped out the throat of another man near the back door. She barreled through it into the hallway, bounding away.

Two gangsters turned to chase her, but Alison downed them with a few quick shots. She hissed as the others continued to fire at her, straining her shield.

Stupid AMDS. A year ago I would have been able to break that oath spell and kick these guys' asses without breaking a sweat.

Her pistols clicked empty, and she tossed them to the side and leapt at a wall, running along it with the help of shadow hooks near her feet. She flung energy bolts at the surviving gangsters, ignoring the Daimyo, who was watching the whole fight unfold with a faint look of amusement.

His minions lacked his defenses. Her magical attacks knocked her targets back with new burns in the centers of their chests.

Alison completed her run and jumped off the wall to

tackle a man. Two quick punches knocked him out and gained her his pistol. With fewer people in the room, her shots became more measured but remained quick. Two rounds to center of the mass, one round to the head, just like Mom had helped her practice so many times.

Several more gangsters fell before her latest gun ran dry. She threw it at a man across the room and the heavy gun smacked him hard in the head, and he collapsed with a groan.

Alison threw out a shadow line to pull herself across the room and escape the continued barrage of the few remaining men. Every part of her body throbbed now, but the pain was manageable and her shield was holding.

When she hit the wall, she leapt off it and rolled across one of the tables, snatching a gun from a fallen gangster. She put two rounds in each of the six remaining men.

Her breathing ragged, Alison swept the room with the gun. She wasn't sure if anyone was left alive, but at least no one was moving.

"Wait a minute," she muttered. "Damn it!"

The Daimyo was gone and the other door open. Alison tossed the gun to the ground and sprinted toward the door, hurdling the edge of one of the tables. She hit the exit and jerked her head both ways down the hall, looking for the fleeing leader.

Not so tough now, are you, asshole?

Heavy footsteps sounded down the hall, so Alison ran that way. When she hit the corner, the heavy door to the stairs at the end of the hallway thudded closed, the sound echoing through the corridor.

Coward.

Alison charged the stairs, head down, heart thundering. The Daimyo couldn't escape. She wouldn't let him.

She crashed into the door shoulder-first, her shield protecting her body. The door flew open, and she spotted the man hitting the first-floor stairs.

She jumped over the railing. The Daimyo pushed out of the first-floor stairwell as she landed on that level, her shield flashing and a pulse of pain shooting through her body.

After a deep breath, Alison rose and rushed to the door. She threw it open and stepped out, ready to finish the Daimyo.

Two dozen men with rifles stood in the lobby area, including the three guards from earlier.

The Daimyo stood among them, his knife in hand.

"Kill her," he shouted.

Their rifles sprang to life. Overlapping bursts of fire filled the air with bullets and muzzle flashes. She gritted her teeth and backed up, the assault relentless.

I need to finish this shit quickly before one of these guys gets lucky or my shield fades.

Alison raised her arms and narrowed her eyes. She did her best to ignore the gunshots and the pain as she drew on her magic. Her hand moved in a series of quick jerks, a small white orb appearing with each movement and hovering. A few seconds later, a row of twelve orbs hung in front of her.

She yelled and swept out her arms. The orbs flew all over the room, exploding on contact with men, walls, and the display cases lining walls of the lobby.

Alison waved her hand to clear out some of the smoke

now filling the room. Small fires littered the lobby. Burned bodies were scattered about, some overlapping.

The Daimyo stood, his charred flesh regenerating and hatred in his eyes. "You can't win. Don't you see? I can replace those men. You've done nothing, and I can smell your weakness."

"Screw you."

Alison took several deep breaths and shook out her hands. She ached all over, but she was not in agony. The other gangsters had been incidental; she was glad she had saved enough power for the real threat.

"How can you be so damned arrogant?" she called.

"It's like I told you: natural selection." He flung his knife.

Alison scoffed. "You won't get through my—"

Agony blasted from her shoulder as the knife embedded itself. She fell to her knees, and her shield vanished.

The Daimyo shook his head and stalked toward her, producing another knife from his torn and burned jacket. The new knife was engraved with Futhark runes.

"Do you think you're the first with power to come at me? When your father destroyed the Harriken, I vowed to never be weak again. I vowed to destroy all who challenged me, and I've spent the last ten years gathering what I need for that."

Alison fell on her hands and knees, her vision swimming. Even if she drank her healing potion, it'd take too long with the Daimyo coming at her.

She rocked back on her knees and glared at the

approaching enemy. "You took the wrong lesson from what my dad did," she replied through gritted teeth.

"Wrong lesson?" He stopped. "What are you talking about?"

"If some powerful badass killed everyone I knew, I'd take it as a sign that I should switch jobs. Maybe become a florist or a mime."

The Daimyo snorted. "That is the difference between men of ambition and those who are weak." He continued his advance. "Don't feel too disappointed, Little Brownstone. You did far better than I thought you would. I'm sure your father will enjoy it when I mail your head to him."

Have to think. I did what Dad would do. What the hell would Mom *do?*

Alison screamed and yanked the knife out of her shoulder, a shockwave of pain shooting from the wound. She ignored it and the residual throbbing from her magic use and threw the blade at the Daimyo's head.

The man's eyes widened, but it was too late. The magic knife pierced his head, and he stumbled back.

Alison pushed to her feet and materialized a shadow blade, then rushed over to the Daimyo and decapitated him with one quick stroke.

"Come back from *that*, asshole."

The Daimyo's body and head fell to the floor.

Alison released the magic and dropped to her knees. She pulled her last healing potion out of her pocket and downed the contents. Either she would have to find a supplier in town or make one herself, and she didn't have the time or the materials on hand.

The wound in her shoulder sealed itself and the pain diminished, but the throbbing remained. She stood and took a few deep breaths, her limbs heavy.

"Okay, most of them are dead, and the boss is dead. I think we're done here."

Alison stumbled toward the front door but paused at the front desk. Her confiscated gun lay on the top. She holstered it and stepped outside.

A loud roar came from above, and she looked up. Two VTOL dropships with flashing red and blue lights hovered above, both marked Seattle PD.

Doors in the back of both ships opened, and a dozen officers in gleaming silver power armor with jetpacks leapt from the opened doors. Their jetpacks flamed to life at the last second, breaking their fall. Some of the men and women carried massive railguns, others conventional rifles, and a few a smattering of non-lethal pulse rifles.

A translucent crystal was embedded in the center of the armor—an anti-magic deflector. Alison had no doubt that even the police carrying normal rifles were using anti-magic bullets. They might be expensive and needed to be enchanted individually, but it was a must for the type of people advancing toward her. Their heavy armored boots thudded to the ground in unison.

The black lettering across their armor explained exactly who they were: SEATTLE AET. The anti-enhanced threat team, anti-magical SWAT. Much like conventional SWAT, the AET team concept had started in Los Angeles and spread across the country and the world.

They'd started with simple armor, then moved to exoskeletons, and finally power armor for the better teams in recent years. Not every city could afford to field a decent AET team, but the power armor, dropships, and anti-magic deflectors proved this city fielded a rich tax base.

Police drones swarmed overhead, and multiple sirens sounded in the distance.

"This is the Seattle Police Department Anti-Enhanced Threat Team," broadcast one of the AET officers through his helmet. "You are to drop any current spells, go to your knees, and place your hands on your head. Any use of magic or sudden moves will be considered hostile action and you will be fired upon."

Alison sighed. She ached, and fatigue sapped her muscles.

This sucks.

She dropped to her knees and put her hands on her head. The cops had annoying timing, but they were just doing their jobs.

The AET team advanced on her, their weapons ready.

Alison chuckled and shook her head. "I surrender."

CHAPTER TEN

Alison sat in a small white cell admiring all the glowing glyphs and sigils suppressing her magic, including the magic in her glasses. The bright light from the magical symbols on the walls kept her from darkness as she reclined on the hard cot. Her muscle fatigue had dissipated over the hours she'd spent in the cell, and the throbbing had faded to a dull ache.

Hrmm, not bad. Cleared out an entire building filled with gangsters, plus killed a guy with a bunch of artifacts. Not quite to Dad's level, but getting there, and that's with my AMDS.

It seemed like Hana got out okay. Didn't see her anywhere, and the cops didn't mention her when they were yelling at me about all the guys I'd killed or wounded.

The metal door slid open. The magical suppression spell deactivated, and her glasses-aided vision returned.

A uniformed officer with a stun rod glared at her from the open doorway. "Turn around and put your hands behind you, Brownstone."

Alison complied. The cop cuffed her and pulled her out

of the cell. Another police officer trailed them, stun rifle in hand and an anti-magic deflector hanging around his neck on a chain.

I suppose I should feel honored in a sick sort of way. Trying to remember if Dad was ever actually arrested by AET. Will he be happy or pissed? Oh, crap, how am I going to explain it to Mack next time I see him?

They led her down a long hallway to an open door. The metal plate next to the door read INTERROGATION ROOM B. She entered at their prodding.

A shaven-headed middle-aged man in a black suit sat behind a table inside the room. His hands were folded in front of him, and he looked bored.

Trust me, I don't want to be here any more than you do.

The two cops jammed Alison into the chair across from the man. She was still handcuffed, so it wasn't the most comfortable position.

The man in the suit looked up at the police. "Leave us."

"She's a high-risk prisoner," one of the cops replied. "We can't leave her unattended."

"Get out now," the man in the suit ordered. Despite the harsh comment, his tone was measured and even. "This woman is under my jurisdiction now. Go check your paperwork or eat some donuts or something."

The cops snorted and walked toward the door.

"Fucking feds," one of them muttered before he stepped out and slammed the door.

Alison glanced over her shoulder at the closed door and back to the suited man. "I'm guessing you're with the Paranormal Defense Agency."

He nodded. "Yes. I'm Agent Latherby with the Seattle

PDA field office." He leaned back in his chair and stared at her, his fingers steepled. "You, of course, don't need an introduction. You're the great Alison Brownstone, daughter of James Brownstone, the famous Scourge of Harriken." He rubbed the skin beneath his nose. "Or maybe I should be bowing, Your Majesty." He stood and gave a mocking bow. "Oh, all hail Alison Brownstone, Drow Princess of the Shadow Forged."

Alison rolled her eyes. "Are you this much of an asshole naturally or do you have to practice?"

"I thought that was pretty funny. Oh, well." Agent Latherby sat back down. "Let's get to business. I don't have to answer your questions, but you have to answer mine."

She sighed. "Okay. What do you need to know?"

"Why are you in Seattle, Miss Brownstone?" He leaned forward. "Did you come to destroy the Eastern Union?"

Alison shook her head. "I kind of stumbled into that. Weird scenario; met someone and things kind of just happened. I'm here on a security-related job."

"Would you care to share the details?" He gave her a tight smile.

She frowned. "No. My clients expect confidentiality, and I'm not at liberty to discuss the low-level details."

Agent Latherby nodded slowly. "How long do you plan to stay in Seattle?"

Alison shrugged. Her wrists were starting to ache. "A few weeks at most, maybe a few days. Depends on how quickly I can find certain relevant parties and convince them to cooperate with me."

"I see," the agent replied. "And when you find these relevant parties, will it involve more destruction and death? Is that how you're going to convince them to cooperate with you?"

She gave him an abashed look. "Not necessarily, but shit happens."

He arched a brow. "Not necessarily? Shit happens? Is that how you explain what went down with the Eastern Union group you attacked?"

Alison nodded. "I wasn't trying to cause trouble, but come on. You're PDA; you know how this goes. If a guy with magic surrenders, it's easy. If he fights, it can get messy fast." She snorted. "I guarantee you I'll always do my best to make sure no innocent people are hurt, but I'm not going to get too bent out of shape if assholes who are kidnapping women off the street with the aid of magic and forcing them into prostitution end up with a few extra holes or dead."

The agent chuckled. "Quite the self-righteous vigilante, aren't you?"

She frowned but didn't respond.

"Let me point something out to you, Miss Brownstone." Agent Latherby aimed a finger at her. "You don't have an active bounty hunting license. It's expired, and it has been for some time."

She shrugged. "I know that. Is that supposed to be a big impressive gotcha?"

"Can you explain why you think you can kill whoever you want just because they have bounties?" He raised an eyebrow.

"You mean those Eastern Union assholes?"

"Yes. Many of those men had bounties, though not their leader, surprisingly enough. I'm assuming you felt that a few bounties justified you killing those men." Agent Latherby stared at her again as he awaited her reply.

"That's not what happened." Alison sighed. "And those guys were bad news. I don't feel terrible about what I did. They tortured a woman right in front of me and threatened to torture her to death. If I had done nothing, I wouldn't be able to sleep at night."

"Oh, I'm aware of their moral turpitude." Agent Latherby inhaled deeply and sighed. "I should note that self-defense laws are strong in Seattle, especially in regards to magical incidents. Things aren't as contained here as they should be, for several reasons. That said, if a woman happened to be in an office building and known criminals attacked said woman and she was forced to defend herself while intervening to save a third party, it wouldn't make sense to arrest her for simply defending herself."

Alison blinked several times. "They did try to shoot me a whole lot. And the Daimyo stabbed me, too. I think I can justify killing him for what he did to my…associate."

"I've already identified the other woman as Hana Sugimoto. You're not accomplishing anything by not using her name." He shrugged. "I've reviewed the security camera footage, and it is consistent with what you're saying." He cleared his throat. "That said, sometimes a little electronic failure can be helpful in introducing ambiguity to this sort of situation. That can be helpful for discouraging follow-ups by the authorities—something you could consider in similar situations in the future."

"What are you getting at?" Alison frowned. "Are you telling me to purposefully destroy evidence?"

"I'd only note to you, Miss Brownstone, that whenever

there's ambiguity, it's always to your advantage if the other party strikes first. That allows for a stronger self-defense claim, which can short-circuit a lot of otherwise cumbersome legal processes. Or you could look into getting a new bounty hunter's license, but then again, as I noted, not all the men involved in the current incident had bounties. That said, my initial suggestion is probably a better strategy overall if you want less grief."

Damn. Now I feel bad for smarting off. Seems like he wants to help me.

Alison sighed. "I get that. What's going to happen in the current situation? Am I going to be charged with something?"

"The district attorney has been encouraged not to pursue charges." The agent pursed his lips. "And the police have been similarly encouraged to give you a wide berth if you're engaged with already...disruptive elements. I'm sure you've heard of our reputation. That Seattle is the Wild West. It's truer than I'd like, which means the local AET don't always have a problem with...let's just call it 'magical self-regulation.'"

Alison chuckled. "You're saying they don't care if I beat down scumbags?"

"I'm simply noting that he who lives by the sword, dies by the sword." Agent Latherby shrugged. "And the more the AET can be made to see it, the better it is for everyone. Especially you."

"Who did all this encouragement? You?"

He shook his head. "You'll find that the PDA and local AET often clash. They resent our heavy involvement in their activities, but since this area is far less controlled in terms of magic than many other similar metro areas, it requires special attention from the PDA. I've been able to gain temporary jurisdiction over this matter only because the Eastern Union was involved and we've been helping the FBI track some of their involvement in the artifact black market, but that's not always the case. The PDA can't order the AET or the district attorney's office around."

Alison frowned. "If you and the PDA aren't the ones telling the cops to lay off me, then who is? And why? Is this because of my dad?"

"No." Agent Latherby shook his head. "Your father is irrelevant in this case. Someone powerful is pulling strings for you. That's a useful advantage to have at the moment, but don't depend on it, Miss Brownstone. That support could vanish in an instant if you cause too much of a scene, and you might end up in a cell for much longer than a few hours."

"Who is this powerful benefactor of mine?"

The agent stood and walked to the door. He paused there and looked over his shoulder. "That's not for you to know at the moment. I suggest you don't push your luck. The police should be processing your release now. You'll be free to go soon."

"Good." Alison forced a smile. "I still have to check into my hotel."

Alison yawned as she collapsed onto her soft hotel bed. It'd been a damned busy day. Constructive in a way, even though she'd made no progress on the McKenna job thanks to Vincent's busy schedule. Taking down a former Harriken satisfied her. With the Daimyo out of the picture, the police and FBI would be able to dismember the rest of his Eastern Union group. They weren't the only Eastern Union group in the city, but they had been the largest.

I think I helped tame the Wild West a little.

She rolled onto her back and rubbed her arms. The muscle fatigue was almost completely gone now, along with the pain.

I can manage this disease. Sure, it might have been a tougher fight if someone other than the Daimyo had magic items, but I'm not my dad. My average job shouldn't involve me clearing out a multi-floor building full of heavily armed men. Even his didn't, for most of his career.

She furrowed her brow, wondering how many of the Daimyo's Eastern Union forces had survived. She'd presumed the rest of their men had rallied to the first floor, but it wasn't as if she'd done a census before showing up to kick their ass. She hoped they learned a more valid lesson from their brutal defeat than their leader had.

A sigh escaped her lips as she thought about the knife in her shoulder. She rubbed the area, grateful for the healing potion. She'd been channeling her inner James Brownstone a little too much. That cockiness had cost her, and she'd been fortunate the Daimyo hadn't finished her off with a hit to the throat.

It's like Mom said. We all have our strengths, and I need to focus on using mine, especially if I'm going to be taking on more than a small number of guys at a time.

Alison sat up and rolled off the bed. She headed into the bathroom.

After turning on the shower, she removed her clothes. A day's worth of sightseeing and ass-kicking worked up a lot of sweat, and she stank.

Her thoughts drifted back to Hana. The woman was a self-admitted con artist, but Alison had looked directly at her soul. Hana wasn't evil, just someone who'd let their mistakes trap them. The woman had not been able to go through with trying to charm Alison even before she realized what was going on.

Alison stepped into the water, enjoying the warm spray on her tired muscles. "I hope she's okay."

After a few silent minutes in the shower, Alison laughed. "And I hope tomorrow isn't so busy."

CHAPTER ELEVEN

A couple of days later, Alison stepped out of a Currus and stared at the glowing and rotating words in front of the squat building in front of her: The True Portal.

"Could have just gotten a sign instead of using magic," she mumbled as she approached the red carpet leading to the door to the dance club.

I hope this isn't annoying. Vincent sounded a little too smug this morning when I called him. Why couldn't the asshole just give me the information I needed over the phone?

Two huge humanoid creatures stood near the entrance on either side, each over eight feet tall. Although they had two arms and legs and wore impressively-tailored blue suits, stone impregnated with various small crystals formed their bodies. Their faces lacked a mouth or nose, and glowing blue eyes peered out of the center of their heads.

Alison blinked. Halicans. She'd heard of them on Oriceran, but she'd never seen one on Earth. They were rare, probably as rare as nine-tailed foxes were on Earth, although she could see their appeal as bouncers.

One of the Halicans threw up a rocky hand as Alison approached the door. Thumping bass sounded from inside, promising a bone-shaking good time to those who loved techno and a hellish torture session to others.

"Insufficient," the Halican rumbled, its hollow voice coming from its chest and not its head.

Please don't make me fight one of these things.

Alison frowned. "Huh? What do you mean, 'insufficient?'"

"There is a standard." The brightness of the Halican's eyes changed. "Your clothing is insufficient. You lack visual appeal, per the standards of our employer."

"Lack visual appeal?" She laughed and flipped her hair. "Are you serious?"

"Yes. This is a most serious matter."

Alison looked down at her outfit. While her jeans and a red denim jacket couldn't be called a man-catching club uniform, the whole outfit was cute enough while remaining functional for ass-kicking. She admittedly hadn't thought to dress up for a night at a club. She didn't plan to dance, after all. This visit was business, and she didn't need to show her ass to get information from an informant.

She sighed. "Come on, guys. Cut me a break."

Wait, should I be calling them guys? The voice sounds male by Earth standards, but that's probably just a spell. Do they even have genders?

"It is our duty," the other Halican rumbled. He pointed down the street. "You may not enter until you are sufficient to the current standards. We can recommend websites focused on fashion if you lack understanding. Your choice of abnormal hair color suggests some under-standing of enhancing your appearance."

"Okay, this is just painful now." Alison rolled her eyes. She'd never been told she wasn't sexy enough by two rock men before. Or rock women. Or rock whatevers. It stung in any event, but she needed to get into the club without causing a ruckus.

I hope that bastard was telling me the truth.

She crossed her arms. "I'm here to see Vincent. He told me if there was any trouble to mention his name, and that he was expecting me. So, yeah, take that." She shrugged.

The two Halicans exchanged looks, their eyes flickering. From what she'd heard, that was their natural form of communication on Oriceran.

Just let me in, you judgmental assholes.

One of the Halicans moved forward with a heavy step, tilting his head. "You are Alison Brownstone."

She nodded. "That's me. I can show you my license if you want."

"Unnecessary. We know."

Alison blinked. "If you know, then why didn't you let me in to begin with?"

"You must confirm." The Halican straightened his head, his eyes dimming. "You may enter. Please consider still visiting the fashion websites to become sufficient."

"I'm on the job, okay? I've got plenty of dresses at home. Jeez. I thought you guys were bouncers, not fashion consultants." Alison rolled her eyes and stepped into the darkened club. "Everyone's a damned critic," she muttered.

"Bet they don't even know why they're wearing those suits."

Loud techno attacked her ears, electronic beats mixed with samples from complex twisting melodies and layered harmonies that couldn't have come from Earth instruments. A wailing female vocal popped in briefly. Alison didn't recognize the language but thought it was from some species of elf.

The massive dance floor dominated the bulk of the first floor, with a small number of tables on the edges and a neon-heavy bar near the back. Wide stairs on either side led up to a second floor.

Alison lifted her hand and concentrated. A slight glow encased her ears and the massive sonic assault of the music quieted, even as the bass continued to rattle her bones.

Strobe lights pulsed as dancers of several species thronged on the floor. Mostly humans, but many Oricerans also mixed with the crowd, including elves and dwarves, but no gnomes that she could see.

She chuckled at a sudden thought.

I would pay good money to see a breakdancing gnome.

Several members of a reptilian species Alison didn't recognize clustered in a corner, their movements erratic and painful-looking. A few winged arpaks enjoyed the heavy beats. A massive Kilomea danced in the center of the floor, everyone giving him plenty of room.

Streams of light flittered overhead, leaving slowly-fading trails. Alison wasn't sure if they were spells or something more exotic from Oriceran, a planet where intelligence was defined by glorious diversity.

She pushed deeper into the club, the sea of people and creatures deepening.

A man in a mesh shirt broke away from the crowd and grinned at her. His dilated pupils and red face suggested he'd chosen the fun of drugs to enhance his night. "Hey, babe," he shouted. "Love the hair. Totally makes you stand out."

Alison shook her head. "I'm not here to dance or meet anyone. Sorry."

He leaned forward. "Oh, come on, babe. You're hot, and I can show you a good time. I'd like to tap that."

She sighed. "Just leave me alone." She gestured to her outfit. "I've got my insufficiently sexy outfit on and everything."

"Like the way those jeans cling to that nice rear bumper. Great face. Great lips." He nodded. "Nah, I like what I see, and I'll like what's under it even better, I'm guessing." He goosed her ass. "Tight and firm."

Before he could pull his hand back, Alison grabbed his wrist and bent it back. He fell to his knees and the people around her stepped away, forming a circle.

Alison glared at him. "One simple rule that applies to most women: no touching without permission." She raised an eyebrow. "Understand?"

"Yeah, yeah." The man grimaced and bobbed his head. "I'm sorry, I'm sorry."

She released his hand and rolled her eyes before pushing past him and striding toward the stairs. Vincent had told her that he'd be on the second floor. He'd refused to send her a picture but told her that he was blond and would be in a dark purple suit and wearing gold chains. He also insisted he was handsome.

She jumped as someone whispered into her ear despite no one being close.

"Looking for me, Alison?" came Vincent's familiar smooth voice.

She narrowed her eyes and looked up the stairs to the second floor. Dozens of tables lit by individual floating light orbs filled the floor. A man waved at her from the table nearest the stairs.

Blond, check. Purple suit, check. Gold chains, check. Is he an informant or a pimp?

Alison nodded. She had to admit that Vincent had a handsome smile, not that she would tell him that.

She bounded up the stairs and dropped into a chair across from him, passing through some invisible barrier that made her skin tingle. Questions about the nature of the spell never came out, as there was an instant change up here: not just quieted music, but no music at all. Even the thump of the bass was gone.

That's handy.

Alison dropped her ear-protection spell and nodded at the man. "Just to be sure, you're Vincent?"

He bowed over his arm in his seat. "The one and only."

"I need the lead on McKenna." Alison frowned. "Mr. D told me you'd help me, but you've been pretty stubborn so far."

Vincent picked up his appletini and took a sip. "Yes, it's even your lucky week, because he's dropped a lot of money on me to earn my assistance. Normally this might involve more hoops and exchange of payment."

Alison gestured at the dancing crowd below. "Don't know why we had to meet here. Why couldn't you have just given me the information over the phone? You've already been paid, so there's no reason to make me jump through hoops."

He set his glass down. "Part of being a businessman is providing a bit of flair, don't you think?" He gave her a bright smile. "But more to the point, this is a safe place to meet and guarantees certain things on my end. Plus, they don't mind if I set up a few spells for business."

"Like the silence spell?"

Vincent nodded. "And the truth spell."

She narrowed her eyes. "What truth spell?"

He grinned. "That's what I love about this place. So much concentrated magic, it's hard to distinguish any particular spell unless it's super-obvious, but there are so many magicals that if someone tries something stupid, they'll pay for it. I don't think there's another place in Seattle I'd rather do business."

Alison snorted. "I'd feel it if you used that kind of spell on me directly. It's passive then—some sort of general lie detection."

"Clever as you are beautiful."

"The bouncers didn't think so."

Vincent laughed. "I wouldn't be too concerned about what some walking quarry has to say about a woman's beauty."

Alison nodded. "Good point, now back to the spell. What's the deal?"

He held up the appletini. "It changes color when people lie, you *or* me. How's that for transparency?"

"Fine, but I'm not answering any questions I don't want to." Alison crossed her arms. "I still think we could have done this two days ago over the phone, but whatever."

"Ah, would that be before you annihilated the Daimyo and his men in a manner that I can only describe as Brownstonian?"

Alison winced, not sure how Vincent had known. The news report had only mentioned that "gang warfare" had resulted in the deaths of the Eastern Union gang. Given the police knew exactly who she was, she assumed only that her mysterious benefactor had pulled strings with the media in addition to the police.

Maybe Vincent had contacts in the police. That might be useful for the future.

She cleared her throat. "I offered the Daimyo the chance to surrender. He was...stubborn."

Vincent chuckled. "How magnanimous." He waved a hand. "But that's in the past. You're interested in the present and future, and specifically in Terrence McKenna. I'll have you know, Alison, that one of the reasons this meeting had to be delayed was so I could verify certain information about Mr. McKenna."

"Why didn't you tell me that before? I wouldn't have been annoyed."

"Sometimes you need to look a person in the eye to know if you could trust them." Vincent stared at her with his blue eyes.

Alison shrugged. "Says the man who uses truth martinis."

"Touché." Vincent sighed. "Now for more transparency:

the simple fact is, I don't know where Terrence McKenna is."

"What?" She frowned. "Then why the hell are you wasting my time? I need to find this guy, not sit here and play games with you in a dance club."

"Calm down." He held up a hand. "I don't know where he is, but I know where you could find someone who does."

"Okay, that's better," Alison replied. "And where is that?"

"A new group of wizards came into town a few days ago." Vincent licked his lips. "Word is they're dark wizards. I hear you're not a fan of dark wizards, Alison."

"You could say that," she muttered back through gritted teeth.

"I'm not a fan either." Vincent shrugged. "Dark wizards tend to be bad for business. A properly functioning economy requires stability from consumers and producers, and they tend to interfere with all of those. These wizards showed up the morning after McKenna rolled into town and have been asking about him."

Alison gave Vincent a curt nod. "Sounds promising. Where can I find these wizards? I want to have a lively chat with them."

Vincent's smug smile finally left his face. "Before I tell you, I want to warn you that these guys are trouble. You've proven you're more than a pretty face and a name, but the Eastern Union were mostly normal humans with guns. These dark wizards aren't going to be easy prey. Not only is this not your town, but you're new here so you might want to be careful which fights you pick."

"Just tell me where they are," Alison replied, her voice almost a growl. "It's my life to risk. They won't know how I found them."

"Your funeral, but if you die in Seattle, I'm spreading a rumor in LA to trick your father into believing it was at the hands of some fuckers from Portland so he'll tear up the wrong city." Vincent scoffed. "They're at a place called the Sunshine Room. It's a bar in Ballard. The leader of the dark wizards is a guy named Alex. They practically live there right now."

Alison smiled and stood. "Thanks, Vincent. I have to go pay some wizards a visit."

CHAPTER TWELVE

S he was going on quite the tour of Seattle nightlife.

The Sunshine Room lacked a Halican bouncer to complain about Alison's insufficient sexiness, but more than a few men and hard women looked her way as she stepped into the cramped dive bar. Heavy rock played over the speakers, but it didn't overwhelm her ears like the music at the club had.

Half these people look like they want to punch me in the face for stepping in here. What, I was insufficiently sexy before, and now I'm insufficiently biker?

Magic also didn't choke the area like at the dance club, making it easy for Alison to home in on the side of the room where a half-dozen men sat scattered over two tables, their long coats draped over the backs of their chairs and their wand holsters obvious.

Even though there was no reason for wizards to hide their nature in modern society, something about the brazenness of the men irked Alison.

If you're dark wizards, you should stick to the shadows, assholes.

She rubbed her cheek and sighed.

Okay, should I be doing a Mom-when-she's-not-pissed or a standard-issue Dad?

Alison frowned and took a deep breath. Just because there were wizards in a seedy bar didn't mean they were dark wizards, and if she didn't get the right group of wizards, she might lose her trail to McKenna by the time she figured out what was going on. Whatever magic he was using was powerful enough to block direct tracking spells, so running him down the more complicated way was a necessity.

"Hey, Alex, catch," one of the wizards shouted. He tossed a bottle of beer to a dark-haired man across the table.

That was all the confirmation she needed.

"Thanks for making this easier," she mumbled under her breath.

Alison sauntered to the table and laid a hand on Alex's shoulder, fluttering her eyelashes. "Hey, I noticed you when I came in. I think you're my type. Maybe we could go have some fun."

He shook her hand off his shoulder. "I didn't say you could fucking touch me, bitch."

Alison kept a smile on her face.

Bet Hana could have pulled that off.

"Sorry," she replied. "You just look like the kind of guy who knows how to have a good time. Guess I was mistaken."

Alex stood, his tall frame forcing Alison back. "You think I'm a fucking idiot, Alison Brownstone?"

She sighed. "Oh, you know who I am? Now I'm kind of embarrassed about the whole easy chick act."

"Yeah, I know who you are. It's not like you're all that obscure." He gave her a toothy grin. "And I know someone who knows you. I never thought I'd run into you, but I've got a message for you."

Alison narrowed her eyes. Did McKenna already know she was on his trail?

"What message?"

"Robert says hi," Alex answered and laughed.

Alison's heart rate kicked up and she swallowed, stumbling back. Robert was the dark wizard who'd put Tanner in a coma when they were at the School of Necessary Magic.

"What did you say?" Alison spat, her hands clenching.

"I said Robert says hi, bitch. He also wanted to know if Tanner ever stopped drooling?" He laughed, and the other wizards joined him. "Or did they have to pull the plug on Vegetable Boy?"

The rest of the room grew silent. Several patrons left, and others moved to the other side of the room, curious looks on their faces.

Alison let out a dark chuckle. "If you know who I am, then you know you shouldn't be talking to me like that, right?"

Alex whipped out his wand with a grin. The other wizards rose and readied theirs.

"You think this is some bullshit like at your little school, girl?" He shook his head. "And you think we're scared because you've kicked the crap out of a few weaklings? You Brownstones are all the same. You get big heads, but it's all smoke and mirrors and reputation."

Alison snorted and narrowed her eyes. "I've taken down more than a few dark wizards since leaving the school, asshole. If you think I'm not all that, bring it on and I'll give you a lesson on why you don't screw with a Brownstone."

"Like I said, weaklings." Alex tapped his wand against his forehead. "Me and my friends are having a good time here and I like this place, so why don't you turn your little ass around and walk out of here, Brownstone? Otherwise, we're going to make what happened to Tanner seem like a vacation in comparison to what we're going to do to you."

Her gaze cut around the room and to the bartender. "You own this place or do you just work here?"

The bartender grunted. "I own it."

"Insurance?"

He shrugged. "Some." He shook his head. "Not enough to cover a magic fight."

"I'll pay for any damages," Alison announced.

The bartender snorted. "Why should I believe that?"

"Because I'm Alison Brownstone. Didn't you hear?" She nodded toward Alex. "If you don't believe me, ask yourself why this asshole is trying to get me to walk away."

The bartender's eyes widened. "No cops, then. Do what you need to. I'm hiding in the back." He rushed into the back room.

Alex and his gang laughed. "You cocky little bitch. I'm going to enjoy this."

Alison turned back toward him, summoning a shield

around her body. The wizards spread out, all pointing their wands at her.

She reached into her jacket and pulled out a knife. "Just bought this. Was traveling a little light for this job. Not sure why. Maybe I figured it'd be a day in, day out kind of thing." She shrugged. "You never know what's going to happen, right? Should have just brought the full kit."

Alex scoffed. "Am I supposed to be afraid of a knife?" He made a few quick movements with his wand, and the air flashed around him. "That all you got, Brownstone? A knife and a mouth?"

"No. I just kind of like it. Pearl grip. Shiny." Alison shrugged. "Okay, you get one last chance, asshole. You can apologize for what you said and answer my questions about Terrence McKenna, and I'll forget how much you pissed me off."

"Fuck off, Brownstone." Alex spat at her, but the fluid bounced off her shield.

Alison shrugged. "Standard-issue Dad it is."

Alex blinked. "Huh?"

She threw the knife into the air. The wizards all looked up.

Alison didn't even bother going for her gun. Their defensive spells would easily deflect bullets.

She rushed toward Alex, summoning a shadow blade. With her other arm, she fired a shimmering white bolt toward another wizard.

The knife clattered on a table as the white bolt struck the wizard's invisible shield, spreading across it and dissipating. The man winced and stumbled back. Alison thrust her shadow blade toward Alex. The dark blade of pure magic hit his shield but slowed as it pierced the barrier.

The wizard spun out of the way, only narrowly avoiding a new hole in his chest. Alison swept out with her free arm, and an arc of dark energy blasted toward the first wizard she'd attacked. He yelled as the attack penetrated his shield and lacerated his chest.

Not just a name, assholes.

Energy orbs blasted from the wizards' wands. Some missed, but a stray red ball exploded against a table behind Alison. The remaining attacks struck her shield, forcing her back. Some pain flashed through her but the spell held firm.

The rest of the patrons dashed for the exits. Alison layered shadow magic onto her shield, the shimmering color dulling but the wizards' attacks straining her less.

"Is that all you've got, Alex?" she taunted.

Alex gritted his teeth and backed up, then flicked his wand while muttering an incantation. Two metal tables flew toward Alison, but she sliced them in half with quick slashes from her shadow blade.

Alison threw two quick spells, a light magic bolt and a shadow arc blast, this time not against the wizards but the windows around them. The windows shattered, raining down glass shards around all the wizards.

Fool me once, shame on you. Fool me twice...

Their defensive spells kept them unharmed but not undistracted. Alison charged the nearest wizard, the one she'd originally attacked. This time her blade passed through both his shield and his chest.

She pulled it out and rounded on the next closest man.

Alex stepped back farther, now behind all his comrades, chanting and making quick movements with his wand. Dark pulsating glyphs appeared in the air, arcs of black and purple energy flowing between them.

Shit. That doesn't look friendly.

Alison summoned another shadow blade in her free hand and slammed both her weapons into her closest enemy, sending him to the floor screaming. She released the blades and bounced off a snap-summoned shadow acceleration disk to hurl her past the wizards pelting her with magical blasts from their wands.

The blows stung, not from the attacks but from her increased strain. She snatched the knife from the table as she passed it. After landing on the floor in a roll, she fed energy into the knife, a purple glow surrounding the blade.

A sudden blast of seven-different-colored twirling rays shot from a wizard's wand and smashed into Alison.

She groaned, her shield flashing and the attack flinging her across the room. She slammed into the bar, denting it. Hissing, she flung the infused knife at the wizard. The blade struck the shield and a wave of dark purple energy erupted, knocking the wizard and another close to him down. Their heads slammed into the tile floor hard.

Alison ducked and dropped to her knees as another wizard fired a rainbow ray. The side of the bar behind her exploded in a shower of wood.

Still on her knees, Alison swung both her arms, launching several curved blasts of pure shadow magic at the chanting Alex. His eyes widened.

What, thought I'd just let you build up a big spell to finish me?

The dark wizard jerked to his side to avoid the attack but slipped, and his wand twitched up. His glyphs all flashed, and the bright light blinded Alison.

The smell of charred flesh filled the air. She blinked her eyes a few times, and when her vision cleared, it took her a moment to realize that only Alex's smoking legs remained.

"That works." Alison bounded toward the last conscious dark wizard. She concentrated energy in one hand, a white glow building.

He blasted her with a fireball. Her shield held, but the now-familiar painful throbbing returned. She slammed her hand into his shield, and the glow vanished.

The wizard backpedaled. "That didn't hurt."

"Yeah." Alison yanked out her pistol and put three rounds into his chest. "The point was to get rid of the shield."

Her victim fell forward, surprise on his face.

Alison sighed and marched over to the two surviving wizards on the floor. One groaned, blood trailing down the side of his face. The other was unconscious.

"And now the easy part."

She dropped her shield, but that didn't do much to help with the pain pulsing through her body.

Alison crouched next to the groaning wizard and placed her gun at the back of his head. "Feeling chatty now, or do you have something you want to say about Tanner and Robert?"

The man groaned. "Please don't kill me. I don't even know who Tanner is. I just laughed because Alex was laughing."

"I should kill you because you're a dark wizard, but I

need you for the moment." Alison snorted. "You want to leave this place alive, asshole?"

He nodded.

"Then tell me where Terrence McKenna is. I'm in a really bad mood right now, and you guys just made it a lot worse."

"I don't know." The man swallowed. "I really don't know."

Alison laughed and pressed the gun into his head. "You seriously want me to use lie detection magic after what I just went through? Playing games isn't going to help you get out of this."

"I'm telling the truth. We were supposed to meet with him. He was going to sell us something. I swear I'm telling the truth."

Alison nodded and kept her gun flush against the man. "Sell you the gem?"

The wizard swallowed. "You know about that?"

She rolled her eyes. "Give me a little credit. Why did you think I was looking for McKenna to begin with? Anyway, what happened? He call it off?"

"No. He just never showed up. The bastard skipped out on us. We went to the apartment where he was supposed to be hiding, but he wasn't there. We tried calling him, but he wouldn't answer. Tried tracking him, but our magic wouldn't work. I don't even know if he's still in Seattle."

"Your magic failed because he already knew exactly what to expect from you. Wonder why he called off the sale?" Alison chuckled. "Oh, I get it—he found someone who would offer more. Who would have ever thought a piece of shit would betray other pieces of shit?"

The wizard frowned. "The bastard."

"Whatever. Where's the apartment?"

The wizard rattled off the address.

Alison pulled her gun away from the man's head. He sighed in relief. She stood and glared at the wizard.

"Get the hell out of Seattle, because if I run into you again, I'm going to kill you. Maybe you're lying about knowing about Tanner. I don't care to find out right now, but if you do know Robert, you tell him that when I find him, I'm going to kill him. Understand?"

The wizard nodded and pushed himself up, eyeing Alison the entire time, fear on his face. He reached for his wand and Alison fired at it, snapping it in two.

"Get the hell out of here before I change my mind, and take your friend," Alison shouted.

The wizard scrambled for the door, dragging his unconscious compatriot.

Alison holstered her pistol and rolled her shoulders. She needed to rest, but there was no way she could pass up a strong lead.

What's a little pain and magical strain? Maybe I'll find out that Terrence is dead in his bathtub and was just using magic to hide his body.

She surveyed the destruction and shook her head. After recovering the knife, Alison pulled out a business card and left it on what remained of the bar.

Doing things the traditional Brownstone way was expensive.

CHAPTER THIRTEEN

Alison crept down the darkened hall of the apartment building. The light strip on the ceiling flickered as she closed on her target's doorway. She hadn't sensed any magic since entering the apartment building, but given McKenna had already been savvy enough to use anti-tracking spells, she wouldn't put it past him to conceal his magic from casual detection.

Her pain had lessened in the thirty minutes it'd taken her to get from the bar to the apartment. Taking on a single wizard shouldn't prove much of a problem, or at least she hoped it wouldn't. If McKenna could unlock the power of the gem, the situation might get more complicated and annoying.

He can't be that badass, or he wouldn't be hiding.

Alison stopped in front of the door, then summoned a shield and placed her free hand on the door. She tried to open it, but the door was locked.

"What?" she murmured. "Did those assholes check this place and lock up after?"

It was time for something a little more complicated than ass-kicking magic. She took a quick moment to silently thank her teachers at the School of Necessary Magic. Even if they hadn't taught her every non-light and shadow magic spell she'd used since leaving the school, they'd instilled the baseline understanding she'd needed to learn them.

After taking a deep breath, Alison traced a glyph over the door and murmured an incantation. A bright yellow glyph appeared, and the lock clicked.

She readied her gun.

Three, two, one...

Alison flung the door open and swept the room with her gun. No dark wizard. No gem. Nothing threatened her but a rank odor from a pile of unwashed clothes on the couch.

She wrinkled her nose. "Not exactly living the big life, huh, McKenna?"

Alison moved farther inside, her gun still at the ready. It was just a normal studio apartment with a couch, a television, and a tiny kitchenette. A cot stood in the corner with a black comforter hanging half off it and a blue pillow near the head, a few stray brown hairs on it.

The bathroom door was closed.

Maybe he is dead in the tub after all.

Alison moved toward it and slammed her boot into the door. It flew open—another empty room with no wizard corpses in the tub.

She holstered her weapon and sighed. "Of course he's not here. Time to search. Who knows? Might get lucky, and he just happened to leave a powerful artifact lying around that somehow a pack of wizards didn't find."

Alison didn't get lucky. Thirty minutes of searching yielded nothing magical. The only interesting finds included a flyer for the Sunshine Room and a card for a local escort service.

She sighed. The Sunshine Room was already trashed, and she doubted she could get the escort service to admit McKenna was a client. Placing the women in danger wasn't fair either.

"The wizards said he'd skipped out, and it doesn't look or smell like anyone's been here for a couple days at least. Has to be a clue I can use. Something. *Anything.*"

Alison frowned and walked back to the cot, her gaze drawn to the hairs.

She smiled, then picked up a hair. "Sloppy, McKenna. You went through all the trouble of setting up anti-tracking spells but left this to find? Surprised your friends didn't notice."

Alison headed into the kitchenette. The missing wizard had been kind enough to leave a glass. She half-filled it with water and placed the hair on the surface.

Now I'm coming for you, McKenna.

She half-closed her eyes and gripped the glass, holding up a hand and whispering an incantation. The hair straightened and spun for a few seconds before stopping, pointing rigidly in one direction.

Picking up the glass, Alison grinned. McKenna might have shielded himself against tracking magic, but leaving a hair behind made him vulnerable to sympathetic magic-fueled tracking. She now had herself a nice compass pointing straight toward the man's current location.

The only problem was he might be a hundred feet away or twenty miles.

"Shit. This is what I get for not renting a car when I first got here." Alison laughed.

A Currus wouldn't do, or anything self-driving, really. She needed an actual human, someone who could deal with changing directions. She pulled out her phone to call a Lyft.

The driver looked over his shoulder, confusion on his face. "You really don't know where you're going?"

"I know the direction." Alison held up the glass. "We just need to follow this. It's a magic thing. Don't worry, I'll give you a huge tip for dealing with the inconvenience. I know this is annoying."

"I've had a lot weirder fares. At least you're human." The driver shrugged as they pulled away from the curb.

Alison stared at the rigid hair in the glass. "Take the next right."

The driver complied, and the hair shifted direction.

"So," the driver began, "magic, huh? I get a lot of witches in this neighborhood. Is there some sort of rental discount or something if you know magic? Or is it one of those things where the real estate agent is a witch, so she encourages other witches to move into the neighborhood?"

Alison chuckled. "I'm not a witch. I'm half-human, half-elf."

The driver glanced into the rearview mirror. "You look a lot more human than most half-elves I've seen, not that I've seen a huge number. You got that white hair, but a lot of girls have crazy hair these days with no more magic than hair dye." He shrugged. "Keep going this direction?"

She nodded. "Yeah."

"Do you mind if I ask what's this is about? I mean, I've got no problem if this is about you tracking your ex who knocked you up or something, but I can't be involved in anything illegal. The company's kind of intolerant of that."

Alison chuckled. "Nothing illegal. Not on my end. I'm just looking for someone who stole something destructive from someone else. I promise to not get you involved in anything dangerous. I just need you to get me to the guy I'm looking for."

"Oh, so you're a bounty hunter?"

The hair started turning. "Take another right. And no, not a bounty hunter. Security consultant."

The driver made the turn. "Sounds fancy. You work for a lot of rich guys?"

"Yeah, I guess you could say that." Alison frowned. "I try to work for people who aren't total assholes, though. It's not about the money. Not completely, anyway. Not like I'm working for free." She laughed.

He laughed. "No judgment, sister. I drive everyone around in this car. It's not like every passenger is a good person, but I haven't driven anyone to a crime yet." He frowned and glanced into the mirror. "You only have the general direction? It doesn't, like, glow brighter as we get closer?"

Alison shook her head. "Just think of it as a compass that points to the person instead of north. It's starting to turn, probably going to need another right soon, but keep going."

"You're not from Seattle, are you?"

She shook her head. "From LA originally, live in DC now. Went to school a few different places."

The driver checked his mirrors and rearview camera. "I might not be magical, but I'm guessing we're going to need to get onto the 90. Any chance the guy you're looking for is rich?"

"Not right now, but he could end up that way." Alison furrowed her brow. "He might want to deal with a rich guy. Why?"

"I'm going to head to the onramp then." The driver changed lanes. "The 90 connects to the bridge that'll take us to Mercer Island. Lots of rich guys there. Scott Carlyle lives there, even."

"Scott Carlyle? Where have I heard that name before?"

The car slid onto the I-90 onramp. Alison watched the hair finish moving. They were going in the right direction.

The driver laughed. "You messing with me? You really don't know who he is?"

Alison shrugged. "I recognize the name, but I can't place it. I don't always pay the best attention to the news."

"He's is CEO and founder of Advanced Magitek

Systems, which is pretty much the most valuable magic-technology fusion company in the world. The dude is one of the richest men in the country. He has more money than Derek Chesterton. You know him?"

Alison nodded. "He also runs a techno-magic company, right? I think I saw a news article about him a few weeks back about military contracts. Something about minor defensive artifacts for Special Forces."

"Yeah. The real kicker is that Chesterton started his company before AMS, but Carlyle's been dominating the sector for the last few years. It's got to burn that a guy twenty years younger than him is eating his lunch." The driver shrugged. "Once you end up a billionaire, though, it's kind of all the same, wouldn't you think?"

"Don't know. Not a billionaire." Alison shrugged.

The driver laughed. "Preach it, sister."

They merged onto the massive multi-lane floating bridge over Lake Washington, the water inky-black under the night sky. Another bridge ran parallel to theirs, the traffic moving the opposite direction.

Alison stared at the hair. "This is definitely the right way. Rich asshole it is."

How much is a dangerous, unstable gem worth? Millions? Tens of millions? More?

She smiled. McKenna was probably sitting in some contact's house, smug and secure that he'd escaped the attention of Mr. D and the dark wizards.

You shouldn't have been so cocky, McKenna. We'll be seeing each other real soon.

"You've got to be shitting me," the driver muttered, eyes wide as he stared out the front window.

They were on a private road, the car idling in view of a massive mansion. The grounds were enclosed by a tall and ornate wrought iron fence. The gate was currently closed, and there was no obvious checkpoint or call box.

A huge lawn spread in front of the mansion, with a few small stands of trees along the edges of the property. A fountain graced the center of the lawn, surrounded by a garden, glowing wisps zooming around and illuminating it. Brick pathways cut through it.

All the flowers were in bloom. Considering the chilly temperatures and time of the year, magic was likely involved.

Alison glanced down at the glass in her hand. The hair hadn't twitched on their final approach down the private road. "He's definitely in there.."

The driver laughed. "Jeez, you really *are* from out of town. You don't know whose house this is?"

She shrugged. "Some rich guy's house."

The driver shook his head. "Not just a rich guy. Scott Carlyle."

"Huh." Alison shrugged. "That's interesting, and it might complicate things." She pulled out her phone to pay the fare and entered in a massive tip. "Thanks for accommodating an unreasonable request. After I get out, I think you should get the hell out of here as quickly as possible."

The driver looked over his shoulder at her. "You going to do something the PDA and AET are going to question me about tomorrow?"

Alison shook her head. "Don't worry, I've got an existing relationship with the local authorities. Just, things might get a little...explode-y, and I don't want innocent people hurt."

"Explode-y?" His brow lifted.

She opened the door, glass still in hand. "Yeah. I hope not, but you never know. Thanks for the ride." She waved and closed the door.

The driver stared at her for a few seconds before backing up and turning around.

Alison blew out a breath and advanced toward the gate. Now that she was outside, she noticed the half-dozen drones circling the area. There was no obvious security roaming the massive lawn, but also no obvious way to get in contact with the house from the gate.

"Huh. This the kind of place they expect you to call ahead?" She eyed the gate, wondering if she should climb, jump, or fly over it. It'd be trivial, but there was no way some billionaire with a magic fountain and a half-dozen obvious drones wouldn't take offense.

The job wasn't to piss off Scott Carlyle. The job was to find Terrence McKenna and get the gem from him.

Another option would be to wait Terrence out, but that could take hours or days. Even if this wasn't his mansion, she doubted it was the kind of place where people made late-night AM/PM runs.

She shrugged. If she was going to get their attention either way, might as well be polite about it. At least this way she could flush out McKenna.

Alison waved an arm at one of the lower-flying drones,

then put down the glass and sheathed her hands in cycling colors with the help of a little magic.

The drone descended and hovered about thirty feet above her, its rotor whirring quietly.

"Identity yourself immediately or security will be employed," a man's harsh voice shouted from a drone speaker.

Alison released the color magic from her hands. She smiled and waved at the drone.

"Hello, my name is Alison Brownstone. I'm a private security consultant on a job. This job involves tracking a very dangerous wizard named Terrence McKenna to this location. That wizard is associated with said job. I'd like to come inside and ask a few questions. If he's not present, I'll be on my merry way."

"Wait there."

Alison crossed her arms and tapped her foot. She hoped Terrence would panic and rush outside to confront her—that would make things easy. She could take him down before the cops showed up.

Shit. What do I do if he decides to stay in there? I'm not a cop or PDA. It's not like I can force them to let me in, and kicking in the door of one of the richest men in the country is not a great idea if I'm trying to avoid ending up in an ultramax.

The gate suddenly swung open.

"Enter and walk straight to the front door, Miss Brownstone," the voice commanded. "Any deviation from this will be considered an attempt on Mr. Carlyle's life and you will be dealt with accordingly."

Alison blinked. Of all the possibilities, she'd never thought they'd just let her in.

Okay, McKenna's probably not in there. If I'm careful about this, they might be able to give me a hint, or maybe they're ready to throw him under the bus. Even evil rich dudes don't like incompetent guys.

Alison stepped through the gate and followed the brick path across the lawn and around the garden, enjoying the thick floral scents. She closed on the front porch, which was larger than her entire apartment in DC. She could afford a bigger place, but she wasn't sure if she would enjoy a place this big.

The front door of the mansion swung open to a brightly lit foyer, exquisite sculptures lining the walls. A handsome and fit dark-haired man in his mid-thirties stood there in a silk suit. Her eyes narrowed on his tie. Several arcane glyphs were sewn into the tie in red and white thread.

She might not have recognized him without the conversation in the Lyft but, her mind now primed, she found herself blasé about meeting one of the richest men in the world—maybe because of who stood to his side: a scowling dark-haired man with his hand inside his jacket. He clutched a black wand.

Alison laughed. "You look just like your picture, Terrence." She glanced at the other man. "Nice to meet you, Mr. Carlyle."

"You can call me Scott," he replied, disaffection under-lying his voice. His gaze flicked to Terrence. "You've made a serious accusation, Miss Brownstone. Care to elaborate?"

Terrence's face twitched, but he didn't move or use any magic.

Alison glanced at Scott and Terrence. The billionaire

seemed calm, but the wizard looked like he'd try to kill her at any second.

She sighed. "Okay, here's the deal. I'm not technically after Terrence. I'm trying to recover a magic-amplifying gem he stole from a client of mine. If Terrence surrenders the gem, I'll go without any trouble although I'm sure he's done some awful things. But like I said, I'm here for the gem, not Terrence, so I'm sure we can all come to an agreement to handle this without anyone breaking anything." She held up a finger. "Oh, by the way, the gem is very dangerous, and not something that should be out in public anyway."

Terrence snorted. "Do you have any idea where you are?" He pointed at Scott. "If you try anything in this mansion, you'll be answering to a billionaire and a billionaire's security team." He grinned.

Alison frowned. The bastard was right. She had no evidence that Scott had done anything wrong other than talk to Terrence, and if she hurt him, the AET wouldn't be stopped by her mysterious benefactor. Whoever it was probably didn't have more local influence than the CEO of one of the most valuable companies on the planet.

Scott rubbed his chin. "That's a good point. Any sort of battle in here would risk damaging my home." He gestured to the door. "Please fight outside. Don't worry about the fountain. That's easy to replace. My people won't get involved. This isn't my problem."

Alison blinked. "Huh?"

"Outside. Fight there." He shrugged. "Simple enough."

Terrence stared at him agape. "You can't do this to me."

Scott gave him a cool look. "Do you want me to summon the security team you just mentioned?"

"We had a fucking deal, and now you're selling me out to this bitch?"

"Not necessarily, unless you're presupposing she'll win, which is telling." The billionaire adjusted his tie and shook his head. "And I do so hate uncouth people, Mr. McKenna. You know what I also hate? People who blame others for their self-made problems." He shook his head. "You see, I wasn't aware that I would be dealing with stolen property. That means I need you to leave, and it also means that I'm going to have to fire someone for incompetence."

Terrence's dark glare shifted between Scott and Alison. "You've made a big mistake."

Scott shrugged. "You could always give her the gem." He glanced at Alison. "You promise you will let him leave if he hands over the gem?"

Alison sighed. "I don't want to but I will. I'm being paid to find the gem, not take him down." She held out her hand. "Give it to me, Terrence, and this ends. No fuss. No blood."

The wizard sprinted for the door and rushed outside.

"They always run," Alison observed.

Scott pursed his lips. "I can imagine. Please handle his matter before it spills out to my neighbors. I understand that a certain amount of collateral damage is inevitable, but I'd truly appreciate it if you could avoid damaging the main mansion."

Alison blinked at the man. "Uh, sure. I'll keep that in mind."

She ran after Terrence, her confidence building. If he

had been trying to sell the gem, that meant he hadn't unlocked its full power. Her residual strain shouldn't slow her down too much in a straight duel with a cowardly wizard.

This was going to be fun.

CHAPTER FOURTEEN

Alison emerged from the mansion to find Terrence standing about fifteen yards away, his wand out and several glyphs orbiting him at different levels, linked by shimmering lines. His eyes glowed bright white, and he grinned from ear to ear as he held up his free hand. He had a small dull gem in his palm.

"You lose, Brownstone," he shouted. "You should have left well enough alone."

She sighed and summoned a shield, building several quick layers of intertwined light and shadow defensive reflection spells over her body. They left her cloaked in a shifting cloudy haze.

It would have been nice to have combat artifacts of her own. Like the Aegis Pendant, several had been destroyed in battles over the last few years, and she'd been slow to replace them. In some cases, she'd even given them away as her confidence with her magic grew, especially after training with the Drow. The idea of a virus sapping her ability had never even occurred to her.

Probably a good thing to have spent my money on, but it doesn't matter. Just one guy. I can take one guy, even if he's all powered up.

"You shouldn't even be using that thing," Alison called. "It's dangerous. If it blows up, you'll die too."

Terrence snarled. "I know. I figured I could offload it, but you've ruined that, you stupid bitch. I won't go too far."

"The guy who blew himself up earlier today probably thought that too." Alison shook her head. "All you have to do is give me the gem, and I go away. None of this has to be a big deal. I'm not here for you. I'm here for the gem."

"Do you have any idea how much money you've cost me?" Terrence thrust his wand toward her. The porch exploded, sending Alison flying. She slammed into the ground and rolled with a grunt. "My freedom was in my reach. I've been waiting my entire life for a score like this. Carlyle was ready to buy it."

Alison hopped to her feet and laughed. "Did you really think you could steal something like that and get away with it? You brought this on yourself, asshole. Don't cry to me."

She threw out her arm to launch a curved shadow blast. The attack disappeared, but one of Terrence's glyphs dimmed. Two more quick attacks followed before Terrence waved his wand and shouted an incantation.

A bright arcane circle appeared beneath Alison. Glyphs of light rapidly filled it.

Alison rolled her eyes. She ran forward but bounced off an invisible field. "Shit."

"See you in hell, Brownstone," Terrence screamed.

A massive explosion erupted from the circle. Agony

shot through Alison as she tumbled through the air, light burns on her hands and face, her defensive spells shredded and gone. She shook her head and realized she was a good forty feet up and heading back down to an inevitable reunion with the ground.

Alison grimaced and concentrated. The shadows behind her pooled into wings, arresting her fall a few feet from contact. She hovered above the ground for a few seconds and then released the magic, quickly layering a few more shields.

Her vision wavered and her body burned, but she was still in the fight.

He's a cocky bastard. I can use that. He's convinced he'll win.

Huge chunks of rock and dirt ripped up from the ground around her. Alison rushed forward, alternately flinging energy bolts of light magic and shadow toward Terrence. His glyphs continued to dim with each hit, but he didn't move. He remained there, chanting incantations.

The chunks shot toward Alison, narrowly missing her as she advanced on the wizard. She flung out a shadow line toward the fountain a few yards behind her opponent and flew toward the structure. Terrence's face scrunched in confusion.

Alison took the opportunity to yank out her gun and open fire, but her bullets bounced off her enemy's shield. The dimming of his glyph was so slight she barely could tell.

Yeah, should also stock up on a few more anti-magic bullets.

The wizard frowned and pointed his wand at the fountain. The entire marble structure shattered into thousands of pieces, and dozens slammed into Alison like a shotgun blast fired by the Fremont Troll.

She grunted as she crashed into the ground, rolling several times. Her gun flew out of her hand. Her shields held, but her vision continued to swim. Fiery pain pulsed through her body.

That damned gem is feeding him too much power. Shit. I underestimated him. Think. Have to think.

Her breathing ragged, Alison formed a shadow blade. She'd have a better chance if she could close on him and disrupt his defensive layers one by one.

Alison hissed as another explosion knocked her on her back.

A few seconds later she regained her bearings, and she lay on the ground taking shallow breaths. She wished she had a healing potion, but it wouldn't do anything for the AMDS strain anyway.

"I'm enjoying this," Terrence shouted. "The great Alison Brownstone. You're not so tough. Maybe I'll take this down to LA and take out your dad next. I'll be the man who killed Alison and James Brownstone."

You just said the wrong thing, asshole.

Alison gritted her teeth, forcing her mind to focus on Terrence and ignore her pain as she stood and wiped blood off her face. She narrowed her eyes and crouched, focusing on the smirking wizard in the distance as dark energy circled her legs and more flowed into a long thin shadow lance in front of her.

She allowed herself a pained grin as she thought about everything she'd learned in her short visit to the Drow. The

School of Necessary Magic had unlocked her potential, and the Drow had helped her refine it.

Terrence laughed. "Don't you get it? You can't win. I'll admit it, Brownstone—if I didn't have the gem, you might have had a chance, but I'm not some pathetic group of gangsters. Right now I'm pretty much a god. An angry, vengeful god."

"Keep telling yourself that." Alison flung out her free hand, and dozens of white orbs exploded in a bright rainbow shower of sparks. Terrence hissed and stumbled back, squinting. She released the energy building around her legs with an earsplitting boom and her body hurtled toward Terrence as she shoved more energy into her blade.

The wizard stumbled a few steps, blinking his abused eyes.

The shadow lance hit Terrence's shield. His glyph layers vanished, but the impact dissipated the energy of Alison's weapon. Her body continued moving forward, and her shoulder slammed into Terrence's chest. They sprawled to the ground.

Alison slapped the gem out of his hand into the nearby grass and pulled the knife from an inside jacket pocket. She whipped her arm around, going for his throat, but he threw up his arm and screamed as she drove the blade into it.

With a quick yank, she sent his wand flying. She found the strength for two quick face punches. Blood spurted from Terrence's nose and he groaned, his eyes rolling up.

Alison managed to stand although her knees kept threatening to buckle. A few steps came next, but she'd lost the dull gem in the darkness. Every part of her hurt, but she'd won, even though the bastard had had the gem.

A haze spread in her mind, and she blinked to keep herself conscious. Passing out would end her pain, but she needed to find the gem first.

Alison scoffed and faced Terrence. "Small-time wizards should stay small time." She hissed in pain and took deep breaths. "I didn't want to do this. You know how much magic you and your asshole friends made me use today? You were going to lose anyway. You should have just surrendered, damn it." She flung her hands into the air. "And now look at you. No gem. No wand. Broken nose. Knife in your arm!" She laughed but winced at the stinging flare that followed. "You threw everything you had at me when you were on magical steroids, but I still won. Brownstone isn't just a name, asshole. You and every other piece of shit out there who gets in my way better remember that."

Terrence groaned and rolled to his side. He managed to sit up. "You...haven't won, bitch. I'll get the gem, and I'll kill you. What can you do? You can barely stand."

"At least I'm standing, which is more than I can say for you."

She kept her voice confident, but it was hard to focus on the man now. Everything grew blurry and indistinct.

A harsh buzz sounded behind Alison and a blue-white bolt zoomed past her, making her skin tingle. The shot struck Terrence in the chest.

His mouth opened to scream but no sound came out, probably because of the huge hole where his lungs had been. He stared at Alison in surprise for a few seconds before slumping.

Alison blinked and looked behind her. Scott Carlyle advanced toward her, a sleek silver rifle covered in golden glyphs in his hand.

She blinked several times, trying to clear her vision and ignore the agony screaming from every cell in her body.

Sorry, Mom. Sorry, Dad. I didn't plan for the billionaire ambush.

Alison pitched forward with a groan, the darkness taking her.

CHAPTER FIFTEEN

Alison groaned and opened her eyes. She was staring up at a high, angled ceiling and lying in a massive bed without a blanket. The mattress molded to her body with the perfect melding of resistance and give.

I should get one of these.

She patted her face. Her glasses were still on.

With a groan, she sat up and rubbed her eyes. Her boots and jacket were off, but she was still wearing her dirty, ripped, and charred clothes. She sighed at the now-familiar dull throbbing ache of excessive magic use.

A quartz-topped nightstand sat next to the bed. The gem lay on the top.

"So the billionaire's ambush was a billionaire's rescue? Huh. Didn't see that one coming."

Her survey suggested a small but elegant guest room with an oak desk and dresser along the wall and a comfortable looking recliner near the desk. Her jacket was folded in the chair.

Alison checked her body. Despite the damage to her

clothes and the AMDS-related unpleasantness, her other wounds were gone.

Someone else had given her a healing potion or used healing magic.

A light knock came from the door.

"Come in," she called.

The door opened and Scott stepped through, his expression neutral and his hands folded behind his back. He wasn't wearing a jacket. Grass and dirt stained his shirt and his sleeves were rolled up, revealing his toned arms and emphasizing his nice biceps.

Wait, why I am focusing on his nice biceps?

Alison shook her head to clear it. Everything about the day had been bizarre, even by her standards.

His mouth quirked into a small smile. "I was expecting a little collateral damage, not having my entire front yard and fountain destroyed. You do like to make a scene, don't you, Miss Brownstone?"

She sat down on the edge of the bed and shrugged. "To be fair, that was mostly Terrence, and please call me Alison. I kind of figure after I nearly die in a guy's yard, we should be on a first-name basis."

"Very well, Alison." Scott chuckled. "How are you feeling?"

"I'm...fine," she lied. No reason for the handsome billionaire to know about her medical problem.

He tilted his head, a question in his eyes. "Good. I'd hate to think I wasted a healing potion on you."

Does he believe me? I kind of feel like he can see right through me.

"That was you?"

Scott nodded. "I keep a supply on hand. You never know when someone might try to assassinate you."

"That's a very paranoid way of looking at things."

He chuckled. "Considering your past and your family, I would think you'd share my view."

"It's been...better lately." Alison shrugged and managed a smile. "Thanks for the assist. I'm kind of embarrassed. I should have been able to kick a solo wizard's ass with ease."

"Taking the man on when he had that artifact was brave, Miss Brownstone. Foolish, perhaps, but brave. And you did ultimately win." His eyes hardened. "But I felt that Mr. McKenna needed to be finished off. Consider that ruthless if you will, but it's done."

She stared into Scott's dark eyes. "Trying to save me or cover your involvement?"

He offered her a thin smile. "I was not going to purchase that artifact from McKenna. By the way, the PDA has already come and gone. They have his body. Unfortunately, I think your knife was still in it. I hope it wasn't precious to you."

"It was neat, but I'd just bought it. So, they took his body and my knife." Alison glanced at the gem. "But you didn't hand that over?"

"It's not government property." Scott shrugged. "And I'd hate to annoy you for no good reason when you made such a concerted effort to recover it." He nodded to the nightstand. "Please take it back to your client with my regards."

Alison eyed the gem. "I had passed out, and it was in the middle of a wrecked yard. You could have claimed you lost it. Could have told the PDA the same thing. I'm guessing you're the kind of guy who can make them look the other way."

"I could have, but I've found that lying unnecessarily complicates matters. I only lie when there's no better way to accomplish what I need."

"You told them about it?" She arched a brow.

Scott shook his head. "Not offering information isn't the same thing as lying."

She locked eyes with him. "You could also have finished me off and blamed it on Terrence. Not like the PDA would dig that deep, especially given who you are. Why didn't you?"

Scott laughed. "You don't think much of me, do you?"

"I don't trust you fully, no. Something about this whole thing still smells. I have a hard time believing a smart and ridiculously rich man like you would just happen to end up chatting with a scumbag like McKenna." Alison sighed and shrugged. "Look, thanks for helping me and giving me the gem, but maybe I don't like unnecessary lying either."

He nodded, a curious look in his eyes. "I know most people don't trust the wealthy, but I'd expect more from you, Alison. Your straightforward manner aside, I happen to know that you're not exactly poor. Even if we ignore that your adopted father's accumulated bounty money, investments, and business interests make him wealthy by any reasonable standard, your own financial resources aren't insignificant, thanks to your inheritance, your own previous bounty efforts, and his management of your money. It's also come to my attention that you've sold some artifacts as well." He snorted. "You might play the rough-and-tumble streetwise girl, but you're a wealthy child of privilege who went to an elite magic school."

Alison chuckled and shrugged. "It's all relative, right? I'm poor compared to you, and all the magic I have doesn't give me the kind of influence you have."

"It's a difference in degree, not kind."

"How do you know all this? Some of it isn't public information." Alison reached up and pulled her glasses off.

She managed not to frown. A powerful magical aura emanated from the tie, so bright that she couldn't discern his soul colors.

Talk about a power tie.

Scott nodded. "I had appropriate personnel to check into certain things. I thought it prudent given your family connections when I became aware you were in town looking for the gem."

"And how the hell did you find that out? It's not like I told a bunch of people."

He shrugged. "Information wants to be free, Alison." Scott crossed his arms and shook his head. "So I made arrangements."

"'Arrangements?'" She frowned. "What does that mean?"

Scott eyed her for a moment. "It's as you said. I was perfectly aware of who McKenna was, but I didn't think it'd hurt to keep him around me for a few days until you showed up. I wanted to see how you dealt with him, but you arrived much quicker than I anticipated." He shrugged. "I wasn't planning to interfere in your job. I just took an opportunity where we both could get something we wanted: you the gem, and me firsthand experience of your capabilities. I was confident you could handle him."

Alison stared at the man, bile rising in the back of her throat. She had been playing checkers with a chicken while the billionaire was playing three-dimensional chess.

"Still," Scott continued with a sigh, "all this makes me even more puzzled by you."

"Puzzled?" She furrowed her brow. "What do you mean?"

Scott walked over to the chair. He grabbed her jacket and tossed it to her before taking a seat. "You know the earliest lesson I learned in business?"

Alison shrugged. "Buy low, sell high? Don't reason from a price change?"

He chuckled and shook his head. "No man is an island. I would have thought you already knew this. Your father went from hunting men by himself to establishing an entire bounty hunting agency, arguably an army. You have the resources to build a team, so you don't end up fighting a wizard alone and relying on the generosity of your local CEO. No matter how powerful your magic or artifacts, it's good to have someone who has your back."

Alison shrugged. "Shouldn't a woman know herself before she tries to lead others?"

What is his angle? There has to be something I'm missing.

"We grow by leading others. Waiting for perfection is waiting for eternity." Scott threaded his fingers together and rested his chin on them. "Or is it that you're afraid?"

"Afraid?" Alison scoffed. "I'm a Brownstone. I just took on a crazed wizard with a ridiculously powerful artifact, and that's not counting the half-dozen dark wizards I took out earlier when I was looking for the guy."

"Not afraid for yourself. Others."

Her stomach knotted. "What do you mean?"

"Risking one's own life is trivial. Risking another person's life is the true test." Scott leaned forward. "There's no shame in caring about others and wanting to protect them, Alison, but destroying yourself in the process will leave those you care about with one less protector."

Alison blinked several times and looked away. She wanted to tell him he was wrong, but she didn't know if that was true.

All my magic and I couldn't save Tanner. Mom says I shouldn't feel guilty about the wish, but even if I used that, it's not mine, really, just an inheritance.

Izzie's on the run, and I can't do anything to help her. Maybe this guy's right. Damn, he's good. Damned if I'll tell him that.

She sighed. "I've got my reasons for the way I do things."

"I understand that, but I'd encourage you to consider your options." Scott shrugged. "You have the resources to at least begin to explore them, but I'll admit I'm biased in this case."

"Biased?"

He nodded. "I want to make sure I've made a good investment. Even though your presence in Seattle is temporary, I don't think it's a waste of resources to make sure I'm on your good side. We could have future dealings both here and in other places. That was why I used my influence to convince the authorities that harassing you wasn't wise, especially since all you did was clean up an infestation they'd failed to handle."

Alison narrowed her eyes. "Wait a second—*you're* my mysterious benefactor? Why? What are you hoping to get out of it in the future?"

Scott laughed, the sound unusually merry compared to his previous attempts. "'Mysterious benefactor?' You make this sound like a Dickens novel. As for why, you're the daughter of James Brownstone. Not only that you're royalty, a real-life elven princess."

She shrugged. "I've trained with the Drow, but I don't have any influence over them."

"I'm a self-made man, Alison. Part of the reason for that is because I've learned to sense advantageous opportunities, and I think you're a good opportunity. Every instinct I have tells me that."

Alison snorted and shook her head. "What do you even mean? You research and produce techno-magic. Yes, I've got magical ability, but I'm sure you have plenty of magicals working for you. What could I possibly bring to the table?"

"As I just told you, you have a unique background and are unusually powerful. My business interests often put me into conflict with dangerous people." Scott inhaled deeply through his nose. "And yes, I do have money and can hire people, but it's difficult to find people who demonstrate great promise that I know I can trust. I consider the confrontation with McKenna functionally an interview where you demonstrated several aspects of your abilities and personality that confirmed you would be a useful asset. You're a security contractor, and I might need you on occasion."

"Asset?" Alison narrowed her eyes. "I'm a freelance security contractor, just to be clear. I'm not going to be anyone's personal lackey."

Scott chuckled. "Of course not. I wouldn't have it any other way. I'm a big believer in the holistic evaluation of people. I also understand that you currently live in DC. All I'm suggesting is that I might occasionally throw some business your way. I'll also help facilitate the fast-tracking of paperwork to set up an official security firm. Even if you don't hire anyone, trust me, it's easier for my accountants this way. When I steer work your way, it'll be from me and other people I know might be compatible clients."

Alison rubbed her cheek. "Honestly, that doesn't sound so bad."

"Real business is win-win, Alison." He shrugged.

"I have to get the gem to my client now, but I'll think about it."

Scott smiled. "Good." He stood. "I'll go ahead and initiate the paperwork."

She frowned. "I haven't made a decision yet."

"It's my time and money to waste." Scott headed toward the door. "And I suspect it won't be a waste."

CHAPTER SIXTEEN

Alison stepped off the elevator and headed toward the hallway leading to her hotel room. She stifled a yawn. It was too damned late, and her body ached. The couple of hours of rest she'd gotten at Scott's mansion weren't enough. Once she got to DC, she'd need to spend a week in bed to fight the exhaustion weighing her body down.

She turned the corner and stopped, blinking.

Hana sat on the floor, her back against the door to Alison's hotel room, her legs out. Although she still had her long black coat, her asymmetric green cocktail dress and matching monster heels were just as inappropriate for the season as her previous outfit had been.

Huh. Maybe nine-tailed foxes run hot?

Hana stared at her phone, occasionally swiping and chuckling to herself. "That's so stupid."

Alison marched over to the woman and stared down at her.

Hana didn't seem to notice her at first, but after a long

moment she looked up and grinned. "Hey, girlfriend. Long time no see." She hopped to her feet.

Alison shrugged. "A few days. Not that long."

Hana nibbled her lip, worry in her eyes. "And you're okay? You look a little tired."

Alison laughed. "Yeah, I had a busy day, but this has nothing to do with the Eastern Union. Other…assholes, but I've finished what I came to this city to do." She reached into her pocket and rubbed the gem before pulling out her keycard. "Let's talk in my room."

The fox-woman nodded.

Alison swiped the card and opened the door. She motioned inside.

Hana entered and threw herself on the bed, spreading her arms and legs out. "This is so comfy. I'm always afraid to charm myself into expensive places. They're more likely to have some other magical around who'll figure out what I've done."

Alison chuckled and closed the door before sitting in the single chair in the room. "I wasn't sure if you got out okay. I saw you kick a little ass, but I ran into trouble on the first floor so I couldn't be sure."

"I can use the claws when I need them, but my preferred weapons are my beauty and charm." Hana sat up with a smile. "But you, though—you're the real deal. I might have a few tricks hidden in my tails, but if a bunch of guys shot me, I'd die."

A frown crept onto Alison's face. "And you're completely okay? You haven't racked up a new gambling debt with a vicious criminal gang or ended up oath-bonded to a complete sonofabitch?"

Hana rolled her eyes. "Ouch, girlfriend. *Ouch*." She tapped the side of her head. "No, I'm fine. I can learn a lesson or two. I've asked around, and no one in the Eastern Union gives a crap about little ol' me. They're worried about you, though. I'd watch your back. I even heard one guy call you the Scourgette." She laughed.

"I'm not my dad. I'm a little more restrained." Alison sighed.

The other woman stared at her, her dark eyes wide in disbelief. "You, like, killed most of the guys in a building." She held up a hand. "Not that I'm bitching. Those bastards would have tortured me to death. Just saying, if that's restrained, I don't want to see you off the chain."

Alison shrugged. "I can't help if they didn't learn their lesson." She groaned and laid her head on the back of the chair. "Now I sound like my dad."

Hana laughed. "There are worse things than having a badass dad."

"I guess that's true." Alison sighed. "Look, not trying to be a bitch—"

Hana cut her off with an eye roll. "That sentence never ends with the person thinking you're not a bitch."

"Sure. Fine." Alison shrugged. "The point is, why are you here, Hana?"

The dark-haired woman sighed, her smile fading. "I tried to screw you over." Her face scrunched in disgust. "But I'm free now because of you, despite lying to you from the beginning. I owe you. I might occasionally lie or convince people to give me things they shouldn't, but when someone helps me, I pay them back."

"You don't have to. I didn't take down the Daimyo for you. I took him down for personal reasons."

Hana scooted to the edge of the bed and let her legs hang over. "Oh, is that how you're going to play it?" She grinned. "Tough-as-nails Alison Brownstone just happens to help out the con artist fox who tried to screw her over? Mighty convenient for me."

"It's the truth," Alison insisted.

"You took the time in the middle of the fight to tell me to escape." Hana smirked.

"I was just pointing out a possibility."

Hana rolled her eyes. "Then you shot two guys to cover my escape. That meant you weren't sure you were going to win, or you would have told me to stay put until you finished everyone off."

Alison frowned. "I knew I could win."

"Maybe." Hana shook her head. "But you weren't posi-tive, so you wanted to make sure I got away, if only to give me a few hours more to find a way out of my problem. No one has cared about me like that for a long time, not since..." She blinked and looked down. "I wasn't lying about my parents. When I lost them, I was young and screwed. Say what you will about humans, at least there's some solidarity. I can't say the same about every magical. The few who showed any interest in me wanted to use me for my power, and it didn't help that I was hot even as a teenager." She looked up. "What can I say? It's weird to me. Plenty of guys have done nice things for me even without the charm, but they didn't know what I was. They thought I was just a cute girl who's funny and fun. You knew I was bad news, and you still gave a damn."

Alison pointed to her glasses. "Do you know why I wear these?"

"To see better?" Hana shrugged. "Isn't that why anybody wears glasses?"

"I was born kind of blind," Alison announced.

"Huh?" Hana blinked. "What do you mean, 'kind of blind?'"

"I couldn't see what normal people see, but I could see magical energy and souls." Alison ran her finger over the frames of her glasses. "These let me see what everyone else sees, but without them, I can still see what I did before—souls. You can't hide your soul. I see the truth of it when I want to. It's how I knew James Brownstone was a good man when everyone else just saw a tattooed thug." She offered Hana a smile. "I could see the pain in your soul, Hana. I know you've got a long way to go, but I also know you're a good person. You didn't deserve what that man wanted to do to you, and more to the point, you had already proved you were a good person."

"What? By running away when you were surrounded by an entire gang?" Hana shrugged. "Yeah, give me an award."

Alison shook her head. "I don't know if your charm magic would have worked on me, but I only don't know because you stopped yourself. You started to use it and you realized it was wrong to turn me over to the Daimyo, even with your own life on the line."

"I've...done a lot of bad things in my life, Alison." Hana sighed. "I don't know if you can say I'm a good person because I stopped myself from helping sell a woman into sex slavery. That's a pretty damned low bar to clear."

"Like I said, I can see your soul. We all deserve our

chance for redemption. My dad and mom taught me that." Alison smiled.

Hana stared at Alison for a moment. "You're telling the truth, aren't you? About all that soul stuff? I kind of wondered what was going on. I knew something magical was involved, but I didn't want to make you mad when you might kill me."

"Yeah. It's the truth. Just saying, don't be so hard on yourself."

Hana's smile returned. "I still owe you. Maybe I've been bad about my gambling debts, but not life debts. You said you're not into oath magic so I won't offer, but if you're ever in Seattle and you need help with something I might be useful for, call me. I'll give you my number. Or, heck, if you just want to hang out and have a good time, we can do that too. I still need to take you to Maneki." She placed her palms together. "It's closed right now, but what about tomorrow?"

"I've got to head back to DC first thing tomorrow. I have a client eagerly awaiting delivery of an item."

"Oh, that sucks. Well, like I said, if you're ever back in Seattle, give me a ring." Hana hopped off the bed. "I'll set you up, girlfriend. I promise." She rattled off her phone number.

Alison pulled out her phone and entered Hana into her contacts list. "I don't doubt it. Try and stay away from gangsters in the meantime."

Hana laughed and saluted, then strode to the door in her killer heels, her smile growing and becoming infectious. She grabbed the door handle. "I looked some stuff up on you the other day. I'd heard of you because of the adoption thing, and everyone's heard of your dad, but I was pretty young when that went down, so I didn't know a lot about you."

"Oh?"

"Are you seriously a princess?"

Alison groaned. "Um, technically yes. I'm the Drow Princess of the Shadow Forged."

Hana laughed. "You sound so depressed by it."

"It's weird. I've trained some with the Drow, but I was raised on Earth and thought I was human until I was fifteen. It's hard to relate to them." Alison shrugged. "I don't think I'm ready to get involved in Drow stuff."

"So now I can go around telling people how not only was I saved by a badass half-elf, but I was saved by genuine royalty." Hana winked, opened the door, and slipped into the hallway. "See you around, princess."

Alison chuckled. "See you around, fox."

CHAPTER SEVENTEEN

When Alison stepped out of the Starbucks in DC, she wasn't surprised to see Mr. D standing in front, his hands resting on a walking stick.

She laughed. "I didn't tell you when I'd be coming in today. You're good."

The gnome offered a thin smile. "With McKenna's death, the spells shielding him from my detection are also gone, and that effectively means the spells hiding the gem vanished. I knew the second you departed with the gem, and I knew when you arrived."

Alison reached into her pocket and pulled out the gem. "Always funny how something so small can cause so much trouble."

"Such is life." Mr. D held out his hand. "I'm impressed, Miss Brownstone. I thought it might take you weeks to recover this, and there was a high probability it would cost your life. I'm still surprised you faced him successfully when he was drawing on its power. Even if he were less effective with it than he could have been, many people would have fallen before him."

"I'll admit things got a little close for comfort, but I had everything under control." She leaned over to put the gem in the gnome's hand. "And there was no way I was going to let that guy beat me."

The gnome closed his hand. When he reopened it the gem was gone, the faint tingle of magical energy in the air.

"I've already transferred the rest of your payment to your account." Mr. D offered her a polite nod. "Thank you again for your assistance, Miss Brownstone. You've saved the world, me, and my cousin potentially serious trouble. I can assure you the best spells and men will take care of this problem so that your services aren't required in the future."

Alison nodded. "If you ever need help again, give me a call."

"Of course." He set off down the sidewalk.

Alison watched the gnome for a few seconds, thinking over recent events. She'd thought DC with its politicians and dangerous underworld was an out-of-control place, but the whole city was quiet and sleepy compared to the craziness of Seattle.

I don't think LA was that bad back in the day. Did losing the kemana mess things up that much?

She shook her head and walked toward a waiting Currus, pondering Scott Carlyle's suggestions. They echoed her mom's advice, which gave them credibility, and Alison could logically understand the appeal of having a team backing her rather than continuing as a solo operation.

If anything, her time at the School of Necessary Magic

had taught her how strong people could be when they backed each other up.

She sighed. It'd also taught her the pain of losing people.

Alison opened the door and slipped into one of the seats. The Currus pulled out of the parking lot, and she tried to refocus on her business plans.

A firm, huh? Dad had his reputation and credibility to convince people to work for him. I might be a Brownstone, but I'm not James Brownstone. Even if I pay well, I can't run a company if people don't respect me and see nothing but a spoiled little twenty-five-year-old princess they think is child of privilege. And it's not like Izzie can come out of hiding to help me, or Lily's going to quit tomb raiding to become a security contractor.

She stared out the window at the passing buildings. Her lifestyle for the first fifteen years of life had been far from wealthy and privileged. Even after that, although the School of Necessary Magic was an elite and select school, it focused on talent and potential, not wealth. Her dad's house was a modest two-story in a very modest neighborhood. It had become gentrified in the previous decade, if only because all the men and women in the neighborhood worked for the Brownstone Agency and dumped their money back into their local community, following the example of their boss.

Child of privilege? I shouldn't let Scott get into my head like that. Just another way he's trying to manipulate me. I should focus on the firm.

It didn't matter. The first thing she wanted to do was take a shower in her own apartment.

After a quick shower and a change of clothes, Alison went to her Fiat. Her thoughts kept returning to the conversation in Seattle. Even if Scott helped her, it didn't mean he owned her. Taking minor advantage of a generous billionaire wasn't a bad thing.

Like he said, good business is win-win.

She slipped into the driver's seat and frowned. Scott wasn't just a generous billionaire, but a man looking ahead and planning for people's reactions.

"There's just something about that guy. I can't decide if I want to punch him in the face or get to know him better. It's not like he stole the gem, but he didn't mind cozying up to a guy just to get me to show up. Who does that?"

Alison chuckled and started her car. She could figure him out later. Right now it was time for delicious victory sushi.

About ten minutes into her drive, Alison dialed her father and set the call to speakerphone.

"Hey, kid," James rumbled over the phone.

She laughed. "I'm twenty-five now. How long are you going to keep calling me 'kid,' Dad?"

"I'll stop when you're older than me."

"That will be a challenge," Alison replied.

James grunted. "Then get used to me calling you kid forever. I wanted to call you about that disease shit, but Shay told me I'd be smothering you and that you'd call us if you needed help. Wrong move?"

"No, it's fine. That's all under control for now, and I always have the wish if it gets too bad. For now, I'm accepting that it's there and trying to work around its limitations, just like you've had to." Alison did a quick mirror and camera check. "I might have to stock up more on anti-magic bullets and artifacts, though. I think I've gotten a little too used to kicking ass with my magic."

"Yeah, I get that," he replied. "Not like I'd take on someone without Whispy these days if I had to, but a good blade or gun will take you far. You're smarter than me, though. You'll get it figured out."

"The disease is making things tougher, but I just finished up a pretty serious job, and it didn't hold me back that much." Alison decided she didn't want to mention Scott blowing the guy away in front of her to help her. "Definitely going to invest in a good magic knife or two soon."

James chuckled. "Serious job? You blow up that rich douchebag's mansion in Seattle? Shay and I have a bet on that."

Alison laughed. "Saw that on the news? Yes, I was involved, but I wasn't the one blowing it up, and it was mostly his yard. He's not a douchebag, I think. Maybe."

"What's that mean? Sounds complicated."

She could almost hear James frowning over the phone.

"You know how it goes, Dad. You're trying to do a job, and things just get out of hand." Alison changed lanes to get away from a tailgating truck. "And people just won't do the easy thing, and next thing you know some building is blown up or something. Or you're blown up, and you have to get a new coat because your old one is burned."

"That's why I just bought a lot of the same kind of coat, even if Shay hated my choice." James chuckled. "Shit happens. Is that what you wanted to talk about, whatever happened in Seattle? No one's giving you shit about it, are they?" A hint of deep menace underlined his words.

"No one's giving me shit, but I did want to talk to you about something that happened there." Alison sighed. "When I was there, someone suggested I start a security firm and look into recruiting people to help me. Mom has mentioned the same thing, and I just wanted to get your direct opinion on it. After all, you were the original lone wolf Brownstone."

"Think about what you just called me."

Alison furrowed her brow. "Lone wolf? I wasn't trying to insult you, Dad."

He grunted. "Don't give a shit about that. What I'm saying is, wolves are pack animals. Yeah, I was a lone wolf, then I became the alpha of a pack or whatever the fuck you want to call my company, and I became stronger because of it. I also think if you have an official firm, the government will worry about you less. I feel bad that because of who I am and who your mother is they have their eye on all of us, but even taking that into account, they're probably watching you because of your heritage."

Alison made a face. "I've had contact with the PDA in DC and Seattle recently. It hasn't been too bad, though."

"Just saying. The more you play by the rules, the fewer reasons they have to fuck with you. Keep that in mind. I don't want you to have to deal with the kind of shit I had to deal with."

Alison turned at an intersection. She wasn't that far from Washington Union Station and more importantly, Odaiba, where she planned to have her victory sushi.

"So you think it's a good idea to start my own security firm?"

"Starting a company was a good idea for me," James replied, "but I'm not gonna tell you what to do. You're twenty-five now, and way smarter than me. I'll only tell you that starting the Brownstone Agency was the second smartest thing I ever did."

"And what was the first?" Alison asked.

"It's a tie between adopting you and marrying Shay."

Warmth rose in Alison's face, along with a smile. "That's really sweet, Dad."

He mumbled something under his breath. "Don't tell her I said it. She'll bust my balls about it for the next week."

Alison chuckled. "Sure, Dad. I'll keep it to myself. Oh, I'm almost to my victory sushi place, but I wanted to chat about something before I get off the phone."

"You should have victory barbeque," he rumbled. "They don't cook sushi."

"They cook the rice, and not every sushi ingredient is raw."

James sighed. "Enough are. Just saying."

"This will make you happy." Alison laughed. "I actually wanted to talk to you about barbeque."

"Oh?" Hope filled his voice. "You going to join the competitive barbeque circuit?"

"No. I want to talk about a barbeque show. Mom said you're excited about *Nadina: Low and Slow*. Maybe when it comes to LA, I'll come out, and we can see it together."

Alison turned into the parking garage for Washington Union Station.

"It's going to be a good show," James replied. "They've even got some stuff about Jessie Rae's."

"Wouldn't be a proper barbeque show without your favorite place being mentioned."

He grunted. "Exactly."

Alison slowed her car to maneuver through the narrow maze made by row after row of parked vehicles. "I've got to find a parking spot now, and I'm probably about to lose signal anyway. I'll call you in a few weeks and we can talk about tickets. Love you, Dad."

"I love you, too, Alison," he replied.

She ended the call. Her smile grew. After all the death and violence of the last few days, it was good to be reminded of the people who loved and cared for her.

Successful job, took out a few dark wizards, and I have someone helping me set up a company. My victory sushi is well-earned.

Alison passed beneath the huge arches leading into the main food court and ran into an ocean of people. Although many came to the station to take trips on the trains, buses, or airbuses, plenty of people came for the food. It'd become as much a place to find a good meal as a transit hub.

Faint tension suffused her body at the density of the crowd, joining the residual ache and fatigue from Seattle. Alison liked people one on one, but too many people together reminded her too much of what it was like when she had to stare into masses of energy, much of it negative. Despite that, a little discomfort was worth it for sushi.

She continued to maneuver and push past people as she made her way toward the opposite side of the massive arched chamber where tables were scattered in front of restaurant counters, including Odaiba, along with a group of other small pick-up only places.

Her stomach rumbled as sweet grassy notes reached her nose. Saffron, she thought, probably from the nearby Tamil place.

Alison ignored the temptation. She was there for victory sushi. Her mouth watered in anticipation at downing more than a few pieces of fatty tuna, her mind convincing her the delicious juxtaposition of slight bitterness and sweetness was already on her tongue.

A loud screech sounded over the PA system, and a number of people clapped their hands over their ears. Murmurs of confusion joined the piercing sound to become a cacophony.

That's annoying.

Someone slammed into Alison's shoulder. She stumbled and frowned at the oblivious man on his phone. He frowned and looked around.

The screeching stopped, and a series of musical tones played.

"Do we have your attention?" asked a low male voice over the PA system.

The raucous noise filling the area died as people glanced around and listened.

"Our world has become polluted," continued the voice. "The threat was always there, but it was small and manageable. Then Oriceran came. Magic returned in force. A normal world with a normal order was upturned.

Chaos reigned. The world suffered. Crime. Hatred. Violence."

Everyone continued searching the area, confused looks on their faces.

Alison narrowed her eyes. She'd heard a speech like this before.

Shit. No, please, just let it be some loudmouths.

"People have accepted that," the man relayed. "Told themselves that magic is part of the new natural order." He barked a harsh laugh. "Ridiculous. Perverse. The brilliant ability of humanity to adapt has been subverted and twisted into something disgusting by the same force that has corrupted our planet: magic."

A few dwarves standing near the Tamil place glowered.

Alison jerked her head around to look for anyone suspicious, but the thousands of people around her made the effort pointless.

"Let us also be clear," the man explained, "that there's no room for bigotry in our vision. Oricerans aren't inherently wrong. They are welcome on Earth as long as they eschew the dark ways of magic."

Wonder how that works for species that can't survive without some form of magic, asshole?

The murmurs of the crowd returned, fear spreading from voice to voice and face to face. The scattered Oricerans stepped away from the crowd as if worried they'd turn on them.

No, you have to realize what you're hearing. We're all in danger. You've at least heard these assholes on the news, right?

"We've tried educating the masses," the man shouted, "but they've mocked us because they are deeply in thrall to the corruption. We've tried educating the leaders, but they are petty men and women ready to sell their souls for power. We've tried killing the leaders, but another always steps into their place. Every attempt to heal this planet has been pushed back, leaving us with only one option: violent demonstration of the perversity of magic."

People rushed toward the exits, shouting or screaming.

Alison's heart thundered. Too many people. Too many targets.

"We will restore the veil between the natural and unnatural," the man thundered, his harsh amplified voice echoing around the vast chamber over the screams of panicking people. "We are the New Veil, and we will save this planet from itself no matter the cost. We will demonstrate the dangers of magic until everyone turns their backs on it."

The hairs on the back of Alison's neck stood up as she sensed magic. Strong magic, at that.

"You hypocritical bastards," she seethed. "What the hell are you planning?"

She turned and saw a small girl, wide-eyed and crying.

"Mommy!" the girl screeched.

Alison jogged toward the girl. "I'll help you find your mom, but we have to get out of h—"

Multiple explosions rocked the station, blowing holes in the massive walls and collapsing parts of the ceiling. People screamed as rubble hit them or a blast tossed them into the air.

Alison stumbled to the ground, her glasses slipping off her face. She spun toward the girl and summoned a shield.

Orange flames ripped from the wall next to Alison. She

threw herself on top of the girl, hissing as the explosion enveloped her shield.

Alison landed, the sobbing girl still in her arms. Bright magical residue nearly blinded her, but she could still discern the red-tinged terror in the girl's energy. She shook her head and stood. "Are you okay?"

The girl nodded, sniffling.

Alison helped her stand and pointed to the exit. "Go now! It's not safe here."

"But my mom!"

"She'll meet you outside." Alison shoved the girl toward the exit. The mob fled toward the door, but dozens of people lay on the ground, some bleeding and unconscious, other moaning or crying. Far too many not moving at all.

She hissed, the energy of so many panicked people mixing with strong residual magic in the area almost over-whelming.

Damn you, New Veil. Damn you. You'll pay for this.

Alison blinked and spun around, looking for her glasses. She caught the familiar energy a few yards away, but something was wrong. She could only see half the glasses, and the energy was rapidly dimming. Several pieces emitting similar magical colors lay next to the piece she could see. She hurried over and knelt to feel around. Bile rose in her throat.

The glasses were broken, half-buried under rubble. That explained why she couldn't see the rest.

No, no, no. Not now. I need to see normally.

The harsh sound of gunfire and additional explosions sounded from several directions. People's plaintive cries joined in a chorus of misery.

Alison looked up and hissed. Too much fear. Too much panic. All the colors blurred into an indistinguishable blob. A gunshot rang out, and a man dropped ten yards away.

She spun, trying to seek out the terrorist responsible, but all she could see were the colors of panic. She gasped as she passed a hole in the wall. A massive magical wall extended outside the station.

It's a damned kill box.

Alison swallowed. She had to do something.

Think, Alison, think.

A magical pulse would let her see the layout to the room like sonar, but it wouldn't do much to help her identify the New Veil terrorists for more than a few seconds unless they were using magical weapons. The terrorists might have used magical bombs and now a magical shield to seal in their victims, but the rat-a-tat of rifle fire made their weapons of choice clear.

Her pulse pounded in her ears. Her twisted stomach would have emptied itself if it had held anything.

What would Dad do? What would Mom do? I have to save these people.

She gritted her teeth. Shay had commissioned the glasses for Alison so she could live a more normal life, whether that meant enjoying a movie or killing terrorist assholes.

Doesn't matter if there are other magicals in the crowd. It doesn't sound like anyone's fighting back, and it's not like everyone is combat trained.

Shit. AET will take too long to get here, and they might not be able to get through the shield.

If I don't do something, a lot of people are going to die.

185

Alison took a deep breath, remembering something Scott had told her.

Not afraid for yourself. Others.

Her father had cut a bloody swath through LA and the greater world as an avatar of vengeance. She wasn't the same, even if she'd killed the Daimyo in a rage.

There'd been so many people she couldn't save in high school, and college, and in the last few years during her occasional dark-wizard hunts.

Alison clenched her fists. Even if she was still recovering from Seattle, she could win as long as she could see the enemy.

Think, think, think.

Yes. That's it. I want to protect these people, and I still have a way of doing that.

She closed her eyes and took a deep breath, concentrating. The Drow had warned her that even the wish had limits. An attempt to wish the New Veil terrorists away would backfire in some twisted way. Keep to specifics. That was what they'd told her. She needed to respect the wish's power while drawing on it to save the innocent people around her.

No more second-guessing. No more worrying about what her parents would do. It was time to become an avatar of protection.

"I wish for normal sight."

CHAPTER EIGHTEEN

All the sounds of the outside world vanished. Even the soul energy and colors of magic faded. There was nothing but darkness and silence. It was serene and calming in its own way.

The world turned white and a dark-skinned woman with long white hair appeared, a smile on her face.

Alison gasped. It was her birth mother Nicole. Another white-haired woman appeared next to her, her skin as dark as midnight. Then another appeared. Dozens. Hundreds, all Drow.

"YOU HAVE CHOSEN." The Drow women spoke as a single booming chorus. "IT IS YOUR RIGHT AS THE PRINCESS OF THE SHADOW FORGED TO CHOOSE. THE WISH IS EXPENDED UNTIL THE TIME OF CONTINUITY AND YOU HAVE EXTENDED THE LINE OF THE SHADOW FORGED."

The Drow women disappeared.

"Show them the true power of a Drow princess," whispered a voice in her ear. "Let them know your righteous wrath so that they will never again dare tempt your power." An invisible hand brushed Alison's cheek. "We can offer you your sight and a small temporary gift of power. Use them both well."

The station reappeared, along with the gunfire and the screams.

Alison blinked several times. She could see the wounded, the rubble, and the blue barrier trapping the fleeing people as if she still had her glasses on, even though the shattered remnants of her glasses sat a few feet away.

She had what she needed to fight—normal vision—but she'd sacrificed more than a wish. She'd sacrificed her ability to see auras and the truth. The wish had extracted its price.

It didn't matter. She didn't have time for regrets. She had terrorists to kill.

Three men with rifles stood near the burning remains of Odaiba firing into the crowd. She swung her arm forward, pouring energy into a wide-angle shadow blast. The curved energy sped from her hand and cut the men in half.

Alison shook her head and summoned a layered light shield.

Four other men rushed around a corner with rifles and took aim at fleeing people. Alison flung four quick energy bolts into their chests and downed them before even realizing she didn't feel any of the now-expected AMDS strain.

Small and temporary gift, huh? Time to go all-out.

Bright lines of glowing white light extended from her

back, along with tendrils of shadow. They twirled together to form wings.

Alison leapt from the ground and soared toward the corner. Sporadic gunfire still came from that direction. She cut around the corner and summoned a long shadow blade in her hand when she spotted a half-dozen terrorists chasing a crowd of panicked commuters.

"Trouble in the air," one of the terrorists shouted.

They all skidded to a stop and jerked their rifles up. They opened fire, their bullets bouncing off her shield. With a grim smile, she dive-bombed the group, finishing them off with two quick slashes and four jabs to chests.

Alison landed and narrowed her eyes at all the wounded people lying on the ground. Despite the lacerations, broken bones, and burns, most were still breathing. If she could open the shield and finish off the terrorists these people could be saved.

She lifted her head at movement from above. Three VTOL dropships hovered above a massive hole in the roof, floating above the blue barrier keeping the victims inside. Waves of blue energy rhythmically pulsed from one of the ships

Alison pulled her arm back and channeled energy into her hand. A bright lance of pure white appeared, its intensity and length increasing by the second.

More terrorists rushed into the room and opened fire, but their bullets continued to bounce off her shield. She ignored them and strengthened her next attack. It was the best chance of saving the most people.

The men charged her as she thrust her arm forward to launch the lance. The magical projectile zoomed through the air and passed through the blue barrier as if it weren't even there. The lance struck the emission ship and the vehicle exploded in a bright flash, the blast consuming the two vehicles next to it and raining debris through the holes in the ceiling.

The blue barrier vanished.

Now at least people could escape.

Alison spun toward the approaching men. She pooled energy into two bright orbs and flung them at the charging terrorists. The explosions scattered them like trees felled by a storm.

Most people had escaped this part of the station, and some of the shouts and screams were growing distant since people could now leave, but another gunshot made it clear the battle wasn't over.

Alison shot into the air and flew toward the closest sound of gunfire. Two quick trips around corners and down the stairs to a boarding platform brought her face-to-face with three more terrorists and dozens of wounded people. The survivors cowered near walls or hid among the seats of the parked train.

The terrorists paused at her sudden appearance, but she didn't give them any time to react before flinging three energy bolts. The men collapsed to the ground, their chests charred.

Alison looked for more terrorists before bounding up the stairs four steps at the time, aided by a push from quickly-produced shadow acceleration disks. She crested the stairs to be greeted by a hail of gunfire.

Twenty terrorists surrounded her. The bullets clattered

to the ground, crushed as if they'd hit a wall, but didn't make it through her shield.

Alison scoffed. "You're afraid of magic, right?" she shouted. "I'll give you magic to be afraid of, you bastards."

Most of the terrorists ignored her and continued firing, but one of the terrorists stopped. He ejected his magazine and popped in a new one.

With a grin, he aimed carefully and fired. "Die, witch."

"Not a wit—"

Her shield slowed the bullet but didn't stop it. Alison cried out as it ripped through her shoulder.

Anti-magic bullet? Shit.

Another bullet hit her in the leg. She hissed again and backed up before starting to laugh hysterically. She hadn't felt the strain of AMDS since the fight began. She only had a short time to go all-out, even shorter than before.

It was time to attempt something she'd avoided for months because of the strain. Another bullet struck her, and she collapsed to her knees.

The other terrorists ceased fire, and the gunman with the anti-magic bullets smirked and advanced.

"There's always a counter to your perversity." He sneered.

"There's a counter to everything," Alison murmured.

Shadows pooled in her wounds, sealing them. The pain drifted away.

The terrorist jumped back, panic in his eyes.

A quick thrust of her arm sent a curved shadow blast into him, and he lost his head. His comrades opened fire again, but their conventional rounds might as well have been spitballs against Alison's current shield.

She soared into the air, bands of white light and pure dark shadow growing around her hands. The terrorists continued firing, several switching to grenade attachments, the explosions blinding her for a moment and achieving their first successes—a slight sting.

Alison dropped to the ground, her hand smashing through the tile. A wave of white- and black-threaded energy blasted from her and struck the terrorists, flinging their now lifeless bodies to the ground.

Alison hissed as a familiar burning throbbing returned.

Running out of the temporary power, huh? Doesn't matter. Just need to beat these assholes. They can't have many guys left.

She stopped and listened. Although people still sobbed in the distance, there was no more gunfire or explosions. Sirens grew closer; the police and ambulances would be there soon.

"Score one for Alison versus the terrorist assholes," she muttered.

Alison released her shield and took a few deep breaths. A rifle cracked from behind her. Pain exploded through her thigh as a bullet ripped through. Another shot hit her arm. She collapsed to her knees when the next shot hit her other leg.

She rolled over and summoned a shield. A scowling man with hard eyes advanced on her. He snorted and fired again. She cried out as the bullet pierced her chest.

Alison coughed up blood, her vision growing dark. She placed her hand on her chest, trying to not lose consciousness.

The man shook his head. "An anti-magic bullet can do

well against perversity but is a form of perversity. Well, the New Veil must degrade itself to save the planet."

"You're a fucking hypocrite." Alison coughed up more blood. "And a fucking murderer."

"No, you sad, pathetic woman. I am like all of the New Veil—a martyr for the soul of this planet."

She released her shield and gritted her teeth. Each breath hurt now.

The terrorist advanced and slammed the barrel against her head. "Any last words?"

Alison swung her arm and extended a shadow blade, slicing the rifle in half. She happened to take the man's hand with it.

The man screamed and stumbled back, clutching his wrist.

She rose and coughed up more blood. Shadows covered her wounds on both sides, the flesh stitching itself back together, but intense pain spiking through her body. Bonus time was over.

Alison fell back to one knee and snorted. "Too much even with a little help, huh, ladies?" She yanked her gun out of her shoulder holster and aimed at the terrorist. She fired until the gun clicked empty, ignoring the fact that the man had fallen after the fifth shot. "That works too."

She collapsed on her back, groaning. There wasn't a single wound left on her body, but every part of her ached, inside and outside. Fatigue created invisible weights on her arms and legs.

Alison turned her head at the sound of heavy clanking steps. Squads of armored AET officers closed on the area, followed by conventional SWAT forces. The whir of heli-copters and roar of dropships sounded overhead.

"I think I did enough," she murmured. "But so much for my victory sushi."

Alison stared at the sun through a hole in the ceiling and snickered.

CHAPTER NINETEEN

Alison wrapped the mylar blanket around her shoulders and waved off the paramedic. "I'm fine. I just needed to catch my breath. At least the assholes didn't blow up the parking garage, so my car should be fine." She winced.

The paramedic shook his head. "Ma'am, you might be in shock. You were barely conscious when the police found you."

"It's fine. I don't need to go to the hospital. I just want to get into my car and go home. I'm hungry for one thing." She frowned.

"There's no way I can release you." The paramedic frowned and stared down at the holes in her clothes. "There are blood and entry wounds in your clothes. Were you shot?"

She shrugged. "A few times, but I have magic. I healed myself."

Mental note: never, ever leave home without a healing potion. I'm out of wishes and bonus power.

Alison tried to smile despite the pulsing ache in her body. Whatever extra juice she'd received as a byproduct of using the wish had long since passed. The horror of the battle over, she could admit to herself that she missed being able to access her full power. Several of the stunts she'd performed in the station would have knocked her out under normal circumstances.

I let the AMDS creep up on me so badly that I've forgotten what I can really do and what the Drow helped me learn.

She looked up and shook her head. "I need to leave. I appreciate your concern, but all I need now is rest."

A suited dapper man with a weathered face stepped from the side of the ambulance, flanked by two men in dark suits and mirror shades. "At least catch your breath, Alison."

The paramedic frowned at the man and advanced toward him. "Excuse me, sir. I need to treat this young woman."

The two bodyguards glared at the paramedic.

The old man smiled at the paramedic. "Lots of people with serious injuries, son. Go treat them. I'll be responsible for Miss Brownstone."

The paramedic frowned at the man. "Who the hell are you?"

"Senator Johnston," Alison explained.

The paramedic blinked.

She chuckled. "It's good to see you again. It's been a long time. A few years, I think?"

The senator smiled. "A Brownstone involved in a major terrorist incident is enough to force even my old butt to check into things personally. Every time I think about retiring, something happens, and I remember why I do what I do. I chatted with your dad a few weeks ago. Did he mention me?"

Alison shook her head. "Nope. Is he in some sort of trouble?"

"No, I was just reviewing governmental expectations," the senator explained. "It's good for everyone to be on the same page." He shrugged. "But I'm not here to talk about him. I'm here to chat with you."

The paramedic glanced between the senator and Alison before sighing, grabbing his first aid kit, and jogging off.

Alison rubbed her shoulders and hissed in pain.

The senator arched an eyebrow. "Maybe I shouldn't have sent the paramedic away, young lady."

She shook her head. "This isn't something they can help with. Have you heard of Advanced Magical Deficiency Syndrome?"

Senator Johnston frowned. "Yes, I have. I'm very sorry to hear you're afflicted, Alison."

Alison shrugged. "It's not lethal as far as they know, so I'm still able to do what I need to do."

"Yes, you are." He gestured around. "You see what I see?"

A man wearing an oxygen mask on a stretcher was being carried into the back of an ambulance. Life flight helicopters flew away from the area, along with a few VTOL ambulances.

She sighed. "I see a lot of hurt people. I was too slow. People got hurt. People died."

Senator Johnston snorted. "Young people are all the same."

Alison frowned. "Meaning what?"

"I've been on God's green Earth for far too many years, and I've learned an important lesson: don't make the perfect the enemy of the good." He shook his head. "Yes, Alison, people died. More than a few, but a hell of a lot more people are alive now because you were here. I have no idea if we could have easily knocked down that wall." He leaned forward and lowered his voice. "I've watched some of the surveillance footage. I saw you blow those dropships out of the sky. It was pure Brownstone. Your father will be proud."

"I did what I had to do."

Senator Johnston crossed his arms and stood up straight. "Of course you did. From what I've watched so far in the surveillance footage, you were very impressive. You need to understand, Alison, that there were thousands of people in that station. If you hadn't immediately acted like you did, there might have been hundreds, if not thousands, of deaths. Also because you opened that wall so quickly and finished them off, we are able to help a lot of these people. We're going to be able to save a lot of the wound-ed." He held up a hand. "That's hundreds, if not thousands, of families who don't have to attend a funeral. Not only that, I'll let you in on a little secret. CIA and FBI have been tracking that particular New Veil cell for a while, but recently lost track of them. You just took out one of the best-financed and equipped New Veil cells. They might have pulled out halfway through the attack and escaped to pull the stunt again somewhere else. You did damned well today, young lady. Don't try to convince yourself of anything else."

Alison sighed and nodded. "I couldn't stand by while they murdered all those people."

"Well, we can't always depend on a Brownstone being around when major terrorists show up, but I'm grateful you were here today."

A woman walked by carrying the little girl Alison had protected earlier.

Alison smiled. "She made it."

The senator furrowed his brow. "Who made it?"

"Sorry. Just some little girl from the start of the attack."

"Good, focus on the positive." He looked around and frowned. "Now, I tell you all this because I want you to understand how grateful the US government and the city of Washington DC are for your assistance in this matter. As far as I'm concerned, you're a damned hero, just like your father."

Alison sighed. "I'm guessing a 'but' is coming."

Senator Johnston nodded. "Exactly. I'm not the only person who has watched that footage, not the only person who saw you pull off magic that might have let you beat your dad, even. And that display of powerful magic has attracted concern and attention from some small-minded men, the same kind of small-minded men we always have to deal with whenever great people are around." He shook his head. "Because of what you are and who your adopted father is, a lot of people in the government continue to be very nervous about you. It helps that there are a lot more magicals openly in the government now and helping influence public opinion, but that doesn't mean there are no other people wondering if regular humans are taking the wrong side."

Alison narrowed her eyes. "Meaning what? They think New Veil is right?"

"Not saying they believe that, just that the flashier you are, the more attention it attracts from men who are upset that we don't have you on a leash." The senator frowned over his shoulder at a low-flying news drone.

"What's the bottom line?" Alison crossed her arms.

"The good news for us is that small-minded men are short-sighted in multiple ways." Senator Johnston sighed. "The simple truth is, out of sight, out of mind can do a lot to keep people from getting in trouble."

"I'm not following you."

He scratched his cheek. "It's come to my particular committee's attention that you recently took a rather exciting trip to Seattle."

Alison snickered. "You really *are* watching me, aren't you?"

Senator Johnston shrugged. "Relocating across the country means you'll be away from the people who are worried about you. It's not that they'll forget, but we're working their little cowardly reptile brains here, Alison. If you're thousands of miles away, it'll be easier for me to use my influence to keep the government off your back, even if you get a little overexcited and live up to the Brownstone name now and again." He chuckled. "Not only that, I have it on good authority that you've landed on the right side of at least a few people in Seattle who can help keep you out of trouble."

She looked at the sky to watch the dance of drones. Several medical helicopters and VTOL ambulances landed to load patients. "You ever feel that fate is railroading you?"

HER FATHER'S DAUGHTER

"Fate?"

Alison nodded. "I did one job in Seattle. Never been there before, and now everyone's trying to get me to move there."

The senator sighed. "I apologize on behalf of the nation, Alison. It disgusts me to see you treated this way, just as it disgusted me when some of my colleagues tried to screw over your father."

She shrugged. "Not your fault, and Dad has always said that you are all right for a politician."

He gave her a thin smile. "Damning with faint praise, indeed."

"You really think moving to Seattle is a good idea?"

"Yes, Alison, I do."

Alison chuckled. "I'm going to at least need a few days of rest."

"Take your time. I don't think PDA is going to be kicking down your door in that time." The senator grinned. "If anything, they'd be too afraid after what they just saw."

Alison considered that for a few seconds before smiling. "Good." She hopped off the back of the ambulance. "I think it's time to go find my car and drive home."

Alison waited until the next afternoon to contact Scott Carlyle with a simple text message, but she sat on her couch spending far too long to come up with it.

Turns out you're not wasting your time helping set up that paperwork for me.

201

A moment later he texted back.

I knew I wouldn't be.

Alison blinked a few times and stared at her phone. She'd taken it for granted when he gave her his private number before she left his mansion, but now she was texting a billionaire like he was her bestie.

"Okay, that's a bit weird. Then again, what about my life has been normal?" She chuckled and shook her head. "Time for step two."

Alison dialed Hana and waited.

"What's up, girlfriend?" Hana answered, her voice cheerful. "Missing me already? You barely left."

"I was hoping to call in that favor you owe me," Alison responded.

"Oh." Hana's tone turned sober. "You coming back for another job? More wrath of the Drow?"

"Not exactly." Alison shifted on the couch. "I'm moving from DC to Seattle."

"Wait, were you involved in that terrorist thing just now? The news keeps saying a 'classified government contractor was involved,' but I kept thinking, 'Hey, if some crazy terrorists are blowing up DC, I wonder if Alison's there kicking their asses.'"

Alison sighed. "It wasn't like I was planning to take on a bunch of terrorists. It wasn't a job. I just wanted some damned sushi, but it's been made clear to me that it'd be best if I moved. A bunch of government assholes are scared of me."

Hana chuckled. "Their loss, but I'm glad to have you back so soon. I never did get to take you to Maneki. You'll love the place. But what favor did you need? I can help you kick a little ass, but like I told you before, you're way tougher than me."

"Don't need any ass-kicking help." Alison shrugged. "At least not yet. Something far less dangerous, I hope. Showing me around Seattle when I come back so I can get a better idea of the lay of the land."

Hana whistled. "Now that I can help with. See you soon. You're going to love Seattle. It's not all gangsters and dark wizards."

Alison laughed. "I'm a security contractor. I don't know if I should be happy or sad about that."

CHAPTER TWENTY

Alison sat across from Hana at a table at Maneki gobbling down some *tako*. She smiled at the nice balance of the octopus nigiri. Not too chewy and not too tender. Almost perfect.

Now here's some victory sushi.

Colorful Ukio-e paintings covered the walls, along with framed Japanese calligraphy. Long-nosed masks representing *tengu*, a type of goblin, and tusked *oni*, Japanese demons, also hung on the walls. Several private sliding-door tatami rooms connected to the main dining room, along with a small bar and a dedicated sushi counter.

Unsurprisingly, Japanese *maneki-neko*, the waving cat statues, were a common motif, with several spread around the room, in addition to drawings and wall scrolls.

Hana downed a piece of halibut sashimi and rolled her eyes. "This is *so* good," she moaned. "This is better than sex."

Alison finished her octopus and laughed. "Calm down,

there. You might want to get to know that halibut first before you run off to Vegas to marry it."

The other woman grinned. "Don't give me any ideas." She popped another piece of the halibut into her mouth. "See?" she murmured around the bite of fish. "I told you I would hook you up. This place is great, right?"

A red snapper nigiri went down Alison's throat before she responded, "You did, and you're coming through in a big way. That's one problem with moving to a new city. You have to find new favorite places, but I'm liking Seattle. I've been here a few days, and no one's tried to kill me, and I haven't stumbled into any large concentrations of dark wizards or gangsters who are trying to pick a fight with me."

Hana winked. "You were just unlucky last time. I know we have a bad rep here, but it's not that bad."

Alison smirked and crossed her arms. "Sometimes one's luck is affected by encounters with certain foxes."

"You wound me, girlfriend. You truly wound me." Hana lifted her teacup and took a sip. "You've got a point, though. While you were busy kicking ass and taking names, I've spent my time productively since you left town."

"That can be dangerous."

Hana's eyes widened. "I know, right?" She shrugged. "Anyway, I've been trying to think about, you know, honest work."

Alison nodded. "And that's what you've been doing since I left? Honest work?"

"Semi-honest." Hana gave her a shrug and a lopsided smile.

"And what does semi-honest mean, exactly?"

Hana held up a finger. "So, let me give you a scenario. If you rob a robber, is that robbery or is it actually a type of heroism?"

Alison sighed. "Are you giving the stuff the robber took back to the original victims?"

"Well, no, not in this case, but, you know, say you robbed a robber, but you didn't know where his ill-gotten goods came from." Hana picked up some red snapper. "So you kept it yourself. The robber's still worse off, so maybe it encourages him not to steal anymore, and it's not like you're stealing it from the original victims. They wouldn't have gotten it back, so they're no worse off, but the bad guy is."

"That is such a convoluted excuse it hurts my head. I don't understand. Are you stealing from thieves?"

Hana tossed the red snapper into her mouth and shook her head. After she finishing chewing and swallowing, she grinned. "I have been conning con men. Totally meta and awesome, right? Sort of like you kicking the asses of criminals."

Alison shook her head. "I don't go looking for fights. I do what I need to do to protect people." She sighed. "And conning con men is going to end up with you being targeted by someone who you can't escape with a little charm. I don't know if that's safe, Hana."

The nine-tailed fox's smile faded, and she slumped. "I know. I don't really know what kind of work to do. Plus, you'd be surprised, but a lot of people in this town don't trust magicals. They say it's a lot better than other places, but it doesn't stop people from lying to you and telling you they'll call you back for a job and never doing it, or saying they have no openings and hiring some boring non-magical person the next day." She snorted. "They say it's supposed to be illegal, but how do you prove that they didn't hire you because of that? Truth magic's not admissible in court."

"Why not just get a job at a place that's magical-friendly?"

"I've thought about that." Hana forced a smile back on her face. "The funny thing is, humans don't trust me because I'm a magical and they don't know what to expect of me, and a lot of magicals don't trust me because I'm a nine-tailed fox and they always think I'm going to trick them."

Alison sighed. "Now, not to sound like a bitch, but you *are* a con artist."

Hana rolled her eyes. "What did I tell you about starting sentences with that phrase? Not cool, Alison. Not cool." She shrugged. "I know what I am, and I'm trying to kind of, you know, turn over a new leaf. Reincarnate without dying. The simple truth is, most magical beings get by on some level by hanging out with their own kind. I'm the only nine-tailed fox in Seattle, so it's hard to fit in, and hard to avoid people who just want to use me like the Daimyo did."

"Fitting in?" Alison grabbed a chunk of her hair and lifted it. "I can understand that. This is my natural color, you know. Part of being Drow."

"Don't hate it. You rock the white hair. Besides, everyone probably assumes you dye it, right? Half the girls in this town dye their hair." Hana puckered her lips. "Hey, but if you worry about it, why not dye it a more natural color?"

"I've tried. It always goes back to white within a day. Since I went to a magic school, it wasn't as bad an adjustment there once I realized what I was. I was ashamed of being a Drow for a while, but my friends accepted me." She shrugged. "Going to regular college and living in the rest of the world is a different situation."

"Friends accepted you?" Hana replied wistfully. "I haven't had a real friend in a while. When you're always trying to play people, you start to think everyone's playing you. Projection—that's what they call that, right?"

Alison picked up a salmon nigiri. "I'm not playing you."

"No, you aren't. Hey, wait a second." Hana narrowed her eyes and leaned forward to stare at Alison.

"What?" Alison shifted in her seat.

"What happened to your cute magic glasses? Whoa. Are you going through the whole conversation only with your soul sight? Are you looking for lies?"

Alison shook her head. "Not exactly."

Hana leaned back and tilted her head. "Not exactly?"

"I can see normally now without the glasses." Alison pointed to her eyes. "Same as you, I suppose."

The other woman blinked. "I can see really well at night." Her eyes shifted to yellow with slitted pupils for a few seconds.

Alison laughed. "In that case, I *can't* see as well as you, not anymore."

"How did that even happen?"

"Wish." Alison shrugged.

Hana arched a brow. "Seriously? As in, magic wish?"

"Seriously, but I don't want to really talk about it. It brings up a lot of painful memories." Alison shook her head. "Let's go back to talking about your job search and how you should get a job other than conning con men."

"What about it? I'm okay for now." Hana smirked. "And if you can't tell if I'm lying, then maybe I'll just con a few more con men and lie to you about it." She winked.

Alison laughed. "Or I could give you a job, at least for a little bit."

"Doing what, exactly?" Hana snagged the last piece of halibut and put it into her mouth.

"Helping me search for apartments or condos. I can look online, but I just don't know the city that well yet. I'll pay you to help me, kind of a daily stipend thing since I'll be keeping you busy." Alison smiled. "Plus, it's nice to have a friend to chat with in a new city."

Hana finished swallowing and smiled back. "That sounds like a good deal. What kind of budget are you looking at for your place?"

"Budget's not really a concern." Alison shrugged. "Want a nice view more than anything."

"Money's not a concern?" Hana crossed her arms. "You probably have a lot of money from your job and all those books people wrote about your dad."

"It's not like he got money just because someone wrote a book about him, but I'm...yes, you could say I'm comfortable."

"Comfortable is what rich people say when they can only afford three yachts." Hana glanced at the few remaining pieces of sushi and sashimi on the table. "I was going to offer to pay, but, come on, girlfriend—you're not only a princess, you're a rich princess. *You* should pay."

Alison laughed. "That's fine. I'll pay."

"Good." Hana beamed. "And we're *so* going to find you a kickass place."

Alison stepped inside the wide, dusty space, a frown on her face as she looked around. Angled wooden beams supported a small loft, but the vast vaulted ceiling left a lot of empty space above her. Two massive inert industrial-sized fans hung from the roof.

Hana gestured broadly with her hands. "What do you think, huh? You can walk to some of the hottest clubs in town from this place."

"It looks like a warehouse." Alison tilted her head. "They don't even have any windows that aren't twenty feet up in here. And the ventilation grates are crazy." She pointed to the huge grates.

"Oh, yeah. It used to be some sort of warehouse a long time ago." Hana shrugged. "But they've converted it into an apartment. Has a bathroom with a shower and everything. Think of it as a super-studio apartment."

Alison frowned. "That's one way to describe it."

Hana hurried to a nearby door and opened it. She slapped a hand over her mouth and turned away, giggling. "Okay, so maybe there are a few things that might not fit your vibe."

Alison headed toward the door and peeked inside. No

one could deny it was a bathroom. More specifically, a men's bathroom. A urinal hung on the wall, and there were two enclosed stalls. Four different showerheads lined the walls surrounding a large concrete drain area that was separated from the tile floor of the main bathroom by a low lip.

She stepped farther inside to inspect a water fountain, but after a moment she realized the silver box with two spouts was an emergency eyewash station.

"Yes, just what I needed—an industrial bathroom." Alison rolled her eyes.

Hana let out a few more giggles. "Sorry. The pictures online looked a lot different." She pointed to the urinal. "Your boyfriend might appreciate that."

Alison sighed and stepped out of the bathroom. "Even if I *had* a boyfriend, I wouldn't think that was a plus."

Hana followed her out of the bathroom, brushing her dark hair off her neck. "No boyfriend? Just like to keep it light and breezy? I get it." She gasped. "Don't tell me you can't get a man, Alison. You're cute, rich, and a princess."

Alison snorted. "I've dated on and off. It's just..." She shrugged. "When I was a teenager, it was hard at first because of my sight. I didn't go to an actual school until I was fifteen and started going to the School of Necessary Magic. A lot of boys were scared to date me then because of my dad. He always made a spectacle himself when he showed up at school. Super-overprotective."

"That's dads, I guess. Doesn't matter if they are accountants or bounty hunters."

"Yeah, well, I did find someone there, someone I..." Alison let out a nervous laugh. "Someone I fell in love with. At least, I think I did. I was a kid just learning about these kinds of feelings. It's hard now for me to know what was real and what wasn't because of what happened."

Hana gave her a sympathetic look. "All men are dogs, not just the shifters. If he cheated on you, it's not your fault."

Alison shook her head. "It's not like that. My school had problems with dark wizards. I don't want to go into the details, but they were targeting people there, including a good friend of mine."

"Oh." Hana blinked.

"Yeah." Alison looked down. "The guy I liked—his name was Tanner. He was hurt badly by a wizard and ended up in a coma, trapped by dark magic. No healing magic we could find would work on him." She out a long sigh. "He spent years in that coma. The library gnomes never gave up, and eventually found an old remedy in an obscure book locked in their vault that mentioned an ancient artifact. When they could finally wake him up, too much time had passed. He was older, but in his mind, he was still the boy from the school."

She looked over Hana's shoulder with a forty-yard stare, remembering a different time. "I'd already moved on, gone to college, hunted dark wizards, and started doing security contract work." She shrugged, returning to the present, letting it all go as she lifted her chin, a determined look in her eyes.

"That's seriously heavy, girlfriend," Hana whispered.

Alison nodded, straightening her shoulders. "I wondered for years if I should be waiting for him or moving on. What would be best for him, for both of us. Even my best friend, Izzie told me to get on with my life.

My parents told me to try to move on, even as they helped track down the artifact to heal him." She blinked away tears.

Hana reached into her purse and handed Alison a handkerchief.

"Thanks." She wiped her eyes. "I've tried to date other guys, but I don't know—it just never works out." She laughed. "Maybe I'm still that teen girl. It's hard, and I threw myself into school, work, and training. I'm not good at dating, to be honest, so I just don't think a lot about guys."

"Life's about fun. At least, it should be." Hana shook her head. "You can't torture yourself over the past, at least until someone develops working time travel magic, and it's not like you don't have a lot going on to get you a quality guy."

Alison finished wiping her eyes and took a deep breath. She handed the handkerchief back.

"I can help you." Hana grimaced and tapped her lip. "Not so sure I'm down with your semi-biker chick fashion sense, but we can do something about that."

"I'm a security contractor who needs to kick a lot of ass." Alison let out a quiet chuckle. "It's functional."

Hana laughed. "Do you need to kick ass while looking for a place to live?"

"No, but...you never know." Alison winced. Too many years of obsession with dark wizards might have taken more of a toll than she'd realized.

Is it that, or was it so many years of not even being able to see my clothes? By the time I could finally see, did it just not matter much to me?

She shook her head. "What about you? You have

anyone? Uh, guy or girl? I wasn't sure before when you were trying to charm me if you were into men or women."

Hana waved a hand. "I can and do appreciate the beauty of the female form, but when it comes to love, I like me a good man. I'm more about loving and leaving, though." She shook a finger. "Just to be clear, I never enter a relationship with anyone I've charmed. I want something real, but I'm also young. You're young too." She put her arms out and spun, smiling. "We've got a lot of life ahead. I don't know about you half-Drow, but I'm going to live a long time, so no reason to settle down anytime soon."

Alison nodded. She honestly didn't know how long she would live. As far as the Drow knew, she was the only half-human, half-Drow hybrid so they couldn't be sure what to expect. She shrugged.

Hana snapped her fingers. "You need to get back on the horse in a big way. Fate has brought us together for that reason. I'm sure of it." She gave Alison a thumbs-up. "I'm going to make it my personal mission to get you a man."

"Good luck." Alison shrugged. "Like I said, dating's awkward for me. Do you know what it's like to be Alison Brownstone, security contractor and daughter of James Brownstone? Drow Princess of the Shadow Forged? It's hard for men not to be intimidated."

Hana eyed her and nodded. "You just need to meet the right guy." She flicked her wrist a couple of times and wrinkled her nose. "Don't date the small-fry losers. Go straight for the top—some rich, handsome guy who is smart. If he's not a magical, then…I don't know, some powerful-type guy who knows what he wants and goes for it, so he won't be intimidated by you."

An image of a familiar handsome face with a coy smile flashed in Alison's mind. Her body tingled.

What the hell? Why I am thinking of Scott Carlyle all a sudden? He's just helping me set up the business. There's nothing there. It's all professional. Being smart, rich, handsome, and having nice biceps doesn't mean he's the guy for me.

Alison let out a nervous laugh. "I appreciate the help, Hana, but it's not like I have the time to worry about men right now. I've got to find a place to live, get the firm set up, and start looking for a building for the firm. I'm going to be very busy."

Hana gave Alison a sidelong glance. "I won't let you run from fate, girlfriend. Like I said, this is my new mission. Once you get all this other stuff settled, I'm going to find you a man so great that he'll blow even your dad away."

Alison burst out laughing. "So you like hopeless quests?"

Hana grinned. "They're more fun."

CHAPTER TWENTY-ONE

Alison smiled as she stared off the back deck of her condo into Elliot Bay. A huge tanker sailed at a glacial pace through the water. Various drones filled the skies, along with the occasional air taxi or helicopter. She could even see the Seattle Great Wheel in the distance. There was something festive about always being able to see a Ferris wheel.

Chilly air caressed her face and dark clouds hung on the horizon, no doubt eager to deliver rain to the city. She'd escaped rain during her first visit, but now that she lived in Seattle, it was as if the city needed to make up for lost time.

"I keep forgetting how close this is to Pike's Place and the pier where I met you," Alison called over her shoulder. "Although I'm still not sure how I feel about a high-rise ocean-view condo."

Hana was in the living room, pulling blankets out of a box. She rolled her eyes. "You're rich, so you might as well have a nice place. Besides, I benefit, too. As your friend, I get to hang out at your swanky condo." She winked. "Nicer than my place, although I've been trying to avoid it in case anyone from the Eastern Union comes sniffing around."

Alison stepped inside and slid the deck door closed before rubbing her cold shoulders. "I thought you sold me on this by touting access to nice restaurants without being too touristy and closeness to Maneki."

"You can have several reasons for buying a place." Hana pulled out a thick quilt and set it on Alison's maroon leather sectional sofa. "And I figure as long as I'm not hurting you, it doesn't matter if I occasionally get something out of it."

"And I thought you told me before that the Eastern Union guys were done with you." Alison frowned.

Hana shrugged. "It's not a big deal, just something someone mentioned to me the other day. I figured I should be careful. Never hurts."

Alison nodded and glanced toward the bay again. "I've got plenty of room. Why don't you just stay with me for a while?"

Hana blinked. "Seriously?"

"Yeah. It's nice to have someone to talk to." She shrugged. "I almost forgot how nice it is. Didn't really have much in the way of friends in DC. I think I've spent more time talking to my parents the last couple of months than friends."

"Thanks." Hana smiled. "Now I'm far more motivated to unpack your crap."

Alison laughed and knelt beside a box marked PHOTOS. She pulled it open and smiled softly at a framed picture of her standing with James and Shay at her UCLA graduation in cap and gown. Various other photos came out next, and she stacked them on her coffee table. Most were pictures of her family or friends from the School of Necessary Magic and UCLA, although she had fewer of the latter.

"You going to get some ceiling mirrors for your bedroom?" Hana asked as she set a few more blankets on the sofa.

Alison eyed her. "Huh? Why would I do that?"

"For a little fun in the bedroom." She waggled her eyebrows. "Just seems like something a rich person would do."

"A rich perv, maybe. And yeah, because I so seem like the type." Alison laughed.

"New city, new you, girlfriend. Other than ass-kicking, no one has a lot of expectations." Hana finished making a nice stack of blankets on the sofa. "Why not reinvent yourself?"

Alison picked up a picture of her as a young child standing next to her birth mother. "Why do I need to reinvent myself? I like who I am, don't you? I'll admit I've had a lot of questions these last few months, but after what happened with the New Veil, I get it. I'm Alison Brownstone, and I kick ass to protect people. I like that person, and I don't want to lose her. I have a lot of confidence in that person."

"Huh. That's cool." Hana considered the topic for a moment and shrugged. "I don't even know who I am half the time." She dropped onto the couch and crossed her mostly bare legs. The temperature had plummeted in the last few weeks as November gave way to December, but miniskirts still dominated the fox's wardrobe. "But I'll admit that when you're not running around killing gangsters, you're pretty fun. That guy at the club at the other day was totally checking you out, by the way. You should have tried harder to give him a chance."

Alison's cheeks heated, and she sat next to her friend. "You can't meet people at clubs. Not really. Not the kind of people I *want* to meet."

"Sure you can, as long as all you want is a good time." Hana wagged a finger. "And you never know. How did your parents meet? I doubt they met in church."

Alison laughs. "Actually, my dad has gone to the same church all his life, but my mom is convinced she'll light on fire if she stays in one for too long."

Hana snickered. "Seriously, though, where did they meet?"

"They met in LA, but they got to know each other during a job. Not exactly romantic. It involved feeding warlocks to alligators at one point." Alison grimaced and shrugged.

A few days before, she'd admitted to Hana that her mother was a professor by day and a tomb raider by night. Shay didn't mind since the firewall between Shay Carson and her Aletheia tomb raider persona had been thin for years now, but Alison had still insisted on a truth spell, and Hana didn't object.

Hana laughed. "So we need to find you a cute guy who'll feed bad guys to alligators for you. That seems doable."

Alison groaned. "He didn't do it for Mom. It was a bounty thing. He didn't have enough room to bring them all back. You have to understand that my dad is very...

practical." She shrugged. "Jeez, makes him sound terrible, but in his defense, the warlocks were evil guys who kidnapped children."

Her friend shrugged. "Assholes get what they deserve. I'm not going to judge." She stared at Alison, her lips pursed. "I'd bother you more about men, but I know you're just going to tell me the same thing you always do." She switched her voice to be more high-pitched. "I have to find a building for Brownstone Security before I worry about my personal life."

"Is that supposed to be me?" Alison laughed. "I don't sound like that. If anything, you have a higher voice than I do."

Hana crossed her arms and smirked. "That's my official Alison voice, so deal."

"Whatever, but I do still need to find an office. I can't operate out of my condo if I'm going to have a team." Alison nibbled on her lip. "Also need somewhere defensible and maybe slightly isolated."

"Why?" Hana asked.

"If I've learned anything from my parents and my dealings with dark wizards, it's that when you are involved in a high-risk career, you attract a lot of nasty attention. I don't want to have to worry about a bunch of companies suing me if some wizard blows up the building. I can't fight my way out of a lawsuit." Alison shrugged. "This place at least has decent extraordinary magical damage insurance."

Hana tapped her lip. "Does the office have to be in a nice neighborhood?"

"Not necessarily."

"Then I've got some ideas, if you want me to help you look? Least I can do since you're letting me crash here."

Alison smiled at her friend. "You've been nothing but helpful. I'd love your help, Hana."

The nine-tailed foxed beamed, her perfect white teeth almost gleaming. "I'm practically your administrative assistant now."

"You know, that's not a half-bad idea."

Hana blinked. "What do you mean?"

"The whole point of establishing Brownstone Security, LLC is so I can build a team." Alison shrugged.

"Oh, I see what's you're saying. I appreciate the offer, but I wouldn't be a good administrative assistant. I was just joking."

Alison shook her head. "Not as an administrative assistant. I still need to work out the formal titles, but I was thinking more an assistant investigator."

Hana tilted her head, her brown eyes fixed on Alison as if she were trying to see through her. "I hate to have to run myself down, because let's face it, I'm hot and awesome, but I'm not you. I can't clear out forty guys and bounce bullets off me like it's nothing."

Alison smiled. "I'm running a security firm, not a bounty-hunting agency. My dad mostly needs people who can kick ass, but half of what I did before I last came here was investigation. If I have someone who knows the city and can charm answers out of people, it'll help cut down on both time and unnecessary, um, collateral damage. Less insurance. Less me having to pay to have bars rebuilt. I like to be restrained, but a lot of the time I'm forced to not be."

Hana's face brightened. "You are serious, aren't you?"

"Yeah." Alison grabbed a photo from the coffee table. It was her as a teenager standing in the middle of a group of men in dark suits, the original men of the Brownstone Agency. "And you keep saying you're not tough, but when my dad started his agency, his employees were all non-magical humans. I saw your moves. You're not going to go down to some asshole in a bar, at least." She held up a hand. "But to be clear, I'm more interested in you helping me check into situations and occasionally defusing problems. I've maybe picked up a few bad habits from my parents on conflict resolution, and I've also gotten used to being a little rougher than I need because of some of the stuff I've dealt with concerning dark wizards."

"Oh. So I get to be the good cop, and you're the bad cop." Hana grinned.

Alison rolled her eyes. "Something like that."

"Huh. Hana Sugimoto on the side of the good guys, or good gal." She shrugged. "It's kind of weird when I think about it, but I like the idea of using my powers to help a friend, and I know you're never going to work for shitbags like the Daimyo."

Alison nodded. "The occasional douchebag maybe, but not shitbags."

Hana thrust out her hand. "I'm in. Can I run around calling myself Assistant Investigator Sugimoto?"

Alison shook Hana's hand. "If you want to, but you probably shouldn't. Looks like I've got my first employee."

"I don't have to call you boss or ma'am, do I?"

"No," Alison replied with a chuckle. She stared at her friend for a few seconds. "Can I ask you a personal question?"

"Sure. I figure by now you realize that when I'm not in con mode, I'm not exactly shy." Hana shrugged.

"You can...transform, right? Into an actual fox, not just a woman with fox eyes and nine tails?"

Hana nodded. "Yeah, sure. Why?"

"Can I see it?" Alison smiled. "I have shifter friends, but I'm curious if it's different for you. You said you're not the same as a shifter."

"Sure." Hana sighed. "I just don't change that much because it's inconvenient. Need to figure out some way to make my clothes change with me." She winked. "One second."

Alison nodded.

Hana bounded off the couch and headed into the bathroom to pull off her clothes and pile them next to the sink while humming to herself. Her nine golden tails appeared, and vulpine eyes replaced her brown eyes. The nine tails wrapped around her body, followed by a golden flash. When the light cleared, a red-orange fox with nine tails sat in the bathroom. The whole transformation had taken only a few seconds.

Hana padded out of the bathroom and sat on her haunches in front of Alison. The nine tails fused into one in another flash.

"Can't talk like that, can you?" Alison asked.

Hana yipped and shook her head.

"And you can't do the badass claws in that form, either?"

The fox shook her head again.

"Someday that's going to be useful, though." Alison laughed. "I don't know how because we're in the middle of a huge city, but I know it's going to be. One nine-tailed fox investigator successfully hired. I think the next step will be getting an actual administrative assistant. What do you think?"

Hana bobbed her head.

Alison smirked. "I think I almost like you better this way."

The fox growled.

"Oh, calm down. You can help with the interviews."

CHAPTER TWENTY-TWO

A few days later, Alison knelt in front of a low Maneki table and smiled at the slicked-haired man in a suit across from her. She'd dragged out her blue suit jacket, skirt, and flats from her wardrobe. It'd been a long time since she'd worn the outfit.

Hana slid the door to the private room closed and walked over and knelt beside Alison.

The nine-tailed fox's outfit had shocked Alison when she'd first seen it that morning: gray pencil skirt, cream shirt, and matching jacket, her hair up in a bun with the help of an ornate pearl phoenix hairpin. The whole outfit was professional, although Alison was amused by her friend's addition of black non-functional glasses and by the surprising fact the fox had an outfit that didn't double as club wear.

Alison almost wanted to ask who she'd charmed to get the clothes but decided against it.

Kind of sucks I don't have my own office to interview people in yet, but I need the administrative assistant to help me with the process. Then again, any excuse for sushi...

She avoided staring at all the delicious fish and rice on the plates in front of her.

Alison glanced at the resume on her phone. "So, Mr. Brown, what do you think you could bring to Brownstone Security, LLC as an administrative assistant?"

He leaned back and smirked. "I know how to get things done, so you can concentrate on looking good and doing your thing."

Hana choked down a laugh. She picked up some halibut nigiri to keep her mouth busy.

Alison arched a brow. "Do you understand the nature of my company? It's a security firm."

Mr. Brown shrugged. "Yeah, sure. I get it. You're the face of the thing, and you hire a bunch of guys. You look pretty and charm the clients, right?"

Hana kept chewing her fish, obviously trying hard not to giggle.

"You haven't heard of me, have you?" Alison asked. "At all?"

"You're new to Seattle, right? Don't worry. I have no problem working under a woman, especially one as attractive at you."

Alison sighed and scrubbed a hand down her face.

This is going to be a long day.

Alison folded her hands in front of her, "So, Miss Ramirez, what do you think you can bring to Brownstone Security, LLC as an administrative assistant?"

The fierce-looking interviewee leaned forward. "Both my clerical skills and my magic."

Hana and Alison exchanged looks. Neither had sensed any magic from the woman, but if she weren't actively maintaining any spells or using artifacts, they'd have no reason to.

Alison nodded. "Miss Sugimoto and I are magicals, so I'm glad to hear you'll be comfortable in that environment. Could you elaborate a little bit on your specific magical abilities and background, and how they might be helpful to the firm?"

The other woman leaned back, a smug look on her face. "As a former disciple of Rhazdon, I bring the power of Atlantean magic. I know you want me as an administrative assistant, but my abilities could help you lay waste to your enemies as well."

Alison blinked. "Rhazdon, as in the Atlantean woman central to the revolt and the Great War on Oriceran? The one who later hid among the prophets as a gnome?"

Miss Ramirez sniffed disdainfully. "Yes."

"And you want a job as an administrative assistant? You might be a teensy bit overqualified as a practitioner of dark magic."

"Your pay is well above the average for the area, and it's a tight job market this season." Miss Ramirez narrowed her eyes. "My powerful magic has allowed me to escape Rhazdon's many enemies. Don't worry—if they come for you, I will destroy them."

"I...see." Alison coughed. "Could you show us some of your magic?"

"The time isn't right. I'm still waiting for the pyramids to charge." Ramirez shot up, glaring at Alison. "Oh, I see what this is." She spun on her heel. "I will not stand for disrespect."

She marched to the door and threw it open before storming out.

Alison blinked and ran a hand through her hair. "That's the fourth one. Why is everyone so weird today? The stupid app was supposed to be funneling us so-called elite candidates." She gestured toward the door. "Not people who think they are Rhazdon reincarnated, sleazeballs, or that idiot who thought she could pitch us a movie script about my adoption hearing. What the hell?"

Hana shrugged. "I don't know. I've never hired anyone before."

Alison's head lolled backward. "Not like I have. By the way, you know how my dad started his firm? How he staffed it?"

"How?"

"He recruited a Marine Corps drill instructor after the Marines helped him with a bunch of hitmen chasing him, and then he basically recruited a whole street gang from his neighborhood and had the drill instructor train them."

Hana laughed. "You want to recruit a street gang? I can point you to a few."

Alison groaned and shook her head. "This just isn't as easy as I thought. Tracking someone down or having an ass-kicking showdown is easy. Maybe I should have taken more business classes in college."

"What did you study?" Hana furrowed her brow. "I never even thought about it, but it's not like you went to magic college, right?"

"Criminology major, history minor. Made both my parents happy." Alison shrugged. "For a long time I figured I'd be a bounty hunter, and I did work for my dad's agency on and off before going in the security consultant direction."

"You could always ask your dad for advice." Hana shrugged. "Or what about Carlyle? You said he helped you with the paperwork."

"No, this is my business, and they had different jobs. Besides my dad's only really good at picking out ass-kickers and pitmasters." Alison frowned. "As for Scott, he—"

"Scott?" Hana interrupted, a huge grin on her face. "You're on a first-name basis with him?"

Alison shrugged. "Why not? I almost died on his front lawn."

"Uh-huh. Whatever you say."

"Don't make me throw this tea on you." Alison picked up her teacup and brandished it.

Hana snickered.

"Besides," Alison continued, "I don't want him to think he needs to hold my hand. The guy's already kind of smug as it is."

Hana laughed. "I'd be pretty damned smug if I were a billionaire too."

"Just saying," Alison grumbled. "At this point, I'd take a chain-smoking overweight pixie as an administrative assistant."

"Maybe you should add that to the 'desired qualifica-tions' list. Wanted: chain-smoking overweight pixie, must supply own cigarettes. It'd be funny."

Alison glanced down at her phone. "We've got one more interview today, but she's not coming for thirty minutes." She swiped the phone. "Huh, that's weird."

Hana glanced at the phone. "What?"

"They don't have the name. The background sounds great, though. She's worked as an executive-level adminis-trative assistant for several huge companies in the area. Some of the earlier stuff got cut off." Alison frowned. "Of course, she could be lying. Rhazdon Ramirez there claimed all sorts of interesting things in her application."

"I wish I knew somebody, but most of the people I know besides you aren't trustworthy. It's almost like living my life as a con artist has put me around scummy people." Hana smirked.

"Maybe we'll get lucky with the mystery woman." Alison shrugged. "If not, guess we keep repeating this until I throw someone through a wall in frustration."

"Sitting in a private tatami room in Maneki eating sushi all day that someone else is paying for isn't my idea of hell." Hana winked.

The last arrival stepped in and offered Alison a polite nod. They exchanged handshakes before the elegant middle-aged dark-haired woman knelt at the other end of the table.

"A pleasure to make your acquaintance, Miss Brownstone," the woman offered, her accent unmistakably English.

Alison smiled. "Likewise. This is a bit embarrassing, but there was a technical glitch. I don't have your name."

"I see." The woman's gaze cut between Alison and Hana. "Ava Garden. Did my qualifications make it through?"

"Most of them," Alison replied. "Ava Garden? Like the old-time actress?"

The woman shook her head. "That was Ava Gardner... common mistake."

Hana cleared her throat, her mouth quirking into a hungry grin. "And you're just a normal person, not a reincarnation of an Atlantean general?"

Ava stared at Hana for a moment, her expression calm and neutral. "Given the state of the world, I can't completely exclude that as a possibility, but to the best of my knowledge, such isn't the case. I'm a non-magical human, but I've worked extensively in both magical and non-magical environments." She nodded at Alison. "Including with elves." She turned toward Hana. "But I can't claim I've ever worked with a nine-tailed fox before. I have worked with a shifter, but it's my understanding they aren't the same as your kind."

Hana blinked. She and Alison exchanged looks.

Alison cleared her throat. "Your corporate experience looks great, but I should note that this a security firm, not a product or services firm, so there is some inherent risk in being affiliated with our company. You'll have to sign personal injury liability waivers."

Ava gave her a curt nod. "You didn't get the early part of my work history, did you?"

"Sorry again. App glitch." Alison shrugged.

"I spent several years in administrative support in the PDA. I was working for them during the destruction of the local kemana by the Galbrathians. They also attempted to attack the local PDA office." Ava folded her hands in front of her. "A very unpleasant day, I can assure you. Set my work schedule behind by weeks."

Alison blinked. "Okay, then. I was about to ask you what you could bring to the firm, but your extensive experience in both the government and private sectors sounds like it'd be great for my firm. You're comfortable with the suggested compensation?"

Ava shook her head. "I'd need twenty percent more."

"That's a definite possibility given your background." Alison smiled. "Do you have any questions for us?"

"It's my understanding that your firm is still looking for an office?"

Alison nodded. "You'd be involved in that process as part of your initial duties."

Ava nodded. "I see. That was all I needed to know." She gave Alison and Hana a thin smile and waited.

"Um, I think that's all I have for you now." Alison looked to Hana. "Miss Sugimoto, do you have anything to add?"

Hana shook her head. "Nothing for now."

Alison smiled at the interviewee. "We'll let you know within the next week."

Ava rose and smoothed her skirt. "I look forward to working with you."

She slid the door open, stepped out, and closed the door.

Alison turned toward Hana. "Is it just me or was she perfect?"

"I know!" Hana clapped once. "Did you hear that accent? That's just what we need, that touch of class for the office. Can you only ask for people with sweet accents to apply or is that against the law?"

"I was thinking more of her extensive experience, including with the PDA. That means she's not going to flinch at the kind of jobs we work." Alison blew out a breath. "Screw twenty percent more. I'm thinking about giving her thirty percent more. I don't think we're going to get anyone more suited for the firm."

Hana nodded. "I don't think any chain-smoking pixies are waiting to apply, either."

"Stiff English woman it is. I'll go get her." Alison tried to stand and winced. "Damn. Been kneeling too long. My legs are asleep. Phone it is."

Hana laughed. "The great Alison Brownstone taken down by kneeling too long."

A few hours later, Hana sprawled across Alison's couch, staring at the ceiling, her jacket on the ottoman. "So you've got an assistant lined up, and me. Where do you go from here?"

Alison leaned against her wall and sighed. "That's the thing. Hiring an administrative assistant through normal means and lucking into you is one thing, but now I need to start considering more specialized stuff. Too bad I can't hire some of my friends."

Hana raised her hand to examine her nails. "Like who?"

"Oh, my friends from my high school, to name a few. All magicals, and all have experience with serious danger." Alison shrugged.

"Why *can't* you hire them?"

"My best friend has…a complicated situation where she can't risk staying in one place for too long. The rest of them have moved on to other things. They have lives. We still keep in touch, but it's not like I can snap my fingers and they'll come running to join my security firm. One of my friends just got elected to Congress last month."

Hana sat up. "Oh, that shifter guy in Virginia?"

Alison nodded. "There's an elven family friend. It's kind of weird—she's kind of like a stepsister since my mom trained her and helped break her into tomb raiding. She'd be great too, but same problem. She's got a good career as a tomb raider, so not a lot of reason for her to leave that to work for me." She marched to the other end of the couch and sat. "Some of this is my fault. A lot of it's my fault. I waffled between wanting a normal college life at UCLA and running around trying to solve my ex-boyfriend's problem and deciding I was going to be a dark wizard hunter for a month before stopping for several. They kind of moved on with their lives while I was running around deciding."

Hana laughed and lay back down. "Says the woman who is opening up her own security firm at age twenty-five and in the last month both stopped a major terrorist attack and cleaned up a sizable group of gangsters in Seattle. You're very hard on yourself, Alison. You need to lighten up."

"I've got to be hard on myself," Alison replied. "It's the only way I'll be strong enough to protect everyone." She lifted her hands. A white orb appeared in her left, a black orb in the right. "This magic isn't just for parlor tricks."

Hana shook a finger at her. "The whole point of the firm is that you don't have to do it all yourself. Let's not focus on the people we *can't* get. No point, right? One thing we need to think about is equipment. If you don't care where we get certain things, I know some people. If you care, I know people who can ask other people."

"Do that. We need a reliable supply of healing potions. I know how to make them, but for various reasons it's not easy or reliable. I'll just hit regular weapons stores for bulk purchases, but I need to get some decent magical weapons, too." Alison smiled. "It'll make my friendly chats with people more interesting."

Hana eyed Alison. "Why do you care about regular weapons anyway? Why not just blow them up all the time with your magic?"

"Oh, I didn't tell you, did I?"

"Tell me what?" Hana frowned.

"I have AMDS. It's this disease that makes my magic harder to use. I was sweating a lot before, but after that terrorist thing, I realized I just have to adapt and overcome. So instead of say, throwing as many magical attacks, I just use a shield and shoot people in the head, or stab them."

"AMDS, huh? Never heard of it." Hana shrugged. "But shooting or stabbing people sounds like it works to me."

Alison nodded. "Yeah. I've gotten too used to doing things a certain way, but I was trained in hand-to-hand combat along with blades and firearms. Just going back to my early bounty hunting roots." She waved a hand. "I've got all that figured out. Had a weapons crate delivered earlier."

"Is that what that was?"

Alison nodded.

"Moving on, then." Hana held up a finger. "Okay, you've got Super Mary Poppins as an administrative assistant, and you're outsourcing accounting, payroll, and HR. You've got your charming and lovely investigator. Probably need a few more ass-kickers, but maybe you should build the firm's rep first. The way I see it, between you and me, we can follow people's trails, but there's one big hole." She frowned.

"What?"

"Computer crap," Hana replied. "I'm not very good with computers." She made a face. "I hate things you can't sweet-talk."

Alison shrugged. "I'm okay, but nothing great."

"We need a hacker, then." Hana held up a hand and her nails extended into claws. "Kicking ass works sometimes, and magic at other times, but this isn't Oriceran. Lots of important crap in computers. You actually can do spells, though, not just specific magic like me. Do you know any techno-magic?"

Alison shook her head. "Not computer stuff."

Hana lifted the side of her mouth. "Hmm. We should be able to find someone. This city is the center of the techno-magic boom, and we've got the best hackers in the world. I know some people, but same problem I have with a lot of people—I don't trust them."

"Am I the only friend you trust?" Alison asked.

Hana shrugged. "Pretty much."

"You know what?" Alison pulled out her phone. "I shouldn't be too stubborn. My parents have some hacker contacts I trust, and I think I'll see if they can point me toward someone." She shrugged. "No hurry, though. We don't have to grab one right away. Not like we have a job."

CHAPTER TWENTY-THREE

Her phone rang, and she looked down at the caller ID. The phone number was local.

ADVANCED MAGITEK SYSTEMS.

Alison frowned. Scott had her number, but his was different than the one calling her phone.

The phone continued to ring.

Hana pointed at it. "Aren't you going to answer it?"

Alison nodded and swiped to answer the phone. "Hello?"

"Hello, Miss Brownstone, my name is Gretchen Keller. I'm Mr. Carlyle's personal assistant. He'd like to schedule a meeting with you to discuss a possible security job."

Alison frowned. "And he couldn't call me directly?"

"Oh, when it comes to official business matters, Mr. Carlyle likes to do everything through me. Now, when are you available?"

Alison stepped out of her Spider into the massive garage containing a dozen different sports cars and two limousines.

Why does he need two limousines?

When the Lyft driver brought her to the mansion the last time he'd stopped at the front, so Alison hadn't realized there was a back entrance that led to a parking garage.

A redheaded young woman waited near the door of the garage. Given her suit, she probably wasn't a housekeeper.

"Miss Brownstone?" the woman asked.

Alison closed the door and headed toward the woman. "You're Gretchen?"

The woman nodded. Now that Alison was a bit closer, she could see a few lines here and there on Gretchen's face that suggested the woman was older than she'd initially guessed.

Gretchen ran her hand over a panel next to the door. The lock clicked, and she held it open.

Alison stepped inside into a long hallway, and the other woman closed the door behind her.

"Thank you for coming on short notice," Gretchen offered. "Mr. Carlyle will explain the details, but this is a very high-priority short-term assignment requiring immediate aid. If you'll follow me." Gretchen strolled down the hallway.

Alison followed. She hadn't seen much of the mansion during her first visit, but the hallway with its paintings and artwork didn't seem that much different than the hallways and rooms she'd already seen.

I've collected pictures, but not much else? Not like I couldn't have had a nice place this entire time. Was it just me convincing myself that there's no permanency?

A few turns brought them to a large but mostly empty office. A massive cherrywood desk dominated the center of the room, although it lacked a computer and had nothing on the top.

Being rich is relative, huh? He's right. I've got millions of dollars to my name, but I have never lived in a place like this. Dad could afford a mansion if he wanted. For that matter, so could I.

She snickered at the idea of James Brownstone living in a mansion.

Gretchen smiled and nodded at the chair in front of the desk. "Mr. Carlyle will be here soon." She retrieved her phone from her pocket. "Mostly I just wanted to get some of the low-level details out of the way." She tapped at her phone. "Mr. Carlyle is offering half of the payment up front and half upon successful completion of the job. Please note the compensation isn't negotiable."

Alison's phone buzzed, and she pulled it out to look at the amount. It was more than she'd been paid by Mr. D for retrieving the gem. Even if she didn't need the money, it wasn't insulting.

"You say that," Alison replied, "but I don't know what the job is."

"I can assure you that Mr. Carlyle took into account the relative dangers and difficulties when he came up with that offer."

Alison chuckled. "Always thinking ahead, huh? And you do realize that I'm not agreeing to do anything until I have the details of the job, right?"

Gretchen's smile didn't falter. "Of course, Miss Brownstone. We'd expect nothing else. Mr. Carlyle understands that Brownstone Security is an independent operation."

"Good." She narrowed her eyes. She needed to ensure that Scott remembered that. A little help with paperwork and permits didn't mean she would follow his orders, but pissing off a billionaire wouldn't help her either.

"Now, if you'll excuse me, Miss Brownstone." Gretchen moved to the door. "I have some matters to take care of. Mr. Carlyle should be here within five minutes."

Alison nodded. "I'll survive." She grinned. "The chair's comfortable enough."

Gretchen let out a soft laugh and all but glided out of the room, closing the door behind her.

Alison tapped out a text to Hana. Might as well keep her up to date.

Carlyle's got me waiting. Half-convinced it's a power play. His assistant is almost creepily cheerful.

Her phone buzzed with a response.

You sure she's not a techno-magic robot?

No, but if she represents the evil robots coming to take over, I could live with it.

Hana responded with a series of different laughing face emojis.

Whatever this is, it seems like we'll have to roll on it right away.

I'll be ready. Hana followed with a salute emoji.

Someone knocked on the door.

He's here. Talk to you later.

Okay.

"Come in," Alison called.

The door opened, and Scott entered. He adjusted his tie, which, though different than the last one she'd seen, was covered with glyphs. He strolled behind his desk to take a seat.

Scott smiled. "Thanks for coming on such short notice, Alison. I wasn't sure if you'd be interested in a job given your recent move and the incident in DC, which wasn't all that long ago."

"So much for the government keeping my involvement under wraps." Alison snorted. "Then again, it's you. I'd be disappointed if you didn't know the truth."

He nodded. "Knowing the truth gives you an edge in business and life, even if it's uncomfortable."

"Not disagreeing. Anyway, I've got my assistant doing a lot of the busywork of looking for a building for me, so if you've got work, I'm interested. I made plenty of money last time you were involved, even indirectly, and I found the whole thing very enlightening in many ways."

"Oh, did you?"

Alison nodded. "It's like you say. It's one thing to hear certain things, another to see them with your own eyes."

Scott stared at her for a moment. "And what did you see that left an impression on you?"

"Influence, power, advanced magical technology, and expert planning." Alison shrugged. "I think you're a far more dangerous man than many people realize."

Scott chuckled. "I'd suggest most people think I'm dangerous."

"But probably for the wrong reasons."

His brow lifted. "Meaning?"

"It's not just the money." Alison shook her head. "The

money's almost incidental. I bet you were almost as dangerous before you were a billionaire, which is why you ended up one."

Scott locked eyes with her for a moment, a thin smile on his face. "As wonderful as hearing someone accurately describe me is, I think this particular week all those traits you mentioned are working against me."

"Why do you say that?" Alison asked.

He shrugged. "Because I'm fairly certain that someone intends to assassinate me in the next week, and I'm dubious that they're doing it simply because they think I'm a good businessman."

Alison nodded. Her heart rate didn't speed up. She'd all but expected him to say something like that. "Someone's going to try to kill you? You're sure? I mean, this isn't just some crazy who sent you a threatening message? I dealt with that for a congressman when I first got into DC. Turned out just to be some intern mad about him not giving her a letter of reference."

"If this were such a minor potential problem, my security team would have been more than sufficient and I wouldn't have had to bring in an outside specialist." Scott shook his head. "My information suggests a credible threat to my life, and it's not the first time. You don't get to be as rich as I am, especially in this industry, without making enemies, and while I do have numerous bodyguards, to be frank, they lack your raw ability and flexibility."

"Okay, makes sense." Alison chuckled. "Sorry. It's just that you're the first man other than my dad who is so nonchalant about mysterious and potentially very dangerous people trying to kill them."

Scott shrugged. "We're in very different industries, but your father and I share the unfortunate reality of people thinking they can take us down. I'm used to it, and in fact, have come to expect it. This time, however, I want to avail myself of a powerful security contractor."

Alison nodded. "What's the plan? From what you've said, it sounds like you already know when it's going to go down. You need me to stick close to you for a week, and I take down whoever comes at you?"

He shook his head. "That's the thing, Alison. I don't go looking for fights, but I like to strike back hard when people come after me. So, yes, I do want you as backup, but your relative freedom and personal abilities mean you could be helpful tracking down whoever is responsible."

Alison furrowed her brow. "Any leads?"

"My people have informed me that a large amount of Trollcoin has changed hands in various dark web forums related to a contract on my life. The money's been distributed in a way that's difficult to trace."

"There's one thing I don't understand," Alison responded. "You know someone's going to try to kill you. You even know approximately when, so why not just call the police or FBI? Maybe even PDA? You have all that influence with them, after all. I'm glad to find someone and kick their ass for you, but the agencies could help." She shrugged.

Scott pursed his lips. "The unfortunate thing is that my company is public. That means any small piece of news about my safety will be of extreme interest to the business community. The incident during your last trip caused an initial ten percent sell-off of AMS stock."

Alison winced. "Sorry. I haven't been paying all that much attention to the news, and everything has kind of blurred together these last few weeks."

He waved a hand. "Not your fault, and it's rebounded since I'm clearly unhurt and the PDA made it clear that the culprit is dead and not associated with a terrorist group or foreign government. The point is, it'll be difficult to involve the authorities at any level in the current matter without something leaking about it, and then our stock price is going to take another major hit. Since the incident is as yet unresolved, there's nothing to reverse the damage, and investors are skittish." He clucked his tongue. "People start stampeding and a lot of people get hurt, not just my company and me. The investors will take a hit. It's bad for them. It's bad for me, and it's bad for the economy." He pointed at Alison. "If you, however, look into this on your own, even if you cause a little collateral damage along the way, it'll just be associated with a Brownstone being a Brownstone."

Alison laughed. "It's not like I purposely try to cause a mess. Not my fault assholes don't know to quit when they're outmatched."

"Of course. The point is, as long as people don't realize you're directly connected with me, we can solve the problem without anyone losing any money or sleep."

"This isn't one of those things where I'm going to dig in and find out you spent years denying your daughter was your child or something, is it?" Alison asked.

Scott laughed. "If I had a daughter, she'd be living with me and being groomed as my successor. I'm not going to lie and claim I've never wronged anyone, but I can state with confidence that I'm doubtful some poor innocent is behind this, if only because of the level of money involved."

"No one who is rich is innocent?" Alison smirked.

Scott smirked back. "At a minimum, wealth makes a man suspect."

"Fair enough." Alison shrugged. "Just wanted to make it clear that you have your standards and I have mine."

"That's part of the reason I trust you on this." Scott leaned back and steepled his fingers. "And I also have full confidence in your ability. I have to give a speech at the Convention Center in a week, and what little information my people have gleaned from the dark web suggests the attempt will likely be made on that day."

"So you need me to find the bad guys in a week?" Alison asked. "What happens when I find them?"

"If you need to deliver them to the authorities at that point, it's fine," Scott replied. "I understand that you're not an assassin, although I also understand that you have no compunctions about defending yourself from violent and dangerous criminals."

Alison eyed Scott. "Neither do you, given what I saw with McKenna."

"I might not be blessed with magic, but that doesn't mean I can't avail myself some of its benefits. The future is a mix of technology and magic, and I will drive the future. Idiots like New Veil or the Humanity Defense League pine for a past that can never be brought back when we should be doing more to integrate the best of Earth and Oriceran."

Alison raised an eyebrow. "A gun represents the best of Earth and Oriceran combined?"

"The Oricerans had a peace that lasted thousands of

years." Scott shrugged. "We haven't had a world war in a century. Peace through superior firepower sounds cynical, but just because something's cynical doesn't mean it's not true." He leaned back with a smile. "Eventually, it's why I suspect your mere involvement in future cases will resolve them without much bloodshed."

Alison shook her head. "I'm not a nuke, or capable of that level of magic."

"Yet." Scott glanced down for a moment before looking at her with a faint smile. "But the far future is by its nature far beyond the week that might be my last. I believe my assistant already went over compensation with you. Is the money sufficient?" Scott raised a questioning eyebrow.

Alison nodded. "Yes, it's fine."

"Of course, I don't think it's unreasonable to withhold the second half of the payment until you've stopped the assassins or, at a minimum, prevented my death."

She snickered. "Yeah, if I let them gun you down, I kind of see how I shouldn't get paid as much. Anyway, I'll take the job. It's basically search and destroy with a side of investigation—closer to bounties."

Scott smiled. "Excellent. I'll send a report on the information my people have gathered. I look forward to finding out who's trying to kill me."

CHAPTER TWENTY-FOUR

Alison and Hana headed up the street toward their latest stop. They had hit several other places during the day but weren't turning up anything other than new people to talk to. Alison had considered asking Vincent for information, but she didn't know how much she could trust the man. He'd taken Mr. D's money, not hers, and he might be more trouble than he was worth.

Hana looked at Alison. "You totally look like an undercover cop trying too hard in that Mariners' hat. Why don't you put on sunglasses too, while you're at it? Wear a shirt that says, 'Totally a bad girl.'"

"My hair stands out too much. It's the best I can do to hide it. I tried dyeing it again before I picked you up, and by the time you got there, it'd already reverted. Never happened that fast before." Alison shrugged.

"Maybe you should consider a wig next time." Hana grinned.

"Maybe, although I don't think I'm going to worry about a hat next time. The only reason I'm keeping a low profile is that I'm still feeling Seattle out. Once I know the city a little better, I'll depend on people knowing who I am more than anything." Alison opened the door to the bar, allowing the loud rock music to spill out. "But I've seen up close how it can be hard to balance reputation in a way that makes people not screw with you without other people seeing you as a challenge to overcome."

The women stepped inside. Given the place's reputation as a biker bar, the large number of men and women in leather jackets and bandanas with guns stashed under their jackets was about as surprising as the sun rising in the morning.

Alison nodded to a scarred and bearded man in the corner. "From what they said at the last place, that's the guy we want to talk to—Frank. He was bragging about something big coming up soon." She shook her head. "He doesn't look like the kind of guy who could go after someone like Carlyle without him seeing it coming a mile away."

Hana adjusted her tube top. "How do you want to work this, the soft way or the hard way?"

"Both." Alison grinned.

They headed to Frank's table. The man sat alone drinking a bottle of beer. Several empty bottles were in front of him.

Alison and Hana sat at the table.

"Hey, Frank." Alison smiled.

He eyed her for a second. "Go back to your station, you fucking pig. You think I can't see an undercover cop a mile away?"

Hana put her hand to her mouth to stifle her laughter.

"You know what? I tried, so screw it." Alison yanked off her hat and shook out her hair. "Do I look like a cop to you?"

Frank eyed her. "You're Alison Brownstone, ain't you?"

"Yep, that's me. I've got a few questions for you, and you're going to answer them or there might be pain involved." Alison frowned at him.

He grunted. "You gonna kill me, Brownstone? I ain't done shit to you. That's how you Brownstones work, ain't it? People stay out of your way, and you stay out of ours."

"Why don't you ask the Daimyo about that? Oh, wait, you can't, because he's dead." Alison shrugged. "I did let a few of the dark wizards survive at the Sunshine Room, so you could talk to them." She looked to the side and ran her tongue inside her cheek. "But I also warned them to stay out of town, so if they *are* still around, I'm going to have to do something about it. Anyway, not talking about dark wizards or dead Eastern Union guys here. We're talking about you, Frank, and what you can do for me."

His face twitched, and fear flickered in his eyes before the arrogance returned. "I don't know shit about shit."

Hana chuckled but didn't say anything.

"Not here to talk about how the educational system failed you, Frank." Alison laid her palm on the table and summoned a short shadow blade. "I'm more interested in big things going down in town. I've got a vested interest in it, you could say, and someone told me you've been running your mouth, so I figured I'd chat with you."

"Fuck you, Brownstone. I ain't saying shit." Frank lifted his chin. "You want to kill me, then fucking kill me."

"Don't tempt me. I'd be doing the world a favor."

Hana sighed and rolled her eyes. She turned to wink at Alison. "I can't take her anywhere. I'm sorry, Frank. She's had a rough life. She can't always relate to people well."

Frank narrowed his eyes and looked at Hana, his eyes focused lower than her head. "And who the hell are you?"

"Hana Sugimoto. Heard of me?" She smiled.

"Nah."

Hana stuck out her lip. "You see? That's just unfair. I don't go around killing buildings full of people, so no one's heard of me. Everyone prefers fighters over lovers." She reached out and put her hand on his forearm. "But maybe we can work a deal." She licked her lips. "You'll find that I'm much nicer than Alison."

Alison kept a hard frown on her face even though laughter wanted to blast out of her mouth.

"What do you mean, a deal?" Frank mumbled.

The nine-tailed fox leaned forward to give him a better view of her cleavage and winked. Her eyes turned vulpine. "We just want to know if you've heard about anything big going down this week. That's all, Frank. Maybe we could have a good time together after talking about it."

The biker swallowed, and his pupils dilated. All the tension vanished from his face. "Good time?"

I bet she didn't even need the charm magic, the way this guy was leering at her.

Hana gave him a winsome smile. "Yes, but if you want me to do something for you, Frank, I need you to do something for me. I need you to tell me about the biggest thing that's going down this week."

Frank blinked a few times and looked at Alison, a frown appearing for a few seconds before it vanished and he looked at Hana again. "Just have to tell you what's big? Nothing else?"

She nodded. "That's all. No taking us anywhere. No giving us anything. Easiest thing in the world." She fluttered her eyelashes. "So, please? For me?"

"Scott Carlyle," he murmured.

"What about him, sweetie?"

Alison looked away to hide her smirk.

"Word on the street is some major money changed hands," Frank mumbled. He kept staring into Hana's eyes. "A hit, that's what people's saying. No one knows who, but they're saying it's an Oriceran, and magic's going to be involved."

Hana made another pouty face. "You sure no one knows who, sweetie?"

Frank shrugged, an apologetic look on his face. "Yeah, babe. That's just the word. No one knows. I asked around, thought maybe I could get in on the action."

She leaned over the table to give him a kiss on the cheek. "Thanks, sweetie. That was helpful. Why don't you take a little rest now and forget you talked to us?"

"Yeah, that sounds good." Frank lowered his head to the table and closed his eyes.

Hana nodded toward the door and stood. The women hurried out of the bar, a few people eyeing them with suspicion.

Once they were half a block down, Alison turned to Hana. "You can put people to sleep and erase their memories? You never mentioned that before."

The other woman laughed and shrugged. "It's not like you gave me a detailed manual of your powers, either,

Alison. The short version is, the charm's like super-hypnosis, but the person has to be in the right frame of mind. One of the reasons I've trained to con people. It's easy to trick people when you get them in a greedy or horny frame of mind. And you know what they say—you can't con an honest man."

Alison frowned. "But what about the memory thing?"

"Oh, it's not that impressive." Hana sighed. "It's not like I can do anything about long-term memories, just short-term stuff. I don't even like to use it that often, because the last thing I need is for people to be told by some friend of theirs they saw them with me and have them come asking questions."

Alison nodded. "Understood. Damn it. The few pieces of info we got pointed us at Frank, and he was clueless."

Hana tapped her bottom lip. "I could go to Vincent and try to charm him."

Alison shook her head. "He'd see that coming, and it'd be bad for both of us. We need to look in a different place."

"What do you mean?" Hana replied.

"Scott's people found some stuff on the dark web, but they couldn't find much more. That's where we need to go. We need a hacker." Alison nodded, her satisfaction with the idea growing with each passing second.

"Girlfriend, I hear you, but how are we going to find a decent hacker who's better than anyone Carlyle has? He's a billionaire." Hana shrugged.

Alison grinned. "Some things money can't buy, and I know a guy who was good enough to run circles around the US government. Got his current number when I called my mom earlier. Let's head back to the condo, and I'll call him."

While Hana went to take a shower, Alison pulled out her phone and dialed the number. The phone rang a few times.

"As I live and breathe," the man answered in an exaggerated Southern accent. "Alison Brownstone."

She chuckled. "Hey, Peyton. It's been a while."

"Yes, it has." His voice returned to normal, faint hints of New York and Connecticut in his accent. Nothing remotely Southern.

"How's the company doing?" she asked.

"Great. Hard to go broke running a cybersecurity company these days." Peyton chuckled.

"I can imagine." Alison smiled. "You ever miss running backup for Mom?"

Peyton sighed. "I'd be lying if I said I didn't, but enough about boring old me. I doubt you called to play Twenty Questions. I've heard you've started a boring non-cybersecurity company."

Alison walked over to the couch and took a seat. "Yes. That's kind of why I'm calling. I was wondering if you could give me some help."

"What? Subcontracting or something?" The sound of chewing came over the line.

Alison laughed. "Let me guess, you're eating pizza?"

"Once I graduated from mere Pizza King to Pizza Emperor, I vowed I'd never be far from a pizza."

Am I that crazy about sushi? I don't make it myself, so I'd say no. Maybe. I hope not.

Alison blew out a breath. "I need a good hacker for my firm. It's like yours, all nice and aboveboard, but I need someone who can get down in the mud if necessary. Preferably someone I can grab as soon as possible for a job I'm working. I need someone to dive into the dark web to sniff around for me."

"I'd offer my services at least as a stopgap, but I understand something very important," Peyton replied. "And I want to make sure you understand it as well."

Alison frowned. "What's that?"

"How much things have changed in the last ten years." Peyton sighed. "It's not just about being a good hacker. Ever since the first real experiments with mixing information technology and magic, things like the Venger dark web system, everyone's realized the power of that sort of thing. Tons of this stuff around. I've got a lot of magicals on my staff, and if you really want to stay on top of the hacking game, you can't just have a world-class hacker, you have to find a hacker who specializes in infomancy."

The sound of Hana belting out a few loud notes from the shower distracted Alison for a second.

"I'm fine with that," she managed between chuckles. "But I need someone I can meet face-to-face. I don't trust anyone I can't look in the eye."

"Fair enough," Peyton replied. "You're in luck, though. Well, kind of. I've got good news and bad news."

Alison sighed. "Okay, what's the good news?"

"There's a guy I know of who fits the bill and lives in Seattle, Tahir Arain. He's a wizard and a hacker. He specializes in info magic, but he's world-class even without it."

"Okay." Alison nodded. "I like that good news. What's the bad news?"

Peyton laughed. "How to say it? Um, he's what we'd politely call a quirky asshole. Because of who you are he probably would be interested in working with you, but he won't agree without you playing some sort of game first. That's his thing. Games. Challenges."

Alison frowned. "What sort of challenges?"

"Usually mental challenges, but I don't know specifically what he'll have in store. Whatever it is, it's going to be at least somewhat annoying. Sorry."

Steam billowed from the hallway as Hana came out in a towel. "We're out of shampoo."

Alison nodded to the phone.

"I'm sorry," Hana mouthed.

"Just answer me one thing, Peyton. Is this Tahir worth it? Is he good?"

Peyton laughed. "Good? I'll never admit it if you repeat this to anyone, but even without the magic, he's better than me."

Alison grinned. "That I can work with. Okay, tell me how to get hold of him."

CHAPTER TWENTY-FIVE

Alison turned her Fiat to the right and moved onto a street with so many holes, she suspected it had not been paved since the truth about Oriceran came out.

"My poor suspension," she muttered as her car shook. "What are they doing to you, baby?"

According to her GPS, she was only a couple of miles from her destination—an abandoned warehouse. Peyton gave her a number for Tahir and she called and left a message, including a generous pay offer for the next week of work. A minute later, she'd received the text with the address and note to "come prepared."

"Come prepared" always meant the same thing to Alison: be ready to kill a boatload of people if necessary. She considered it a practical, not a cynical, attitude.

She'd loaded extra magazines into her tactical vest and rolled out. She also had brought along an entire box filled with grenades in case a little bonus death was needed.

Given what both Mom and Dad went through with their hackers, this might get messy if this guy's in any sort of trouble.

Her phone rang with an unknown number, and she answered it on speakerphone.

"Who is this?" Alison asked.

"The person you're coming to meet," replied a distorted voice over the phone.

Alison rolled her eyes. Hackers were drama queens.

"You in trouble?" she asked.

He laughed. "Trouble? No. Why would you think that?"

"You told me to come prepared." Alison gripped her steering wheel tighter. "I thought you might need a little help with angry gangsters or something."

"I don't get in that kind of trouble. I'm careful, so I don't have to worry about things like that." The distortion in his voice stopped.

Alison chuckled. "And humble, too."

Tahir scoffed. "Are you humble, Alison? Are you going to pretend the average person would have a chance of standing up to you?"

"No, that's just kind of basic reality. A law of physics, you could call it." Alison slowed. Her final turn was coming.

"Good. You understand." Tahir took a deep breath. "False humility is pointless."

"Let's cut to the chase, Tahir. I want to hire you. I hear you're the best, and you say you're the best, so everyone's in agreement. I pay damn well, and you'll be challenged on difficult jobs, like the one I need you for this week. If you want to do your own thing on the side, that's on you as long as it doesn't interfere with any of the work I hire you for."

He sniffed on the other end. "You seem convinced I'll take your offer. I'm not hard up for work."

Alison scoffed. "I don't know you well enough to know if you'll take my offer. I only know that you come highly recommended and I need a solid hacker like yesterday. I'll even tack on a premium for your first job. If you want to turn down me throwing money at you, that's on you, but if that's the case, tell me so I can move on and find the guy below you in the list of badass hackers."

"I'll admit I'm intrigued," Tahir responded. "Most people I wouldn't have called back so soon. I only did because you're Alison Brownstone. I know you're involved in a lot of interesting things besides killing terrorists, and I find myself seeking more interesting challenges to my skills."

"Terrorists?" Alison chuckled. "The government shouldn't have bothered to cover my name up since everybody and their brother seems to know. Okay, so you can dig around. What about the job? And where do you have me going, exactly? Why an abandoned warehouse? If you're not in there about to be shot, then what the hell *is* in there?"

"You have to understand that reputations are just words. They don't prove anything."

Alison scoffed. "Words that talk about what someone's done in the past. They suggest a possible future. They aren't perfect, but they're a good guide."

She slowed the Spider as she approached the address. A brick warehouse stood in a cracked and weed-covered parking lot. The building was discolored, and colorful gang tags adorned almost every square inch.

What, did they bring a cherry-picker to do some of the higher ones? Or maybe used magic? If anyone dares to touch my car, they are going to have a very, very bad day.

Alison laughed. Her obsession with her vehicle was yet another way she'd turned into her parents.

She pulled into the parking lot, looking for any sign of a man, but the lot remained stubbornly empty of anything but trash and weeds.

Tahir let out a low chuckle. "Yes, reputations are a possible future. Not one that is assured, and that's why I've brought you here today. The words 'Alison Brownstone' might mean that you're a powerful half-Drow or they might mean nothing. Smoke your father's blown into the words. Words have only the meaning we give them, and you can give your reputation meaning by demonstrating it to me."

"That is the longest way to say 'Put up or shut up' I've ever heard. Peyton did say you were a quirky asshole."

"Yet you still want to hire me." Tahir snorted.

"Skills are skills," Alison replied. "And I'm not the nice girl I was a long time ago." She blew out a breath. "Okay, I'm here. You want me to prove myself? How? If it's about winning in a hacking challenge, I give up already. I'm not a hacker; that's why I'm trying to hire you. And you already told me you're not in trouble, so this isn't about saving your ass."

"No hacking and no saving," Tahir responded. "I want to test if the rumors about you are true. Test your abilities, and this is the easiest place to do that."

Alison laughed. "You want to fight me? I get that you're a wizard, but you're an info magic specialist. Trust me, you can't win against me one on one. That is another of the laws of physics things."

He scoffed. "Of course not. I'd never be so stupid as to take you on myself. My main weapon is my brain, not my fists or a gun. No, I have something else in mind. Tests in the warehouse; dangerous, including facing things like remote-controlled weaponized drones. Your life may be at risk if you don't live up to your reputation. If you're just smoke, Alison, turn around, leave, and never call me again."

"So you want to attack me, but you want to do it from the safety of your home? Long-distance ass-kicking is never as satisfying." Alison grabbed her phone and stepped out of the car. She canceled speakerphone and brought the device to her ear. "I have to admit I'm not impressed if that's what this is about. I don't need help with ass-kicking, even if you can fly combat drones. I need dedicated hacking, cracking, and deep-dive computer research-type help. I need someone who is about information first."

"It doesn't matter what you want," Tahir responded. "You'll attempt my test or this conversation is done, even if you are Alison Brownstone and you are offering a lot of money."

Alison circled to the back of her car and popped her trunk. She grabbed several EMP grenades from the trunk and hooked them on her tactical vest. "You watching me now, Tahir?"

"Of course. Look behind you."

She turned around. A half-dozen drones flew several hundred feet up in the area, not unusual for any random neighborhood in Seattle, although two of them seemed to be circling the area.

Alison waved. "So your test is me blowing up your weaponized drones in the warehouse, I'm guessing? This kind of thing used to be my summer vacation."

Tahir snorted. "No, the drones are just obstacles. This is a hunt for a golden keycard. I've hidden it in the warehouse, and you have to find it. You have one hour. If you fail, we're done, and I'll ignore your attempts to contact me again, and even go out of my way to use my abilities to make your life harder."

Alison gritted her teeth. She didn't like being threatened, but it wasn't like the guy was around to kick in his teeth. Time to get petty instead.

"A golden keycard?" She snorted. "Okay there, Willy Wonka. This will be easy. I see any Oompa Loompas in there, they're getting a 9mm to the head before they can sing any songs about parents raising their children to be violent."

"Easy?" Tahir replied. "We'll see. You have one hour... starting now."

Alison yanked out her 9mm and charged toward a side door in the warehouse. She summoned a shield and touched the door handle. The door wasn't locked, and she yanked it open and backed up with the door.

Nothing exploded. Nothing fired through the open doorway.

Huh, was at least expecting a grenade or something.

Alison peeked around the corner. Boxes half-eaten by rats filled the main warehouse floor, along with several small pools of stagnant water discolored by oil and chemicals leeched from the ground.

She crept through the door, her gun at the ready. The

whir of a drone sounded from above, a stun rifle attached to the bottom.

Really, Tahir? That's all you've got? I was expecting military-grade shit.

A blue bolt ripped from the drone and struck her, her shield absorbing it with ease. She felt only the slightest sting. This level of magic was trivial even with her AMDS.

Alison rolled her eyes and downed the drone with a single shot. A riot of buzzing filled the warehouse as a dozen more drones rose from behind boxes or fallen shelves like a swarm of angry metal bees.

Bullets blasted from small-caliber cannons on some of the drones, joined by stun bolts from another. Rockets hissed toward Alison from two. Alison ducked to the side, the minor explosions pushing her but not doing much against her shield.

Let's be efficient about this, shall we?

She grabbed one of the EMP grenades from her vest, primed it, and tossed it toward the swarming drones. A harsh buzz sounded, and sparks played across all the remaining drones as they crashed into the ground, smashing into dozens of pieces.

Alison tossed another EMP grenade into another corner of the warehouse just to be sure. Nothing crashed or thudded on the ground that she could hear.

"If you can hear me, Tahir, I'm almost insulted," she shouted. "If you know about what happened in DC, you should know the drones are a joke. I was taking out drop-ships in DC."

His laugh came from a hidden speaker.

So he EMP-hardened at least some of this.

"I just got done telling you how words are nothing until proven," Tahir taunted. "You're beginning to prove you're at least interesting, but being good with a gun and having magic isn't everything. I'm also testing your soul."

"Please. I can tell you a few things about souls. I doubt you know the first thing." Alison snorted.

"Perhaps," he replied. "Then let's just say I'm interested in testing your spirit."

"You better be worth it when this is all over. Don't I get some sort of hint about the keycard? Even if you weren't flinging toys at me, it'll take more than an hour to search this warehouse since I don't have any clue where the keycard is." Alison kept her gun up, sweeping back and forth as she moved toward the smoking remains of the drones. "My reputation is for ass-kicking, not puzzle-solving."

"You should be able to figure it out based on what you know about me. That's part of the test."

Alison inspected each destroyed drone, but there wasn't a keycard, golden or otherwise, near or on any of them. A quick jog around the warehouse floor didn't yield anything interesting.

"Forty-five minutes left," Tahir announced.

"Oh yeah, this crap is timed," Alison grumbled. "Wait a minute. I keep forgetting the whole point. I'm not interested in you just because you're a hacker, but because you're an infomancer."

"So? What's your point?"

Alison held up a hand and concentrated, sending out a pulse of magic. Years ago, she'd used the technique to "see" a room without the glasses, but she was looking for a subtle return of energy to mark low-level magic she couldn't easily sense at a distance. She felt nothing.

So, not on the main warehouse floor, huh?

Multiple doors led outside, but an open door led to a short hallway that turned off.

Alison jogged over to the hallway and sent off another pulse. She nodded, pleased. Subtle magic meant no strain.

Not everything's about clearing out a room of gangsters, as fun as that can be.

She narrowed her eyes when she detected a faint magical residue around a corner.

There we go.

Alison crept forward, her gun at the ready and rushed around the corner. A huge steel wall blocked her path.

"You've got to be fucking kidding me," she muttered.

A thud sounded from behind Alison, and she spun. A wheeled sentry bot stood right behind her, the open door to a hidden compartment right behind it. The pulse rifle at its side came alive, pelting Alison's shield a few times.

Alison tossed her gun into her left hand and extended a shadow blade from her right. She stomped forward, ignoring the slight strain of repeating stun bolts hitting her shield before reaching the sentry bot.

"Now I am just straight-up pissed. This kind of crap wouldn't have challenged me in high school."

She fed more power to the blade and whipped her arm down, slicing the sentry bot in half. The halves clanked on the ground, sparks and smoke pouring out of the destroyed robot. The sweet smell of ozone filled the air.

Alison pivoted on her heel and glared at the steel wall.

"You want to force me to carve through the wall? Don't think I won't."

How the hell did that asshole even get that here? Wait. Something's not right.

Alison laughed, released the blade, and holstered her gun before grabbing another EMP grenade. She stepped around the corner and tossed it in front of the wall. Once the buzz sounded, she peeked back around. The wall remained.

"Huh. Here goes nothing, then."

Alison shrugged and walked toward the wall, resisting the urge to break into a sprint. Her right foot contacted the wall and passed right through. A few more steps and she was on the other side, between two tall black tripods—holo-emitters.

She walked past the emitters toward a collapsed and cracked office door rotting in front of an empty office. A golden keycard sat in the center of the room.

Alison snatched up the card. "Do I get to tour your magical factory now, Tahir, or are Oompa Loompas coming for me?"

He chuckled, his voice coming from an old speaker in the corner this time. "If you had tried to fire or cut your way through the wall I was going to end it. That would have proven you were too rigid to be of interest to me."

Alison shook her head and released her shield. "I don't get this. You have a warehouse puzzle chamber set up in case random women try to hire you?"

"I've got a few places around town where I test things. Theories. Strategies. This is one of them. I've gotten some useful data out of this. Even if you'd failed it would have helped me, so I didn't mind taking the time, even if I decided against your offer."

"Congrats to you, then." Alison stared at the speaker, not sure where else to look. "Just so we're clear, I need your help right away. Not going to press you on it now, but we do need to meet face-to-face soon. That's how I do things, especially given how much I'm going to be paying you. You've checked me out and you know my reputation, so you know I'm not going to sell you out to some piece of shit after."

Tahir snorted. "Fine, but I want to be clear myself. I'm no one's bitch, and if you want someone to fly a drone behind you to wipe your ass, I'm not the right man for that kind of job."

Allison shrugged. "Do I seem like the kind of woman who needs a drone or sentry bot with a stun rifle following me? I need you because I need a person who can hit the dark web hard, including the magical dark web, and dig deep for information when I can't find it the old-fashioned way or by dangling someone off a building. If you're inter-ested in that, we can do business. If you have a problem with that, I guess we part ways now, and we both can laugh about the funny death puzzle warehouse you made if we ever run into each other."

The silence stretched on for longer than Alison would have liked.

"Fine. You intrigue me, Alison Brownstone. You're powerful and intelligent. I'd wondered." Tahir chuckled. "Your father's more renowned for his power than his quick wits."

"He's smarter than a lot of assholes think," Alison

replied. "And it doesn't matter. I'm not my father. I'm not my mother. I'm me."

"So I see." Tahir cleared his throat. "You've made it clear that there's something you want me to handle right away. What is it?"

Alison slipped the keycard in her pocket. "Someone's planning to assassinate Scott Carlyle. I need some leads, and I need them fast. Need someone to dangle off a building."

"Trivial," Tahir replied.

Alison snorted. "Get met the leads, then brag."

CHAPTER TWENTY-SIX

A couple of hours later, Alison was sitting at her dining room table looking through neighborhood delivery menus on her phone when it rang with a message from an unknown number.

"Hello?" she answered.

"It's me," came Tahir's now familiar voice.

Alison chuckled. "Is this one of those things where you'll call me from a different number every time and I have to call you using a different number?"

"For now. I'm willing to meet with you face-to-face when the time comes, but there's no reason to leave an easy trail for others. I don't want to lose the game in an embarrassing way." Tahir chuckled. "Although having you as a friend is helpful."

"Oh, so not so sure you'll never be in trouble after all?"

"Sometimes a man's luck runs out."

Alison glanced at the sofa. Hana was leaning over a selection of knives from the weapons crate. She picked up one and eyed it with a smile.

"What's this about?" Alison asked. "You got something for me already?"

Tahir scoffed. "Of course I do. I wouldn't waste your time. I've done some back-tracing of certain servers and tri—"

"Just give me the executive summary," Alison interrupted. "I need to know what door I have to kick in."

He chuckled. "I'll be sending you GPS coordinates in south Tacoma. Low-end apartments."

Alison furrowed her brow. "What's so special about those? What could they possibly have to do with a plot to assassinate a billionaire?"

"There have been some suspicious money transfers associated with accounts I can potentially link to at least one of the Trollcoin wallets listed in the information you sent me. Those money transfers were funneled through various shells to disguise the fact that every apartment in that complex is being rented by the same organization. That's clear from the electronic signature involved. There are records of occupants and they're decent on the surface, but I've been able to clearly establish that half of them are crap obviously planted in the relevant systems, and I suspect most of the other half is crap, too."

"Huh. Nice job, Tahir. Apparently *your* reputation is real, too."

He sniffed disdainfully. "Of course."

"So what organization is behind the apartments?" Alison asked.

Tahir sighed. "That I don't know. It's been too well hidden."

She blinked. "Wait, you're saying you were able to find

information that even computer guys working for a billionaire couldn't find, but there's still someone who's able to hide?"

"Yes, as much as it annoys me to have to admit that. You're not dealing with a small-time organization if they can rally this kind of computer skill. This isn't just hacking. Infomancy is involved. That limits my ability to do certain things without leading them back to me." Tahir muttered something under his breath. "Whoever's behind this will haunt me at night. I don't like to be outmaneuvered."

"Ego much?" Alison snorted. "As for scary hauntings? They should see me when I get mad. Send me those coordinates, and I'll go say hi to the Nightmare Squad." She smiled. "But thanks, Tahir. Don't feel bad. Now at least we have a lead, and this investigation is alive again. Talk to you later."

She ended the call and stood. "Grab your favorite knife, Hana, then grab a gun from the case. It's time to go apartment shopping."

The other woman looked up with a smile. "Oh, free stuff. Nice." She stood after grabbing a weapon. "You think this is going to get dangerous?"

"Don't know. Kind of hope so. If it's not dangerous, this might be a dead end."

Hana smiled. "Well, at least it'll be interesting."

Alison parked her Fiat in a visitor parking spot in front of the apartment complex's office. At least, she thought it was visitor parking. The faded paint made it hard to read. A few other vehicles were parked in the lot, most too new and expensive for the neighborhood, as well as two white vans.

She stepped out of the car and onto the path leading to the front office. "I think this is going to be more a soft thing. You ready?"

Hana snickered and saluted. "I live to serve."

They marched into office.

A balding man at the front counter looked up, obvious surprise on his face. "Can I help you, ladies?"

Hana slipped her arm around Alison's shoulder. "We want to see an apartment. We're from out of town. My wife and I are relocating from Des Moines."

The man looked between the two women, a subtle expression playing on his face, and shook his head. "I'm sorry. We're full."

"But I've seen empty apartments," Alison lied. "We were looking through some windows with open blinds earlier." She held up a hand. "We're not trying to be creepy; just wanted to see what they look like on the inside."

He frowned. "I'm sorry, ladies, but we don't have any free units."

Alison frowned.

Hana dropped her arm and moved toward the corner with a bright smile. "You must have a tough job, right? All these tenants, people getting frustrated when you're doing nothing but telling them the truth."

The man continued frowning and glancing at Alison and Hana. "You can say that, but I really can't help you."

The nine-tailed fox looked around the counter and

behind the desk as if seeking something and nodded. "I have to admit something. She's not my wife."

Alison blinked.

What the hell is she up to?

The man snorted. "Didn't think so. I can smell bullshit from a mile away. What the hell is this about?"

Hana looked down with an abashed expression. "I'm embarrassed. We were supposed to keep this secret." She sighed and looked away. "I told them this would happen when we came to this complex. That the people working here wouldn't fall for it."

"Oh shit." He ran a hand over his scalp. "You're from corporate, aren't you?"

She shrugged. "Guilty as charged. These were supposed to be undercover evaluations, but I got a little messed up running a training scenario with my new trainee over there." She pointed her thumb at Alison. "Trainees, am I right?"

His face twitched. "Hey, um, I'm just doing my job. I wasn't....come on. If you're from corporate, you understand my situation."

Alison crossed her arms and wiped the frown off her face. She nodded at the man.

He swallowed. "I don't understand. Did I screw up? I thought I was following orders."

Hana leaned forward, her eyes turning yellow. "What were you supposed to do if people came and asked about apartments?"

The man blinked several times and then stared at her. "Tell them they were full."

"Why?" she asked, her voice almost a whisper.

"I don't understand. Corporate told me to keep most of the units clear." The man sighed. "I was just doing what they told me."

Hana nodded. "And why do you think that is? Why do you think corporate wants the units clear?"

The man shrugged. "Smuggling, I guess. Or something like that. We've all heard the rumors, and I know they're doing illegal things at night. I think for the latest one, someone's going to hide out here after doing something illegal. I keep my head down, ask anyone. I've never called the cops on any of the shady stuff I suspected was going on here." He swallowed. "I know they have some guys here already setting stuff up for whatever the next plan is."

"Don't worry. Corporate respects your loyalty and your discretion." Hana smiled softly. "It'll be rewarded."

Relief spread over the man's face. "I thought I was in trouble."

She shook her head. "It's the opposite. Why don't you go to your desk, take a little nap, and forget you talked to us?"

The man nodded, turned, and dropped into his chair. He closed his eyes and let his head fall forward.

Alison nodded to the door and stepped outside. She didn't talk until Hana was outside and had closed the door behind her.

"Erasing his memory isn't going to work," Alison explained. "They've got security cameras all over this complex. If anyone checks the footage they'll know we were here, if they don't already. Given what he just said, someone's probably paying close attention to who shows up here."

Hana shrugged. "Well, at least we know there's something wrong with this place."

Alison strode toward her Spider. "Why the sudden switch to us being corporate drones instead of being married?"

Hana shook her finger. "Let me educate you, girlfriend, about the skill behind conning someone."

Alison crossed her arms and leaned against her car. "Enlighten me, oh great con artist queen."

"You have to use people's weaknesses against them. It's simple in theory, but hard in execution." Hana shrugged. "And you have to be willing to abandon strategies when they don't work." She pointed at Alison, then herself. "We're both hot. The easiest strategy for most men is to take advantage of that. They want to be liked by hot women, even in situations where it's inappropriate. They crave that kind of attention."

Alison nodded. "Like Frank."

Hana nodded. "Exactly. I was hoping to try to short-circuit the manager with the idea of us two hot women living together, but when he pushed back, I realized it wasn't going to work, so that's when I saw the key to why —something that confirmed what I suspected."

"What?" Alison furrowed her brow.

"He had a picture of himself with his husband on their wedding day." Hana smirked.

Alison stared at her. "Did you just assume that since he wasn't into us, he was gay?" She laughed. "What are you, my mom?"

Hana blinked. "Huh?"

Alison waved. "Long story that involves my dad and

when they first met. In her case, she was wrong, but you were right. But how did you guess the corporate thing?"

Hana shook her head. "You're misremembering. I didn't say anything about being from corporate. I just told him we were supposed to keep things secret." She snickered and tapped her forehead. "Let people fill in the blanks and roll with it. That's another major part of conning them. If we weren't on a schedule, I could have probably gotten all of that out of him even without the charm magic." She shrugged. "It's just about managing people's expectations and giving them what they believe should come next."

Alison shook her head and opened the driver side door. "Sometimes you scare me."

Hana winked. "Good. He mentioned some guys here." She nodded toward the vans. "Those kind of look out of place. In most other apartment complexes in this area, the wheels would be gone by now."

Alison nodded. "Let's take off for now. We can come back later tonight and check things out."

Hana furrowed her brow and glanced into the side view mirror and rearview camera. "Alison, I don't mean to alarm you, but I'm pretty sure we're being followed by two vans."

Alison nodded. "I know. This is actually convenient."

"What do you mean?" Hana looked her way.

"We don't have to come back later." Alison grinned. "I was thinking we were standing out too much, but it turns out it was a good thing. I half-hoped someone was watching and noticed you put that guy to sleep."

Hana grinned. "Look at you, Little Miss Manipulation. You have the heart of a con artist."

"I think these assholes don't know who I am and are underestimating me." Alison changed lanes. "Otherwise they wouldn't be so obvious about following me." She patted three linked knife sheaths underneath her jacket. "It's been a while since I used these bad boys. Gnome-crafted, custom-made for my mom back in the day. She gave them to me as a graduation present."

"Your mother gave you knives as a graduation present?" Hana chuckled. "Has she used those to kill people?"

"Oh, loads. But they all had it coming, and hey, you laugh, but they can be very useful. In a world of magic and guns, people underestimate knives." Alison pulled into the cracked parking lot of a long-abandoned, dilapidated building.

She killed the engine and got out. Hana hopped out the other side and circled around.

The vans pulled into the parking lot and stopped a few yards from Alison's car. Men in suits piled out of the vehicles on either side, guns in hand and translucent crystals hanging around their necks—anti-magic deflectors.

Hana whistled. "That's a lot of money on those necks."

One of them stepped forward, his left hand over his right wrist and his gun pointed down. "I'm going to make this easy for you, Brownstone. You stuck your nose into something you should have left alone."

Alison shrugged. "Kind of my thing lately."

The man smirked and patted his deflector. "Don't

worry. We know all your moves, but this doesn't have to go down the hard way. We just want to go talk somewhere." He nodded to Hana. "You come with us, your little friend can drive away and forget any of this ever happened. If you don't, you both die right here and now."

Alison scoffed "Aren't you planning to kill me later anyway?"

He shrugged. "At least this way you have a chance, and your friend lives."

"You know my name, but do you know who I am?" Alison flexed her fingers.

"Spare me the intimidation. We came prepared. Every one of these guns is filled with anti-magic bullets." The man gave her a feral grin. "What's your choice?"

If I take the time to throw up a shield, they might get a shot off. If they've got the anti-magics, they could kill me if they get a lucky shot, but they are close together. Need to put them off-balance.

Alison kept her eyes locked on the man and shrugged. A second later, she whipped out a knife and flung it straight into his eye. The man screamed and pitched backward. The others brought up their guns.

One.

A burst off an acceleration disk sent Alison flying into the men, her two remaining gnome blades in hand. She slashed with both arms, blood spraying from the necks of two more men.

Three.

The glow of Hana's nine tails appearing distracted the men but Alison ignored it, instantly understanding what she was seeing in the corner of her eye. She kicked a gun out of a man's hand before jamming a blade into his heart.

Four.

Hana leapt into the fray, her claws ripping into the throat of a man hesitating between shooting her or her friend.

Alison grinned.

Five.

A man squeezed off a shot, his bullet narrowing missing Alison's arm. She threw one of her knives into his head before leaping up and wrapping her legs around another man's neck, dropping to the ground and taking him with her. They slammed down together, and she snapped her arm over to stab him.

Seven

Alison hopped to her feet ready to finish off the last man. He lay on the ground on his stomach, his back and arm torn and bloodstained, Hana holding her claws to his throat.

"Good catch, Hana." Alison smiled. "Thought I might have made a mistake by not saving one." She wiped her blade on the jacket of one of the men before sheathing it and jogging over to recover and clean the other two.

The remaining man groaned. "You'll never get away with this, bitch. You have no idea who you're fucking with."

Alison rolled her eyes. "You see, it's the opposite. You assholes didn't know who *you* were fucking with. You planned on me relying on my magic, probably using shadow blades or magical blasts, but I've been trained by the toughest man and the toughest woman on this planet." She scoffed. "And those skills are still there whenever magic isn't a convenient solution." She crouched by the man. "So now you're going to tell us who you are."

He shook his head. "Fuck. I talk to you, I'm dead anyway. Go ahead and do your worst."

Alison whipped out a knife and held it to his throat. She nodded to Hana.

The nine-tailed foxed stepped away. Her claws receded, and her tails vanished, but her eyes remained yellow. She knelt beside the man.

"Now, now," she whispered. "No reason for this to end in more violence. We kept you alive for a reason, even though you threatened to kill us." She patted his shoulder. "I wouldn't twitch if I were you, because Alison's hand might slip. You can get away from this situation still. All you have to do is tell us what we need to know."

The man scoffed. "I'm not telling you shit." A few specks of darkness appeared in his anti-magic deflector.

Alison moved the knife and sliced the chain holding the deflector. She tossed it a few feet away. "Try again, Hana."

The man frowned. "Try what?"

The fox stroked his arm. "You're such a brave man. I respect that. Respect how you faced off against Alison Brownstone, who is pretty much a complete badass. You might have even had a chance if you hadn't made the wrong assumption."

"Screw you," the man replied. His tone was already less hostile than before.

Hana smiled. "I know this is hard to believe, but Alison doesn't like to kill people unnecessarily, so you'll be doing us all a favor if you just calm down. Take a deep breath. Yes. That's it. This doesn't have to be a big deal. You can walk away. It's kind of the same offer your boss made. You cooperate, and you don't have to die today."

The man twitched.

"Don't move, asshole," Alison ordered.

The man's head jerked up, and his eyes rolled up. Green-yellow foam poured out of his mouth.

Hana stood. Alison frowned and drew her knife back.

The man twitched and writhed on the ground, blood now joining the foam.

Alison sighed. "Damn. You sense that?"

Hana wrinkled her nose. "Magic. What the hell?"

"I've seen this kind of thing before. Dark wizards sometimes use it, even if it's not this exact magic." Alison sheathed her blade. "This guy probably had some sort of spell on him to kill him if it looked like he was going to talk."

The man stopped moving, his eyes open in a death stare.

Hana frowned. "We have no more leads."

"Nope, plenty to follow up on." Alison knelt and reached into the man's pocket. "Grab their wallets. We'll pass them on to Tahir." She nodded to the deflector. "Grab these as well."

"Won't they interfere with our magic?"

Alison finished pickpocketing the dead man. "Sure, but as I just proved, sometimes you don't need magic to win a fight. Spoils of war." She winked. "Learned that from my dad. We'll throw these in a vault when I have an actual office. Not all of my employees will be magicals." She stood and shook the wallet. "But these are a priority. Oh, and get their phones, too."

CHAPTER TWENTY-SEVEN

Alison knocked on the apartment door, holding a trash bag filled with wallets and phones in her other hand. "I was surprised he gave up the address so easily."

Hana shrugged. "He already agreed you could meet, no reason he wouldn't."

"Don't know. These hacker types can be paranoid assholes." She shrugged.

The door swung open, revealing a tall and fit brown-skinned South Asian man with dark hair, wearing jogging pants and a white t-shirt. "Come in, ladies."

Alison thrust the bag into his arms. "Here's the treasure I need you to follow up on."

Tahir chuckled and took the bag to the couch. "I'm glad to see my lead paid off."

"So am I."

Alison stepped inside the apartment and glanced around. Clean, organized, not a speck of dust. It reminded her of her dad's house.

I was expecting sweaty nerd and hoarder after that shit at the warehouse.

Hana smiled at Tahir. "It was pretty wild. You should have seen her take the guys out."

"I can imagine." He picked up the bag again and carried it over to the desk in the corner where he had a computer and three monitors set up. A VR headset sat on the desk. "A half-day. I'll have the information you need in the morning."

Alison frowned. "How do you know? You haven't even looked at any of that stuff yet."

Tahir shrugged and walked over to his open kitchen to grab a glass and start filling it with water. "Because I've done this kind of thing before. From what you told me before, your client has days left. He can wait one night."

"Unless the killers move up the deadline."

Tahir gave her a lop-sided smile. "He's not vulnerable enough for them to go after him now. If he were, they would have already finished him. No, whoever this is, they're either going to wait until their perfectly planned time or until they're offered something better. So, morning is fine."

Hana patted Alison on the shoulder. "Don't sweat it, girlfriend. We took down a pack of bad guys today. Well, mostly you, but we've got a trail. I bet Tahir will give us the exact coordinates of the bastards, then Scott can bribe the Air Force to drop a bomb on them."

Alison chuckled. "Fine." She pointed at Tahir. "You said morning, so I'm holding you to that."

"Of course." He took a sip of his water. "I don't offer deadlines I can't meet." His mouth lifted in a tight smile. "I have to say, Alison, working for you is already proving interesting."

Alison shrugged. "Glad you like it. Talk to you tomorrow."

She headed for the car. Hana waved at Tahir and followed her out.

Alison frowned. "I think he's screwing with me."

Hana looked between her and the door. "Who, Tahir?"

"Yeah. I think this is a power play. He could probably do it in an hour, but he wants me to know he won't be my puppet."

Hana shrugged. "Does it matter? He's right. We're nowhere near the deadline, and so you might as well let him feel like a big man. You know how these hacker types are, and he's even worse because he's a wizard. All the normal ego amplified by ten."

Alison shrugged. "Okay, let's head back to the condo then."

"Or we could not." Hana rubbed her hands together.

"And what it is that you want to do?" Alison nodded toward the door. "Until he gives us our lead, not much we can do. We already rattled the hornet's nest at the apartment complex. None of those guys are left alive for me to use a tracking spell. Nothing to do but wait."

Hana rolled her eyes. "There's more to life than hunting down ridiculously overprepared assassins."

Alison blinked. "Uh, sure. What are you getting at?"

"The other day at breakfast you mentioned liking music." Hana smiled.

Alison nodded. "Yeah, sure. I grew up blind. Music's a special thing when you're blind. Later on, I went to concerts and realized how my soul sight could make it even more special." She gave a bittersweet smile.

She didn't regret the wish, even if it *had* cost her soul sight. All choices had consequences, and the consequences of hers were that she'd saved a lot of people's lives and was now more effective in battle, even without artifact glasses.

"Why are you asking me about music?" Alison asked.

Hana put on a wide-eyed expression Alison was beginning to recognize as her "innocent little me" face. "So a week back, I scored tickets for a concert from a nice man for the band Atlantis and Doom. They're playing at a small local club."

Alison furrowed her brow. "Atlantis and Doom? Never heard of them."

"Metal band. Got this really hot half-elf drummer, Tommy." Hana shrugged.

"You like metal?" Alison eyed her friend and chuckled. "You don't seem like the type."

"Oh, girlfriend, I'm a like an ocean trench of depth and surprises." Hana winked. "Plus, I'm surprised you don't like it."

"Why?"

Hana shrugged "Metal's all about passion and anger. Seems like it'd suit your personality."

Alison snickered. "Didn't used to be this way. Hey, wait a second, when you say you scored the tickets from a nice man, what does that mean? Do you mean you bought the tickets, you conned him, or you charmed him?"

Hana grinned. "Well, I can say he was a nice man, and he gave me tickets."

"Fine." Alison shrugged. "It might be nice to blow off some steam before I have to go kill a bunch of people."

The heat of hundreds of bodies writhing, jumping, and screaming pulled the sweat from Alison's body. She was no metal aficionado, but it was hard not to admire the ridiculous speed and chord progressions of the guitar player. And even if she wasn't close enough to the stage to evaluate the appearance of the drummer, the tempo of this insane ten-minute drum solo convinced her that magic had to be involved.

Hana bounced up and down, her fist in the air. "This is fun, right?" she yelled over the roar of the crowd and loud metal pouring out of the speakers.

Alison smiled, allowing herself to bounce a little. She couldn't deny there wasn't any tension left in her body. She could see the appeal of metal.

"Yeah, it's fun," she shouted back.

"Want to go to the mosh pit?" Hana asked, gesturing to the dense pack of men and women throwing themselves against each other near the front of the stage.

Alison laughed. "Don't think I'm ready for that. Too many reflexes that might end with me knocking someone's ass out, and then me having to fight bouncers."

The amplified guttural scream of the lead singer deafened her. She couldn't understand how the man hadn't already killed his voice that night.

Dad should have been a metal singer. His voice is perfect for it.

Hana continued bouncing and banging her head.

Alison kept dancing, smiling as she observed the stage and the crowd. There were more than a few dwarves and elves in the crowd, not to mention the half-elf drummer and a certain half-Drow and a nine-tailed fox in the audience.

Music's the real magic, and it's nice to have a night where I don't have to think about shooting someone in the head. You're right, Hana. Seattle's not all gangsters and dark wizards.

CHAPTER TWENTY-EIGHT

Alison woke to the not-so-dulcet tones of her ringing phone. She rolled over to grab the phone from the nightstand, not bothering to look at who the call was from.

Somebody better be dead.

"Hello?" she murmured.

"Jacobsen Associates," replied Tahir over the line.

Alison shook her head to try to clear out the sleep. She tried to remember what it was she had Tahir doing, but her clouded thoughts refused to let the memories connect. She was glad she hadn't taken Hana up on her after-concert suggestion of hitting a bar. "What? I have no idea what you're saying. It's just random words. Banana surgeon."

"Jacobsen Associates. Your dead men," Tahir explained. "Even though their fake IDs and some online records were supposed to make you think they worked for a different company entirely. Clever work, but not enough to beat me."

The words cleared the haze in Alison's mind. She

frowned, trying to associate the name with anything she knew.

"Should Jacobsen Associates mean anything to me?" Alison sat up and stretched her free arm. "It sounds like a bunch of accountants or something. I'm going to be far less smug if I just killed a bunch of accountants. Though, on the other hand, if they were accountants, they were unusually badass."

"They're not accountants." Tahir chuckled. "On paper they're a security firm, just like Brownstone Security."

"What about when you dig deeper?"

"In reality, they are a group of expensive assassins." Tahir snorted. "I can't identify who paid them, but it's got to be someone with deep pockets to afford Jacobsen. These are the kind of people you hire to take out major players: high-level politicians, CEOs, exiled dictators, and that sort of thing."

"Well, it is a CEO we're trying to protect," Alison mused. "Do these Jacobsen men commit suicide when captured?"

"Not that I can find," Tahir replied. "If anything, it's a mild sore point among some in the assassination community. There are competing groups that use such suicide policies as a selling point."

Alison frowned. That wasn't good.

"At least we know who did this." She sighed. "That lets us focus."

"It gets stranger," Tahir replied.

"Stranger? How?" Alison put it on speakerphone so she could stretch both arms.

"The money trail is circular. It all leads back to Jacobsen, including that apartment complex." Annoyance tinged Tahir's voice.

"So basically you're saying it looks like Jacobsen Associates paid themselves?"

Tahir chuckled. "That's one way to think of it."

"Maybe they did," Alison replied, "if someone else paid them first, something valuable and purely analog. For all we know, someone left them a box of gold bars in a building." She sighed. "This is annoying shit. Someone's trying very damned hard to cover their tracks. We have many pieces of the path, but not enough to close it all. How are you doing? Do you think you'll get more if you keep pushing?"

"Unlikely, but I'll keep trying."

Alison smiled. Forward progress was all she needed. "Thanks, Tahir. This is a good start, anyway. I'll go talk to my client and see if this helps with anything. Keep pushing, but keep being cautious."

"I always am. I promise nothing, but I'll call you if I find out anything else."

Tahir ended the call.

Alison fell back in her bed with a yawn. "Deep pockets and assassins? This shit sounds like out-of-control corporate warfare. I think I'm starting to miss the simple venom of your standard-issue politician."

A few hours later, Alison sat on a couch in yet another room in Scott's mansion, a small library. Sealed climate control stacks lined the room. Rare books filled the stacks, some older than the country.

Mom would love this. I wonder if Scott reads any of these books or if they're just for show.

Scott settled in on a chair across from the couch, his phone in his hand. "Please describe your progress to me in detail."

Alison nodded. "The executive summary is that my investigation suggests Jacobsen Associates might be involved with the planned attempt on your life." She shrugged. "But my investigation got me on their radar, and they seem to know who I am and my reputation."

"I see." Scott furrowed his brow. "And you're worried about them coming after you?"

Alison shook her head. "What, that? No. They already tried to go after one of my investigators and me the other day. We killed seven of their men and tried to interrogate a survivor, but some sort of spell killed him. I don't know if it's something Jacobsen did or if it comes from somewhere else." She frowned. "That's one of the few things about this that bothers me. Are you familiar with Jacobsen at all?"

Scott nodded. "Yes, but to be clear, it's not a service I've ever availed myself of. I'm ruthless, but I do have my lines I refuse to cross."

"Best my people can tell, killing themselves isn't standard Jacobsen policy." Alison shrugged. "Which there is even more money involved in this than we think or the people hiring them are powerful."

"If they're so powerful, why operate through a front group?"

Alison shrugged. "A test?"

Scott shook his head. "Perhaps, but doubtful as well."

"Can't say. They did try to scare me off by warning me about stumbling into something big." Alison snorted. "My people can't figure out who hired them, but the Jacobsen hit crew is associated with a questionable apartment complex, and we can link some of the money flowing into that apartment complex back to your hit, so it seems like someone is paying a lot of money to have you killed."

The billionaire leaned back with a satisfied expression on his face. "Impressive, Alison. It seems the conspiracy is beginning to tighten in scope." He chuckled. "Jacobsen Associates. That narrows the list of subjects considerably, given their fees."

"If you have anywhere else you want to point me at," Alison suggested, "please share. I can go have an angry lunch with the person and scare them into confessing or surrendering."

Scott shook his head. "This isn't a case where I think even you can solve the problem directly using tactics like that. You'd never get within ten feet of him. I suspect the man behind hiring Jacobsen is Derek Chesterton."

Alison frowned. "The techno-magic CEO? The guy who entered the industry before you?"

"Exactly." Scott nodded. "He's insanely jealous of me, but half his problem is that his business interests are far more spread out. This wouldn't be the first time he's dealt with Jacobsen. He's maintained plausible deniability thus far. If it weren't for that, maybe you could go at least talk to him directly, since he'd have less reason to hide."

Alison snorted. "You're seriously telling me some CEO has flung assassins at you, and you're worried about plausible deniability versus just going and kicking his ass? This isn't a nasty game of chess."

"I'm aware of that, Miss Brownstone." Scott shrugged. "But the harsh reality is that men like Derek and me have layers of backup plans and contingencies for direct attacks, which is why he has to rely on catspaws like Jacobsen. Certain things I tolerate, but if he openly warred with me, I would be forced to reply in kind, which would in the short term damage my business interests."

Alison groaned. "I get it. You're saying we can't kick down his door, but what about the police? I can have my people turn over the evidence they found anonymously, and the FBI can drag his ass off. He can rot in jail until his trial."

"And we're back to the original problem. Do you have billions of dollars lying around for my shareholders?"

Alison rolled her eyes. "Of course I don't."

Scott frowned. "Then no police."

"Why aren't you more worried about another billionaire paying professional assassins to kill you?" Alison stared at him. "You're the one saying he's so dangerous that I can't go just kick in his door."

Scott shrugged. "Why should I worry? I'm paying you to stop it, and I have supreme confidence in your ability or I would not have bothered to hire you."

"But you won't let me go deal with this guy, and you won't call the cops." Alison snorted. "Why aren't you taking this seriously? It's like you *want* to die."

Scott rubbed his chin. "Maybe that's a good idea, actually."

She stared at him. "Have you been drinking?"

"No, I was thinking." Scott stood and moved to a window, staring out into a dense copse of trees. "If I go to the Convention Center, I'll certainly be killed, or at least they'll try. I won't put it past them to bomb the building, so there's a high risk of collateral damage, but if I skip the event, I won't know the next likely attack window and won't be able to prepare or properly defend myself."

Alison nodded. "Following you there, but I don't get how this ends up with you dying and that being a good idea. You don't strike me as a suicidal type."

"No, I'm far from that." Scott turned to face her. "Now that you've identified the killers, I can better judge their likely forces. I've dealt with them before. They are well-funded but arrogant. That can be exploited."

"I noticed that the other day when I fought them." Alison shrugged. "If they'd been a little more well-prepared, it might have been a far worse outcome.

"Not knowing the killing team made certain strategies not viable, but now that we know it's Jacobsen, it's more practical to feed them the exact information we want."

Scott nodded. "We should spring the trap early; let them know I'll be traveling with a lower number of security vehicles. Their previous losses are going to make them more likely to take the bait. They've got to be twitchy at this point.

"You seriously want to purposely poke these Jacobsen guys into attacking?" Alison shrugged. "The guys who attacked me weren't so tough. Just a bunch of assholes with anti-magic deflectors, although if I hadn't been so close, they might have been able to get some decent shots in."

"Beating them proves nothing." Scott shook his head.

"That sounds more like one of their scout teams. They'll have at least a few magicals on their actual kill team. Much more dangerous, and they'll also understand they might face magicals."

Alison frowned. "Then shouldn't we be worried about innocent people getting hurt? If you're going to leak travel information, it's almost unavoidable."

Scott moved back to his original chair and sat. "It's a matter of leaking the right info and using the right route. My people can assure me a route where there will be minimal risk to innocent people. This is the best plan, especially with your presence. I guarantee that Jacobsen personnel won't have anyone with your abilities. We'll end this in one final battle. I've dealt with Jacobsen before, and if they lose their primary kill team, they disengage from their job pretty quickly. This bloody nose will keep them quiet.

"Fine," Alison replied. "When do you want to do this?"

"Tomorrow," Scott announced. "No reason to delay it any longer than we have to, although it'll take a few hours for certain information to spread. I'll try to convince everyone I'm going out for a little drive tomorrow."

Hana eyed the array of weapons spread out on the floor of the living room. "You know, technically if you blew up your condo with a spell, it'd be covered with insurance, but not one of these weapons. They might fine you for having them here." She laughed. "Half of them are illegal anyway."

Alison knelt in front of a few different rifles. "I'll worry about that later. I have these out because I'm trying to be smart about this. The bastards I'll be dealing with tomorrow should be a little tougher than the guys we fought. If I take them too lightly, I could die."

"Just saying your semi-illegal weapons collection shouldn't be in an apartment complex, and I'm not sure how smart it is to bring work home." Hana shrugged.

Alison laughed. "Yeah, I'll need to get a building for the firm sooner rather than later, and then I'll have to find a place to store things like artifacts. Maybe a storage unit, or a few large safety deposit boxes."

"Why not just get a safe here or at whatever building you end up getting for your firm?"

Alison shook her head. "I still have a few artifacts in storage back East that I haven't brought over because I don't have a good solution. A lot of this will depend on how large the firm grows in the future, but I think I'll have to look into getting a secure warehouse for additional gear in addition to setting up some sort of armory at the firm."

Hana circled the weapons. "By the way, did you want me to join the party tomorrow, boss woman?"

"Boss woman?" Alison laughed. "I thought you didn't want to have to call me anything like that."

"I'm trying it out to see if I like it." She tilted her head and worked her mouth. "Not convinced either way, to be honest."

Alison sighed. "Not going to even pretend this won't sound like me being a bitch, but no, I don't want you coming. Look, Hana, you're brave and you've got some good moves, but this won't be a handful of guys I've surprised and am already cutting to shreds. This is going to be a serious fight with a major team of professional killers, almost certain to include wizards. I think you could be trained, and once we have a building we can look into tactical training for you, but right now you'd be more a liability than a help in this kind of situation. And unless nine-tailed foxes regenerate, you could be killed easily."

Hana sighed and headed toward the sofa. "I wasn't exactly eager to sit around and wait to be ambushed anyway. I…" She laughed and sat, crossing her legs. "It's weird."

"What is?"

Hana shrugged. "How I'm changing. You see, I've always kind of prided myself on being a coward."

Alison stared at her. "Huh? You were proud of being a coward?"

"Exactly. You don't get it, because you're Alison Brownstone and you're a badass Drow princess." Hana shrugged. "If a problem comes you just chop it in half, but for me, being a coward meant being a survivor even when no one else had my back. But now…"

"Now what?" Alison dragged a box of rifle and pistol magazines closer and counted. She had only a handful of anti-magic magazines, but if she picked her shots well, she could make the expensive bullets count. One powerful witch, wizard, or Oriceran could lay waste to dozens of men, depending on the magic used.

Hana smiled and looked away, her face growing scarlet. "What can I say, girlfriend? I was living a perfectly good life as a cowardly con artist, but now that I see you doing your thing, I kind of want to be more like you: a strong, badass chick who kicks ass, takes names, and apologizes to no one." She groaned and rubbed the back of her neck. "Is that totally corny? Shit. I'm embarrassed on your behalf for having to even listen to that speech."

Alison laughed. "Yes, it's corny, but it's also flattering. And yes, I have powerful magic even with my AMDS, but it's not like I was born knowing how to fight. I promise that after this case is over, I can train you until you can always protect yourself, no matter what the situation. I can't have my first employee and only investigator not able to defend herself if I'm not around, can I?"

A warm smile appeared on Hana's face, followed by the most vulpine grin the woman could achieve without shifting to her four-legged form. "I'd say good luck tomorrow, but I don't think you're going to need it. I guess I'll say, sucks to be those Jacobsen assholes."

Alison picked up a throwing knife. "Yeah. Sucks to be them."

CHAPTER TWENTY-NINE

Alison slapped a magazine into her pistol and holstered it. She checked her rifle again before slinging it over her shoulder. The wide space available in Scott's SUV limo was proving to have unexpected tactical value.

Maybe I could get an SUV limo. Wonder what Dad would say about that?

She snickered.

Scott sat on the opposite row of black leather seats, his glyph-inscribed rifle in his lap, ready to provide his last line of defense if everyone else died. Two of Scott's private security detail wearing gray armor and helmets also sat in the limo, but another eight rode in the two SUVs flanking the limo. It was a decent defensive force, but far from enough to repel a serious attack without aid.

"You ever thought about leaking the information and just not coming?" Alison asked. "This could be everything from a curb stomp to them blowing the entire convoy up with a spell."

Scott shook his head. "It's a possibility, but given that the killers likely have wizards or other magic users with them, we can't be sure they won't be able to tell I'm not there. Sometimes you have no choice but to use live bait. I don't relish the role, but I don't mind it either. Forcing others into danger on your behalf without risking yourself implies a certain weakness of character."

Alison stared at him. "And you're really not fazed that your life is in danger?"

He shrugged. "It's not the first time, and I'm sure it won't be the last time. Living a life of worthwhile influence means naturally accumulating enemies. You know that yourself, given the dangerous men you've had to battle."

"The Brownstone family solution has always been to just kill those enemies. That way they don't accumulate." She did a quick check of her vest. Multiple throwing knives were sheathed in it, along with her three gnome-crafted knives. She was prepared for combat at any range.

One of the security detail frowned and looked at Scott. The guard's hand went to the receiver in his ear. "We've got a dropship inbound, sir, along with vans approaching from either direction at high speed. They mean to box us in, sir."

Scott chuckled. "Rather flashy, aren't they? Take us toward the old factory. No reason to keep this on the streets. People still need these streets, but they don't need the factory."

The guard relayed the orders with the help of his throat mic. Alison didn't know how many drones or satellites were covering the area for Scott.

This is it. Time to show these Jacobsen bastards how it's done.

Alison took a deep breath and slowly let it out. She

flexed her fingers as the vehicle turned off the road and came to a stop. "This was a good plan. We're doing everything in our tempo now, not theirs."

Scott nodded. "Exactly. We all have our part to play, Alison, and it's time for you to play yours."

She threw open a door. "Time to see if I'm worth what you're paying, Scott. Don't die in the crossfire."

The security guards rushed out of the convoy vehicles. Several of the guards from the other vehicles held bullet-proof tactical shields. They extended the defensive tools, effectively establishing a base wall ringing the convoy.

Two of the men rushed to either of the temporary ballistic walls and set up tall metal tripods engraved in runes. The runes started glowing and a translucent white field extended between the tripods.

Maybe that explains why he doesn't have these guys running around in power armor when he has toys like that. Little techno-magic goes a long way.

The glint of sunlight off white-painted metal signaled the approach of the vans. A distant roar grew louder by the second. One of Scott's guards pulled a missile launcher from the back of his vehicle, and after sliding in the missile, he held it up, aiming through his VR glasses and waiting for the fuzzy shape closing to sharpen into the dropship.

Nice, Scott. A missile launcher. Need to get a few of those for my company, but first things first. Right now we need to stop everyone.

Alison layered a shield over herself, confidence animating her motions.

Several vans screeched to a halt along the road outside

the abandoned factory. The security guards opened fire, but their bullets bounced off an invisible wall in front of the vans.

Okay, so the magicals are in the vans, not the dropship. Interesting.

The guard with the missile launcher lined up his shot. "Back blast area clear," he shouted and pulled the trigger. His missile roared away, leaving a trail of smoke. It was louder than the gunfire. It cleared the line of vans, the wall not that high. The round closed on the approaching dropship.

This is fun.

The aircraft jinked to beat the missile tracking, but that lasted only a few seconds before the missile impacted and the back of the dropship exploded.

Alison shook her head as the dropship smashed into the ground, the entire thing going up in a fireball followed by a column of smoke.

People complain about me making a scene, but I'm not smashing vehicles into the street.

Two scowling Light Elves stepped around the vans. They held up their hands and chanted something, but Alison couldn't begin to know what it might be given the distance and all the gunfire being exchanged.

Scott's security detail continued pouring bullets at the enemy, but they kept bouncing off the elves' shields.

A few seconds later, a massive fireball blasted from the elves. Alison threw her arm to the side, concentrating energy into a thin but wide shield in front of Scott's guards.

The fireball exploded against the shield. Some pain shot through Alison, but she ignored it.

I can win this.

We'll lose if we just sit trading spells since I'm the only choice they have.

Alison pulled her rifle off her shoulder, ejected the magazine, and slapped in anti-magic bullets.

She sprinted past the edge of the security guard's defensive line. Several bullets from the Jacobsen team zoomed by her, a few striking her but bouncing off her shield.

Time to close on them.

With a burst of magic, Alison leapt toward a street light, twisting before she bounced off the pole, accelerating again. One of the elves rushed toward her, chanting, a glowing nimbus surrounding him. Alison lined up her shot and fired a burst before hitting the ground a few yards from him.

One of the bullets deflected off the elf's shield. Another was slowed to the point it bounced off the elf's arm, but the third ripped into his side.

The elf screamed and fell.

Still alive. Congrats.

Half the killer's forces spun toward Alison to shoot her, but their attacks only wasted ammo. She didn't move forward, hoping instead to draw their attention. She lowered her rifle and aimed it at the elf's head. She fired another burst, and his head exploded.

A lot of anti-magic bullets for one elf. That was a very expensive kill. Not a good way to break even on a job if I'm relying on AMBs.

Alison rushed toward the other elf, ignoring the

humans and their conventional attacks. She switched to single fire and snapped off four quick shots, two of them managing to pierce the elf's defenses.

He collapsed to his knees and coughed up blood. Alison finished him off with a shot to the heart and jumped in front of a van as one of the human killers threw a frag grenade her way.

Her newfound cover didn't fully protect her, so when the grenade exploded it showered her with shards, all deflected by her shield. The pain flashed in her body from the strain, but she continued to push that out of her mind and focus on the enemy.

The residual energy of the dead elves' invisible wall faded, allowing the security guards' volleys to riddle the vans and several of the non-magical killers. Alison slung her rifle over her shoulder and yanked out two 9mms. She spun around the corner and opened fire into the exposed flank of the enemy.

Man after man fell between the hammer of the security guards' attack and the anvil of Alison's point-blank assault.

Too bad, assholes.

A security guard screamed as a bullet ripped through his back. Alison finished off the last of the killers and spun that direction, her brow furrowing as she sought more targets.

Scott's men broke formation and reformed into a circle. Another man fell.

What the hell is going on? Why...

Alison frowned and looked up. Three killers stood on the roof, aiming their rifles.

She holstered her pistols and focused energy into an

explosive orb, gritting her teeth at a spike of pain before launching the attack.

The ambushers turned to run, but it was too late. Alison's orb smashed into their portion of the roof, consuming the men in an orange-white flame. Their bodies tumbled to the ground, charred and smoking.

She winced as several pieces of debris fell from the roof.

Well, it's an abandoned building anyway. Maybe a tiny bit of overkill.

Alison rushed toward the security guards. She leapt into the air, her magic fueling a massive jump as she arced toward the top of Scott's SUV limo. A moment before landing, she spread a layer of magic beneath her. Her legs bent, and the magic helped propel her even farther.

Flying might take a lot of energy, but with simple jumping, physics did all the work for her. Alison flew toward the top of the roof, a pistol at the ready. She landed rolling and popped up after a few feet.

As she suspected, another half-dozen killers were hidden behind the roof's edge, their rifles ready. Their guns came alive.

Alison didn't rush forward. She let the bullets strike her shield as she advanced with narrowed eyes. With careful aim, she put a single bullet in the head of each man until she'd silenced their guns.

She took a few deep breaths and turned, looking around the area from the top of the roof. Smoke curled up from the destroyed dropship and damaged roof. It looked like a war zone, not a simple ambush. That was what it meant to work for someone like Scott.

Alison marched to the edge of the roof and leapt off, releasing her shield but feeding magic into a small layer of condensed shadow a few inches above the ground. She hit her landing pad, feeling nothing. She stepped away from the layer and released the energy.

There was a little heaviness in her limbs, and some pain in her body, but she could have killed another 30 men at that rate. Alison cracked her knuckles. It was good to test her limits again.

Close a door, open a window. I didn't spend all those summers training with the guys at Camp Brownstone for nothing.

Scott emerged from his vehicle, his rifle in hand and a frown on his face. "Causalities?"

One of his guards shook his head. "Wounded, no dead, sir. Healing potions have them back at fighting strength."

"It doesn't matter," their boss responded, looking at the bullet-riddled vans and smoking dropship in the distance. "The enemy's defeated." He frowned. "It ended about as quickly as expected with you here, Alison."

Alison walked over to him. "Something wrong?"

He nodded. "Such carnage, just because Derek is such a shit businessman that he'd kill a rival rather than outperform him. I can't express how thoroughly loathsome I find the man."

"And you seriously can't do something about him?"

Scott shrugged. "It's all supposition. If I had proof, I'd have already used it. You were able to find out more than my people, and we still have no direct line of evidence we can walk a district attorney through. Even if he's a normal human, he's like me and has plenty of access to artifacts and techno-magic. He knows how to cover his tracks, and he owns half the politicians in the state. That means even I have to tread lightly around him."

"Only half? You can't just do nothing. If what you're saying is true, he threw a small army at you." Alison pointed to the burning remains of the dropship. "I get that billionaires do everything bigger and better and more expensive, but that's got to mean something."

Scott chuckled. "Don't worry about it, Alison. We won. In the end, he's learned an expensive lesson about not challenging either of us. I'll be watching him closely, and he won't be able to make any moves for a while, if he dares to at all."

Alison nodded. "And you're not planning on hiring someone and sending them after him? A little payback?"

"Not my style." Scott shrugged. "I'm going to continue to collect what I need to send the FBI and PDA after him eventually." His smile turned cold. "I'd rather he rot in prison knowing I defeated him than get off easy with a bullet to the brain."

"A little sadistic. Remind me never to get on your bad side."

Scott smirked. "I'd say that applies more to you. The fight against McKenna was impressive, but it was just one man, but today you were truly spectacular. Your involvement turned a potentially protracted engagement into nothing more than mild pest control or weeding."

Alison shrugged. "Just doing my job and keeping my client alive. Glad you're pleased with what I've done."

"You were a fortunate gamble."

She frowned. "Gamble?"

Scott nodded. "You're not the only magic user in my employ, but I chose today to use some of the others to protect other important places, such as my primary office and my mansion. I gambled on your skills being sufficient to defend me from the assassination attempt. Your efforts at uncovering the information certainly exceeded my expectations."

Alison grinned. "Come on, Scott. It was more of a sure thing than a gamble."

He laughed. "Perhaps true. You'll be getting a bonus for your performance."

She frowned. "Thanks. Something's bothering me, though."

"What?"

Alison pointed at the column of smoke floating into the sky. "A lot of men just died, major battle magic was used, and someone blew a dropship out of the sky with a missile. I don't see any drones. I don't see any AET dropships. I don't hear any sirens. Even if the police haven't been around, there's no way that a drone hasn't noted any of this."

Scott gave her a thin smile. "I made sure to coordinate with the authorities. While Derek may own half the politicians in this state, I own the other half, or maybe it's more accurate to say I'm on good terms with them."

Alison chuckled. "Nice to have strings you can pull."

"Of course. If you'll excuse me. Thank you for your hard work today, Alison." Scott nodded and walked over to his men.

A couple of the men with obvious holes in their armor

shrugged at Scott. "Healing potions have us back to full strength, sir."

Scott shook his head. "Every one of you risked your life against a dangerous foe who could have killed you. Magic might heal you, but it doesn't stop the pain you feel from a bullet, and it won't be able to bring you back if you die. Thank you, gentlemen. I appreciate your efforts, and I won't forget them come compensation time."

Alison watched with a smile. Not every day ended with such a lopsided ass-kicking, but she was happy to accept the ones that did.

CHAPTER THIRTY

"Sounds like you've got the shit under control," Shay observed over the phone.

Alison laughed. "Yeah. Now that I understand what is going on and have had time to practice, I've been better able to work around it and start taking advantage of all my other training. After all, *you* kick plenty of ass, Mom, and you don't have any natural magic. So even with reduced magic, if I train hard enough, I should be able to outperform you."

"That's a good way to think of it," Shay replied. "I'll admit I was worried when you told me, but what you've done in Seattle is amazing. I know what it's like to be your age and starting a new business in a new city. Don't worry if you screw up, Alison. I made plenty of mistakes before I figured things out. As long it's not a lethal mistake, you can always do better the next time."

Alison smiled. "Thanks, Mom. I'm pretty pleased with the people I've gathered. Hana and Tahir both have their quirks, but they're both good at what they do."

"How long is Hana going to stay with you?"

Alison ran her tongue inside her cheek as she thought that over. "Not sure. I'm paying her a good wage so she can afford a decent place now, but I haven't told her she has to leave anytime soon. Kind of fun having a roommate. Reminds me of high school and college. Nostalgic. And it's nice to have a good friend. Speaking of friends, Lily's talking about stopping by for a visit soon. She said something about hitting Bali and Hokkaido first."

Shay sighed.

"What's wrong?" Alison asked. "Is she okay?"

"Oh, this has nothing to do with her." Shay chuckled. "It's about you."

"What about me? What's wrong with me?"

"You don't understand," Shay replied. "It's the opposite. You sound so damned happy, and that's a good thing. It's not like you were super-sad before, but you had started reminding me of your dad and me when we first met. We were both kind of sad sacks in our own ways. We kicked ass at our jobs, but—I don't know how to say it—our hearts were closed off."

Alison scoffed. "I wasn't a sad sack, and my heart isn't closed off."

Shay laughed. "Just saying it's good to hear you're kicking ass, are happy, and have friends you can actually see. We'll also understand if you can't come down for Christmas this year. If you need to take the time to focus on your business, then do that."

"Not sure about that," Alison replied. "Still figuring out a lot of things and getting to know the city. It might not be as large as LA, but it's damned complicated in its own way."

"Don't ever tell your dad that or he'll never set foot in the city."

Alison smirked. "I'll keep that in mind."

"Take your time with everything." Shay took a deep breath. "And remember we're always here for you, no matter what you need. If that Chesterton asshole starts fucking with you, I'm gonna pay him a visit in the middle of the night. He wouldn't be the first powerful man I've threatened."

Alison snorted. "Don't worry, Mom. If it gets that bad I'll do it myself, money and power be damned. I'm Alison Brownstone, and I don't take shit from anybody."

"That's my girl."

Alison, Hana, and Ava sat around the dining room table in the condo, tablets in hand, a series of different commercial real estate listings on the screens—dozens on each tablet. These included different styles, different heights, different layouts. The only common point was they were commercial buildings for sale.

What's the best choice? Something one story but spread out? Something else?

Hana pointed to a four-story office building available for purchase in the heart of Redmond. "What about this one? Look at all the big name companies nearby. That's got to make the company seem more professional. Probably would help us line up clients more quickly."

Alison shook her head. "That's exactly the problem. The building's not isolated enough. If something big goes down, we won't just have to worry about collateral damage, we have to worry about serious damage to the economy. I don't mind people complaining about a Brownstone occasionally blowing up a building, but I don't want anyone to be able to blame a recession on me."

Hana snickered. "That ego's growing, isn't it, girlfriend?"

Alison shrugged. "Can't help if it's the truth. Being a Brownstone means two things." She held up a finger. "One, kicking a lot of ass." She held up a second finger. "Two, it means you'll end up in a situation where you're required to kick a lot of ass."

Ava rolled her eyes and pointed to three different images. "These all have terrible defensive visibility. Snipers would have a field day. I would recommend against that if you want a building with a lot of windows."

"Good thinking." Alison rubbed her chin. "Wonder if we should avoid buildings where someone could insert troops from a dropship easily? How to accomplish that? Focus on roof design and layout?"

Ava nodded. "It's something to consider, although I'm personally doubtful enemies will attempt to engage you with light infantry in such a scenario." She narrowed her eyes. "It might be possible to get an exemption for your building for point defense that could cut down on that sort of thing. I'm doubtful, but it wouldn't hurt to try."

Hana looked at the two of them and rolled her eyes. "I get the whole 'be prepared' thing, but listen to yourselves. Snipers? Worrying about dropships invading? You're going to be buying a building to house a small security firm. You're not building an Army base."

Alison laughed. "I was in a fight that included a drop-ship not all that long ago."

"I know. Just saying." Hana crossed her arms and rolled her eyes.

Alison shrugged. "Besides, this all relates to what I was just saying. I might recently have participated in pissing off a homicidal billionaire, and that's not counting the terrorists I have upset or all the dark wizards I've hunted. A little proactive defense isn't a bad idea. I know I can handle them, but the better the setup, the less risk to others."

"Homicidal billionaire, huh?" Hana shrugged. "Even if Chesterton blames you, that means you're on the good side of another billionaire, and he's much younger and *much* hotter than Chesterton."

"What are you getting at?" Alison snorted. "Scott's just a client."

Hana waved a hand dismissively. "Sure, sure. I'm just saying, 'tall, dark, handsome, and loaded' isn't a terrible preference to have for a man." Hana grinned. "You can't use the job as an excuse when you're not working for him."

Alison pointed at a listing. "Picking a new building for the firm is part of the job."

"It's your love life. Just trying to point out certain possibilities. Next time you see him, ask him about feeding warlocks to alligators on your first date." Hana winked.

Ava frowned and looked at the two women. Her eyes were more annoyed than confused now.

Alison shook her head. "We're in Seattle. Not a lot of alligators."

"Then go to the zoo," Hana replied. "Use your imagination, girlfriend."

"I'm not…" Alison groaned and scrubbed a hand down her face. "There will be no alligator feeding involving Scott Carlyle and me ."

Ava cleared her throat. "Ladies, we still need to narrow down the choices. It's been a week since the assassination attempt. I would have thought we'd be down to a handful of choices, but there are still dozens of possible candidates. Focus is in order, for the good of the company."

Hana saluted. "Ma'am, yes, ma'am. I will focus on commercial real estate, ma'am."

Alison stood and stretched. "The world's not going to end if we take a few extra days to find a place. I've been so damned busy in both November and December, I deserve to take things a little slower."

Ava pursed her lips. "Without a building, we can't move forward on constructing the training grounds you're interested in, and our hiring potential is limited. Your dining room table is small, Miss Brownstone. How many employees do you intend to hire and have meet in your condo?"

"Can always buy a bigger table." Alison laughed and moved toward her window. The sun was setting, casting the sky in pink and orange, the colors reflecting off Elliot Bay. It was both beautiful and soothing. Going for the expensive condo had been a good choice.

Her first major job since moving to Seattle had been an unqualified success. Her company was firmly established, and building a reputation. She had a friend and the beginnings of a powerful team. Even her administrative assistant was badass in her own way.

Brownstone Security, LLC had come to Seattle, and

Alison wouldn't rest until everyone either respected the name or feared it.

Alison stepped toward her window and placed her hand on the glass. She peered into the distance, focusing on where the ocean joined the horizon.

Not a bad move. Not a bad move at all.

I might even have a chance to build a life here.

The story is far from over. Alison's adventure continues in ON HER OWN.

FREE BOOKS!

WARNING:

The Troll is now in charge.

And he's giving away free books
if you sign-up!

Join the only newsletter hosted by a Troll!

Get sneak peeks, exclusive giveaways, behind the scenes
content, and more.
PLUS you'll be notified of special **one day only fan
pricing** on new releases.

Visit: https://marthacarr.com/read-free-stories/

ON HER OWN

The story is far from over. Alison's adventure continues in
ON HER OWN

<u>**AVAILABLE FOR PURCHASE HERE**</u>

Alison Brownstone is starting out in her life, adulting in the real world. I can relate but it took me a little longer than Alison to have the courage to do it my way. I was 47 when I finally got up and took a bold chance. I packed up everything in a small U-Haul, sold what I could, gave away the rest and took of for New York City singing the Mary Tyler Moore theme song the whole way. No real plans, some money, an apartment in the Bronx waiting for me, and knowing about three people, tops.

It was the only way I was going to leave. I had spent my life up to that point making excuses for why now wasn't the right time. Maybe later. Maybe I can make where I am work. Maybe if I can earn just a little more first, lose weight, meet someone... I had a million excuses. Truth was I lacked courage and trust, mostly in myself.

Years passed and in that time I wasn't completely unhappy – I was surrounded by loving friends and was still writing – but I wasn't really happy either. There was always a part of me on each and every day that wondered about being somewhere else.

The lesson I learned is – Dreams Matter. Doesn't matter if they're bold and grand or small or weird and tailored just for you. They matter...

For some reason 2007 was the year I had enough and just, well, left. It was the only way I could get myself out of one place and to another – New York City. If I had planned anything, I would have talked myself out of it. Very few people thought it was a good idea, so I avoided all of them and relied on my friend Dhyanna who helped me pack, mail boxes and never had a negative word to say about it. Of course I'd be fine just because things generally work out. It's her general philosophy. Didn't understand that at all but I'd nod and hope she was right.

So, if you're keeping track of history you'll have noticed that 2007 was the edge of the beginning of the Great Recession. Who knew? It was just ahead of Bernie Madoff in NYC, making things even economically worse. I ended up in the Bronx, always on the edge of financial ruin and loving every minute of it. It was the first time I had done something that benefited no one but me. I walked everywhere just to be walking in NYC, looking at the sights, amazed to be there.

I pictured Lucille Ball wandering everywhere seeing some of the same things like the lions in front of the library or the façade of Carnegie Hall. Yeah, that's right, Lucille Ball. She was a maverick in the TV business and forged a way for herself in the 1950's.

I also headed straightaway for the same sofa where Dorothy Parker, the writer, held court at the Algonquin with other writers making witty remarks. Sat there sipping coffee, forming different funny things to say. Like I said, I loved it all.

Okay, fast forward to the present day and I'm still working a day job and I'm a full time author and I'm working on when is the right day to leave one job and stake my claim in the literary world. Have to admit, I'm dragging my feet a bit. Might be all those years of financial distress – just paying the rent felt like a big accomplishment some months. There are probably a few reasons rumbling around in my head.

I know it's going to take courage, once again, to pull that trigger. Hopefully, a bit more planning this time. Years ago, the guy helping me move in to that Bronx apartment bailed on me at the last minute and left me with everything I owned on the sidewalk. I had to keep telling people, *not a yard sale*! But I'm venturing out there with the same enthusiasm and delight in the world finally looking for that next adventure. Totally worth it. Thanks to all of you for coming along with me – makes it all so much easier. More adventures to follow.

THANK YOU for not only reading this story but these *Author Notes* as well .

(I think I've been good with always opening with "thank you." If not, I need to edit the other *Author Notes*!)

RANDOM (*sometimes*) THOUGHTS?

So, I'm going to be a (slightly) wicked boy before Christmas. I'm going to relate a behind-the-scenes story, and then (since I lie for a living) I'm going to...um... enhance the story.

Translation, I'm going to lie through my teeth...kind of.

So, early November we had a large Indie Publishing convention here in Vegas. Both Martha (collaborative author on these books) and LMBPN's VP of Operations Stephen Campbell (affectionally known as Zen-Master Steve ®) were chatting at breakfast.

During this breaking of early morning bread, Martha was bemoaning (that was ZMS's statement) her lack of a love life and Steve, thinking he was going to zing her, asked her when she was going to do something about it.

Without missing a beat, Martha retorted, "About the same time you finish your book!"

(This is a book Steve has been writing for what seems like years (probably two) and in editing a good portion of this year.)

So, the two of them made a bet. Either Steve finishes his book (and publishes) or Martha has to go on four (4) dates with the same guy. First one to attain the challenge wins.

Now, that's fine and all, but today we had some issues with (this) book and had to address them. Except, Martha's was nowhere to be seen.

Eventually, she shows up on phone messages saying she is purchasing a mattress. Eventually, she finishes and calls from her car to find out the challenges we had to go through. During this call, I'm talking to Martha on the phone, holding it up to my headphones where Steve can hear her chatting (I was on a ZOOM (like Skype) call with Steve at that time.)

During this time, Martha is chatting with Steve where I have to reply for him, what fun, and mentions the photographer is coming on Saturday.

Now, they have mentioned a bet (I did not know the bet details at the time), a mattress, and a photographer.

So, MY story is Martha is having a boudoir photographer over to take pictures on Saturday and needs to go on dates to win her bet with Stephen.

I'm guessing the photography is going to be a part of her tactics to accomplish reeling in available bachelors.

I have to hand it to Martha. When she decides to win a bet, she goes all in.

[ZMS Edit—Michael's version is far better than the reality that Martha is updating her author photos. However, I do expect her to use those author photos as part of her evil plot to win the bet. (Note to Martha, if you read this, I'm pulling for you :))]

HOW TO MARKET FOR BOOKS YOU LOVE

We are able to support our efforts with you reading our books, and we appreciate you doing this!

If you enjoyed this or ANY book by any author, especially Indie-published, we always appreciate if you make the time to review a book, since it lets other readers who might be on the fence to take a chance on it as well.

AROUND THE WORLD IN 80 DAYS

One of the interesting (at least to me) aspects of my life is my ability to work from anywhere and at any time. In the future, I hope to re-read my own *Author Notes* and remember my life as a diary entry.

Dec 3

I'm sitting at my desk in the Vegas condo typing these notes, waiting for my wife to get home so we can go to Italian downstairs at Crystals. I've had discussions with Stephen about how to handle the *Author Notes* for when I'm gone most of January over in Asia.

Our plan is for me to do audio that someone will transcribe for me as I'm jetting around. Therefore, for those books that publish while I'm away, I'll be able to say something cool like, "I'm in Bali" or "I'm in Bangkok." (*Editor's note: Best tours ever in Bangkok, Judith! https:// bangkokvanguards.com/. And check out Celuk in Bali for jewelry or Ubud for art.*)

(I have to have these experiences for the books, you see. It's all business.)

At the moment, it's just "I'm in Las Vegas…where I am most of the year." I realize that for a LOT of people (and me for most of my life), Las Vegas was a great destination.

Now it's home.

For those who have never considered living in Las Vegas, I'd suggest thinking about it. It is a LOT more fun to live here than I would have guessed. Also, if you are an author, it is becoming a hub of Indie publishing (and general publishing.) I had lunch today with Mike Bray, CEO of Wolfpack Publishing. Wolfpack is one of the biggest Western publishers out there and Mike is a fun person to talk to. If you have ever read Dean Wesley Smith, Kristine Kathryn Rusch, Jonathan Brazee, JN Chaney, SM Boyce, Alex Steele, and many, many others, they all live here in Las Vegas. (*Editor's note: Does an hour and a half away count? It's close enough to come over and smack you about the head and shoulders when you need it!*)

If you know others, just put their names in your review, I'd like to know who else lives in this wonderful city!

FAN PRICING

If you would like to find out what LMBPN is doing and the books we will be publishing, just sign up at http:// lmbpn.com/email/. When you sign up, we notify you of books coming out for the week, any new posts of interest in the books and pop culture arena, and the fan pricing on Saturday.

Ad Aeternitatem,

Michael Anderle

OTHER SERIES IN THE ORICERAN
UNIVERSE:

SCHOOL OF NECESSARY MAGIC
THE DANIEL CODEX SERIES
I FEAR NO EVIL
THE UNBELIEVABLE MR. BROWNSTONE
THE LEIRA CHRONICLES
REWRITING JUSTICE
THE KACY CHRONICLES
MIDWEST MAGIC CHRONICLES
SOUL STONE MAGE
THE FAIRHAVEN CHRONICLES